Strange Recompense

by

CATHERINE AIRLIE

Harlequin Books

TORONTO•LONDON•NEW YORK•AMSTERDAM
SYDNEY•HAMBURG•PARIS•STOCKHOLM

Original Hardcover edition published in 1952
by Mills & Boon Limited

ISBN 0-373-00511-3

Harlequin edition published March 1960
Second printing July 1980

Printed in Canada

CHAPTER ONE

THE GREAT SHOULDER of Cader Idris loomed ominously through a curtain of rain which swept down to the rugged coastline, obliterating everything but the grey sea and towering cliff locked in the struggle of the elements, and the sound of rain and tide was a mighty roar of defiance flung back in the face of the wind. It seemed that no other sound would have been audible on such a night, dominated by the fury of the storm, but it came, fitfully, between the gusts of wind—the sound of a car being driven at speed along the narrow winding ribbon of a road topping the cliff. Then suddenly, out of the night and the greyness, two shafts of yellow light hovered uncertainly, dipping as the road plunged downward and rising again to the headland.

Even here, high up on the treacherous coast road, the car did not slacken speed, plunging on through the rain and darkness in the shadow of the Welsh mountains to an unknown destination with the wind whipping away the sound of it again and again until, with a screeching of brakes, it appeared to rear, arrested, like a terrified animal, before it plunged over the cliff into the angry sea below.

In that split second, as the dark shape hung suspended before that final plunge to oblivion, a figure was flung clear to lie, crumpled and still, on the coarse grass topping the headland. Wind and rain blew over it, a woman's figure, thin and pathetically ill-clad for such a night, lying face downwards on the grass without movement, without any sign of life whatever.

As the first gleam of dawn broke over the bleak Cardigan landscape the storm abated, showing an opal-colored band of sky along the horizon far out into the Channel, and the rugged outline of the bay took vague shape in the rapidly strengthening light. The wind blew cold from the Atlantic, but the rain had ceased and the full fury of the storm had passed.

Slowly, almost imperceptibly, the figure on the cliff stirred, with groping movements of returning consciousness like those of a blinded person seeking the light. The girl turned on to her back and lay there.

Where am I? How did I get here? I can't remember, and—I don't know who I am!

Panic, sudden and terrible, took possession of her at that last thought, and shock reduced her mind to chaos. Desperately she sought about her for an explanation of her predicament, but nothing would come. The past was a reality over which she had no immediate control; the present was danger.

Wildly she looked about her, as if for some way of escape, but she was not imprisoned. There, before her, was the road winding down into the valley, although it ended somewhere behind her where she dared not look.

She would not look at the sea, although she could hear it pounding against the cliffs like an angry animal straining at a leash, and presently her eyes fastened on a narrow pathway straggling off across the moor.

She stood on the cliff top, torn between the two, watching the road almost as if she feared it, and then she plunged downwards through the wet gorse towards the path that led more directly away from the sea.

Quickening her pace as the sun rose and strengthened and the morning star paled above the hills, she covered distance unconsciously, almost running at times as if some stupendous force was compelling her away from the scene of disaster, away from memory, away, even, from final recognition. She had no memory of the accident. She had no memory at all.

"Dear God!" she prayed, "if I could only remember!"

She looked up at last, a desperate sort of courage in her eyes as she struggled to her feet, stiff and sore from the night of exposure behind her. The road was the only way, after all!

She had covered the best part of three miles before the road showed signs of leading anywhere, and then a van passed her bearing an unfamiliar name.

By the position of the sun she knew that it was mid-day, and hunger gnawed suddenly and fiercely. Instinctively she sought the road, walking close to the grass verge when she reached it, although there was no traffic to necessitate such caution, but when the car came up behind her she had no need to step aside.

Ruth Melford would have driven straight past the girl in the navy-blue coat that bright June morning, her mind preoccupied with her own affairs, if she had not been arrested

4

by the vivid beauty of the wind-blown hair. As she drew level something made her turn to look at the girl's face, and what she saw caused her to push her gear into neutral and bring the car to a standstill with a grinding of brakes, several yards ahead of the walker.

The girl drew abreast almost reluctantly, it seemed, her blue eyes darkened by her obvious distress, her pale face and lagging step witness to her utter physical exhaustion.

"Good morning!" Ruth offered lightly. "Can I give you a lift into Glynmareth? I seem to be going your way."

The girl stared back at her for a moment, her forehead puckered as if in an effort to remember, and then her whole expression broke up in confusion and the deep-set, dark-lashed eyes looked suddenly wild.

"I don't know where I want to go," she said desperately, pressing an ungloved hand to her brow. "I—I don't know about anything. I can't remember."

Ruth leaned over and opened the off-side door of the car.

"Get in," she commanded in her brisk, practical way. "You look desperately tired and—ill. Have you walked far?"

The girl seemed to recoil at the thought of entering the car, staring at it as if it might be some monster ready to devour her at a touch.

"I've been walking since—daybreak," she said. "I must have come a long way, but—but——"

"Do get in!" Ruth urged making one of the sudden decisions so characteristic of her. "At least I can run you into Glynmareth and we can see what we can do for you there."

After the barest of hesitations the girl obeyed her, shivering and drawing back into the corner of her seat as they came into sight of the red rooftops of Glynmareth. She appeared to shrink from contact with her kind, and Ruth refrained from further questioning, but her quick glance took in the crumpled dress and the mud-stained shoes which spoke so plainly of a night spent in the open that the first thing to think about was quite clearly food and warmth, followed by a long and healing period of sleep.

"You said just now that you did not know where you wanted to go," she mentioned as the first of Glynmareth's white-washed cottages slipped past and they were driving down the main street of the little town. "I wonder if you would let me take you home with me? You see," she explained carefully, "my brother is a doctor and he may be able to help."

The girl considered her suggestion, saying with a lucidity which made it quite clear that she was completely in command of the present:

"Why should I thrust myself upon you? We are strangers. I must go to the police."

In spite of her effort, her voice trembled, and Ruth took the decision out of her hands.

"Let me see what I can do for you first of all," she said. "The police might quite conceivably bring you to my brother in the long run. He's Medical Superintendent at our local cottage hospital and—forgive me, my dear, but you look very much in need of his care."

The kindness of tone and words stung tears into the girl's eyes. She was clinging to Ruth now, to the idea of protection and shelter and warmth removed from the grim austerity of a police court.

"It may take time—remembering," she said confusedly. "I really ought to remember——"

"Don't try just now," Ruth advised. "It will only have the effect of distressing you further." She knew enough of medical practice to realize how near to collapse the girl was, how thin the line could become which marked the breaking point. "Once you have changed out of these wet clothes and had a good sleep you'll remember all you want to know. Tiredness can make our minds blank—desperate tiredness."

She was studying her companion without the girl's being conscious of scrunity, for the pale oval of the finely-boned face was reflected clearly in the windscreen before them, and she could see the sudden twitching of the firm young chin as her companion attempted to control emotions which were new and frightening. It was a face to command attention, she thought, with its widely spaced eyes, small, neat nose flaring a little at the nostrils, and the generous mouth held in check by that nervous biting of the lips, a face with the decided stamp of character about it.

Ruth turned the car in between the stone gateposts of the hospital grounds and drove off the main avenue towards her home with the conviction that here was no ordinary case of amnesia but one which carried a story with it which might be difficult to unravel.

The Melford villa had been built at the same time as the hospital and looked across a well-stocked garden to the larger building with its wards and sun-balconies, which was Glynmareth's pride. Reached through a well-planned shrubbery, it had all the privacy the Superintendent could desire in what little leisure time he permitted himself, without isolating him from his work, and Ruth drew up at the front door with a sigh of relief.

"Here we are!" she observed briskly, seeing that her companion had drawn back into the shadow of the car as they approached the door. "You had better come in with me and have something to eat while I contact them over at the hospital. They may not even want to take you in there, once you've had a good night's rest," she added encouragingly.

The girl slid from her seat and stood uncertainly in the sunlight. A faint sound, like a cry of protest, broke from the girl's lips as she stretched out her hand to steady herself, and Ruth was just in time to catch her before she fell. Her dead weight was as much as Ruth could cope with and with a sigh of relief she caught the gleam of a apron flitting along the path beyond the berberis hedge.

"Nurse!" she called loudly. "Can you come in here a minute?"

"Do you think you could open the sitting-room door for me?" she asked. "I've picked this girl up on the moor road and she seems to have been caught in all that rain last night. It rather looks as if she might be the victim of an accident."

"We'll lay her down on the settee," she decided, pushing cushions aside as she spoke. "Once I've got her settled I'll slip across to the hospital and see Matron. This may be more serious than I imagined at first." She straightened, looking down on the pinched white face among the cushions. "See what you can do about bringing her round, Nurse," she suggested before she turned away. "There's brandy in that corner cupboard over there. I'll dash across for help, and you could go through her pockets and see if you can find any evidence of identification."

7

The idea behind Ruth's directions was to find her brother, although she realized that he might not be at the hospital at that hour. He had spoken of a consultation somewhere in the town while they were having breakfast together and, as she re-crossed the shrubbery in the direction of the hospital, the thought struck her that she was seeing less and less of Noel these days as he buried himself more and more in his work. Apart from breakfast and a late supper together, their days were spent apart. Lunches he ate out, and sometimes she wondered if he ever found time for dinner at all. He was wrapping himself up in his profession to the exclusion of all else, studying in any spare time available for the extra degrees he coveted and putting in far more hours at the hospital than he need have done.

Left alone with her charge, the seventeen-year-old probationer set to work with four months of experience behind her and a sudden grim fear in her heart. She had never been left alone with anyone who looked so desperately ill before, and she was quite sure that her patient was about to die.

She lifted the brandy and poured a little through the parted lips, but her patient did not appear to respond in any way, and the short period of her training went down before a native superstition. This was something unusual, a stranger brought in from the moors! She was most definitely dying. The fear of death was still very strong in Jill's heart, and in her experience these things happened with terrifying suddenness. She caught at the unresponsive hands, trying to rub warmth and life into them, and after a minute or two the girl stirred and opened her eyes. She looked at Jill and gave her a wan smile, and then she slipped back into unconsciousness again and fear stood once more in Jill's heart.

"You could go through her pockets and see if you can find any evidence of identification."

A senior's words were law to Jill, even although Miss Melford was not actually one of the hospital staff. She was the doctor's sister—the Super's sister, no less, so that she was to be obeyed almost as if it had been Matron herself who had given the order.

There was nothing very much to go on, nothing to establish anyone's identity, she thought, as she laid the articles she found on the table, one by one. A good quality linen handkerchief, crumpled a little, but still clean; a small suede purse with some money in it; a powder compact with a blue enamel lid and—a wedding ring.

Jill looked at the last item as if it were the most important of all, as indeed it must be. It was a nice ring, she thought, reminding her of her mother's solid, substantial gold, and it was evident that it belonged to the girl lying so motionless against Ruth Melford's velvet cushions.

She was quite convinced now that the stranger on the settee was about to die. Little gasping sounds were coming from between the girl's pale lips and the slim fingers were clutching spasmodically at the edge of the improvised bed. Jill had seen those clutching fingers before.

Once again the girl's eyes fluttered open, but they were glazed and unseeing now, and despair took the place of fear in Jill's heart. Convinced that she was face to face with death in one of its most pathetic forms, she no longer felt that she faced it alone. Deeply religious like most of her fellow-countrywomen, she knelt down beside the settee, realizing suddenly that she was still holding the stranger's ring, and the fact seemed a pointer to what was expected of her. She knew, then, what to do with the ring. The girl must not die without it on her finger, no matter what reason had made her take it off before she reached Glynmareth!

Quickly she slipped it on to the third finger of the unresponsive left hand, thinking, with all her native Welsh superstition uppermost, that her patient could now die in peace.

She was still on her knees beside the settee when Doctor Melford came back with his sister, and she rose to her feet at their approach, awed into silence at being even in the same room with him.

He looked human and kind now as he bent over the girl on the settee, but Jill felt that she would have fainted on the spot and utterly disgraced herself for all time if he had spoken to her at that moment. He had such an air of thoughtful dignity when he went the rounds with Matron or came in after hours to a special case, that he seemed to walk perpetually alone, and she knew that he was reputed to be one of the "coming men" in the profession.

9

He stood beside the settee, leaning over his patient with that look in his eyes which inspired confidence, and Jill waited with her heart beating wildly under her starched apron.

"You've given a restorative, Nurse?" he asked as if she was quite capable of dealing with even the most complicated case. "Has there been any reaction?"

"She seemed to regain consciousness for a minute or two," Jill heard herself say with surprising clarity, "and then she lapsed back again. I tried twice," she added more nervously, "with the same result."

"Thank you."

She could see that he was preoccupied and she signalled to Miss Melford that she had left the girl's possessions on the table beside the settee.

Ruth nodded.

"You were going off duty, Nurse," she said. "Thank you for your help. Matron is sending someone across from the wards."

Almost thankfully the little probationer stole away, forgetful of the ring, forgetful of everything but the fact that the Superintendent had actually spoken to her and, what was more, took it for granted that she knew what she was doing. It might be embellished just a little, she thought, when repeating her triumph in the nurses' common-room across the way!

Ruth Melford stood watching her brother anxiously as he made his examination of their patient, feeling a responsibility out of all proportion to her obligation for the girl she had picked up off the moor, trying to read his verdict in his steady grey eyes even before they were turned in her direction.

He dropped the girl's wrist and moved towards the window.

"We must get her to bed," he announced. "I don't want to take the risk of moving her over to the hospital right away, Ruth, and I know you will cope. Let her have the spare room for an hour or two, and I'll get Matron to send someone over to help. I will be able to keep my eye on her for the next hour or so and I believe that will be all-important."

10

"What do you think could have happened?" Ruth asked, still perplexed by the events of the past hour, but quite sure that she had done the right thing by bringing the girl home with her. "She was completely bewildered when I found her, and she seems to be a stranger to the district."

"We'll have to report it to the police, of course," he said, "but for the present I propose to wait. You say she told you that she couldn't remember anything?" he added. "Where she had come from—who she was?"

"Not a thing, as far as I could gather. She was terribly upset about it and seemed almost reluctant to come with me until I insisted," Ruth explained, speaking automatically as she thought of something else. "When you say you are prepared to wait, does it mean that she is all right—that she is going to live?"

"Of course she's going to live!" Noel replied without any hesitation whatever. "She's strong enough to pull through a possible bout of pneumonia, and that's as near to a diagnosis as I can make at the moment."

He straightened, his lean, dark face still thoughtful, and Ruth crossed the room to pick up the girl's personal effects from the table beside the settee.

"This must be all she had in her pockets," she said. "Powder compact, purse and a handkerchief. Not much, really, to go on, and very little with which to establish an identity. Oh! but look here! There's a name embroidered on the handkerchief in blue 'Anna'!" Her thin face flushed excitedly. "Do you think that will be her own name, and will it help?" she asked eagerly.

Her brother took the fragment of linen from her, stretching it out between his strong hands to reveal the embroidered name.

"It's possible," he agreed, answering her first question. "And every little helps if this is a case of true amnesia. We shall find that out when she regains full consciousness, but I don't propose to trouble her with too many questions until she has slept for at least twelve hours."

He glanced down at the settee to find his patient's eyes wide and full upon him, quietly thoughtful eyes, gently inquiring as they lingered on his strong face, and a surging pity welled in him as he recognized her utter helplessness.

"Can you tell me where I am—who I am?" she asked

11

unsteadily, still with those wide eyes fixed on his. "I have lost my memory. I know that someone brought me here in a car, but—before that, I have no memory at all."

"What you feel now may pass as soon as you have had a good rest," he explained. "These are the essential things at present: I am a doctor, and I shall look after you."

Her eyes clung to his for a moment longer, and then, slowly, they closed and a small sigh of utter exhaustion escaped her lips. Noel Melford turned round to where his sister waited.

"Best leave her where she is," he advised as they went from the room together. "She'll mend more quickly that way."

"What do you think, Noel?" Ruth asked. Now that they could speak more freely she was beginning to realize that she had committed them both to considerable responsibility. "Do you think she's likely to get her memory back and—how soon shall we have to tell the police about her?"

"Right away, I think." He took out a cigarette and lit it, blowing the smoke thoughtfully above his head. "Her people may be trying to trace her, and if there's been an accident anywhere the police may be looking for her even now. It's a grim business, this amnesia, difficult to fight at the best of times," he observed, "and generally full of all sorts of complications. How old would you say that child was?"

Ruth considered.

"Older than she looks in the present circumstances, I should think," she decided. "About twenty-three or four. Does age help?"

"Everything helps. Approximate age may help to establish possible reasons for the amnesia, although there are no hard and fast rules. In the morning I shall see what I can do with the one clue we have found—the name on the handkerchief. Anna, wasn't it? If it is really her own name, which is very likely, then the rest may be easy." He moved restlessly about the kitchen, following in her wake as she prepared a meal, as if he sought some sort of assurance from her presence. "We could have done without this."

Ruth turned to put an affectionate hand on his arm.

"I'm sorry, Noel," she apologized. "I've thrust this on you without a great deal of thought, I'm afraid, when you were busy enough in the ordinary way—too busy, I sometimes think." Her eyes pleaded with him to understand. "But I had to bring her home, Noel. There was something about her—not actually pathetic—that's not the right word —but—in need of help." She turned away, not quite sure why she should suddenly feel that she was pleading with him on her own account. "I had to bring her," she repeated.

"Of course you had to bring her!" He put a firm hand under her arm. "Your motherly instinct will out, old lady! Don't worry too much about it," he went on to advise. "We've handled amnesia before. I'll give Tranby a ring in the morning and get him to come over and have a look at your protégée and if she's all right by then we can send her on her way rejoicing."

He had spoken lightly for her benefit, but Ruth knew that he had never taken any of his cases lightly, that the girl she had brought to Glynmareth would remain their responsibility until he had established her identity beyond the shadow of a doubt and freed her from her present bondage.

"Hullo, there, Ruth! I've brought along the necessary help. Fancy you turning the villa into a rival establishment!"

The gay voice drifted in from the garden and Ruth turned to the open door.

"It's Sara!" she smiled "We're in here, my dear—consulting in the kitchen!"

A tall young woman in the uniform of a nursing sister appeared in the doorway, her immaculate white coat and cap dazzling bright in the sunshine as she paused for a moment to consider brother and sister with a satisfied smile. Sara Enman experienced the old thrill of warmth and achievement as she looked into Noel Melford's eyes, although, as yet, she could not lay claim to his affections with any real authority. His eyes were a little remote today, she mused, telling herself that she understood that look because she understood Noel and all that his profession meant to him as no one else could understand. When he was engrossed in a case nothing else mattered to him, and quite often he had taken her into his confidence in that respect, a compliment which Sara appreciated to the full. As second in command of the nursing staff, she held her own small niche in the little community of which he was virtually head, and a sense of power had developed in her out of all proportion to her importance. She was beginning to make herself objectionable to those who worked under her, the martinent complex developing early, but she kept that side of her character for the hospital wards and those times when Noel was well out of earshot.

There were things about Noel she might never know, tender, passionate things that went deep to the soul of the man, but she had assured herself that she could do without these things because they had so many other things in common. She was the sort of person Noel needed, someone who would understand his work and his ambitions and share his interests with him. That, Sara had decided, was really the most important thing in life.

Her friendship with Ruth had been cultivated largely to the end of getting to know Noel in his off-duty hours, a thing which might not have been possible otherwise, and as she came into the kitchen she smiled at Ruth.

"Why the kitchen?" she asked "And where's the patient?"

"Noel wants her to sleep all she can," Ruth explained. "We've left her on the settee in the sitting-room. It's comfortable enough there and there's no point in moving her upstairs at present"

"Not when we'll be moving her across to the wards in the morning," Sara agreed briskly taking charge automatically. "I'll make all the arrangements and then you won't have any more trouble. What's the matter?" she asked, turning to Noel for the first time.

"Amnesia," he said briefly. "She's young. It may only be a temporary lapse."

"I see." Ruth watched Sara's face take on its most professional expression, her grey eyes rather hard, her fine lips firmly compressed as she accepted the cigarette Noel proffered. "Another case for Inspector Evans, I suppose. We've had 'em before!"

"Not like this," Ruth heard herself saying sharply, contradicting the suggestion in the younger girl's voice. "This girl's different."

Sara's carefully shaped eyebrows went up.

14

"In what way?" she asked mildly. "They mostly turn out to have a fairly seedy history, picked up off the street like that."

"This girl wasn't exactly picked up off the streets," Noel informed her quietly. "Ruth came across her out on the moors after she had walked some considerable distance, it seems. She doesn't look—the other type."

Sara glanced at him sharply, then at Ruth.

"This certainly makes a difference," she said in a completely changed voice. "Could there have been an accident, do you suppose? Perhaps she walked away from the scene of it in a dazed condition and can't quite recall what happened. She may have had a blow of some kind, on the head, for instance, which would account for the amnesia," she added professionally.

"We shall take all that into account," Noel said. "We'll know by the time we report the case," he added. "And the police will check up on possible accidents in the district."

"It almost seems as if Noel is reluctant to call in the police," Sara observed as Ruth filled a hot-water bottle at the sink. "I wonder why?"

Ruth handed her the bottle.

"You'll see for yourself in a minute," she said. "Will you carry that in for me?"

The nurse who had come across from the hospital was still waiting in the hall and Ruth smiled as she recognized the girl, glad that "Topsy" Craven was on duty because of a rich quality of understanding in her make-up which she had discovered during her own recent illness, when she had been nursed back to health in one of the private rooms at the hospital.

"Your patient is in here, Topsy," she explained, opening the sitting-room door. "My brother doesn't think she should be moved, so we won't bother to undress her until she has had a long, refreshing sleep."

Sara had preceded her into the room and was standing looking down at the nameless girl on the settee with her most professional expression.

"Young, indeed," she mused. "to have come to this! Loss of memory. One invariably associates it with some sort of tragedy. Well," she concluded briskly, "we should know part of the answer by the morning, if not all of it."

15

For the remainder of the afternoon Ruth found herself chained to the house, "hovering," as she put it, "outside the sitting-room like a broody hen with her first patch of chicks," waiting for any sound from within that would tell her the girl was awake.

Once, when she opened the door noiselessly, she found Topsy dozing in the chair beside the window and marvelled once again at the capacity of nurses in general for hard work and an ever-cheerful disposition. Surely, she mused, they must be born and not made!

Topsy's patient had not stirred, but even Ruth could see that she was sleeping naturally now. She closed the door with a sigh of relief, thinking that it remained only to wait for Noel's verdict when he came home some time after six o'clock.

Wondering why this case should suddenly have come to mean so much to her, she saw her brother's tall figure approaching from the direction of the hospital and glanced hastily at the clock; it was a full hour before his usual time for returning and she knew that anxiety about his new patient must have brought him.

"How is she?" he asked without preliminary. "I thought I would pop over and have another look at her."

"She appears to have been sleeping quite naturally most of the afternoon," Ruth told him. "Nurse Craven has been with her, and there has been no sign of complications."

He nodded, pausing by the closed door of the sitting-room, his face gravely thoughtful as he turned over a possible suggestion in his mind, but he went on into the room without communicating his thoughts to his sister, and Ruth turned back to the kitchen to prepare his evening meal.

She was peeling potatoes when Sara Enman appeared at the back door for the second time that day

"I've just come off duty," she explained, "and I wondered if there was anything I could do for you. About the girl, I mean," she added when Ruth looked puzzled. "Has Noel notified the police yet?"

"I don't know." Ruth felt vaguely irritated by the question for some unknown reason, wishing, almost, that Sara had stayed away. "He's with her now, as a matter of fact. I suppose he'll want to check up on her reactions as soon as she returns to full consciousness."

16

"There's a police surgeon to do that sort of job," Sara returned sharply.

"Oh! Tim won't mind!" Ruth smiled. "Anyway, I believe he's still away in London."

She thought of Tim Wedderburn, slow, stolid, not given to a quick decision, but universally liked wherever he went. They called him Doctor Watson even to his face, and he laughed quietly at their joke and went on doing his job slowly but surely.

"That doesn't exactly make Noel responsible for all the police cases that come in while he's away," Sara remarked dryly "He's far too busy to be bothered with routine stuff like this, and I understood he was operating this afternoon"

"Yes," Ruth said, "but he must have got through early. He came in just before you did."

For the first time in their long acquaintance she was finding it difficult to understand Sara thinking of her unexpected visit as bordering on interference, but that was unreasonable where an old friend was concerned. Ever since her recent illness small details had been apt to take on undue importance, and she made up her mind to speak to Noel about it whenever a suitable opportunity presented itself. A tonic or something was probably all she needed.

"Has she been sleeping all this time?" Sara asked, still determined to pursue the one subject which interested her. "I wonder what line Noel proposes to take. I would suggest sodium pentothal. You get a lot out of them that way."

"The 'truth drug'," Ruth mused. "It always seems—rather cruel to me, dragging a person's secrets from them ruthlessly like that, perhaps against their will."

"One has to be ruthless in our profession on occasion," Sara remarked, examining her well-kept fingernails with minute attention. "Especially with the criminal classes. People who are trying to hide something, for instance, don't react normally to the usual methods."

Ruth flushed. Could Sara be suggesting that the girl she had picked up on the moors was a criminal? Briskly she thrust the suggestion aside.

"Noel expected that there might be a report of an accident when he phoned the police," she said, "but I haven't had time to ask him what he has done. I'm hoping he'll stay over for a meal and not go dashing back to work till all hours without a bite," she explained as she turned to put the potatoes on the electric cooker. "Will you stay, Sara?" she invited. "There's quite enough for four."

"That girl would be far better over in the wards," Sara said decisively, as if she could not let the subject of Ruth's protégée drop even to answer her invitation. "I can't stay this evening," she went on regretfully. "I've got a pile of corrections to wade through, test papers and the usual reports to check. Matron leaves almost everything like that to me these days," she complained. "She takes it for granted that I live only for my work, as she does."

"Never mind!" Ruth consoled. "You'll disillusion her one of these days!"

She was not quite sure what she meant by that, she mused, as she watched Sara walk away in the direction of the nurses' home. Perhaps she meant that Sara would get married quite soon. She had done remarkably well in her chosen profession, rising to the position of ward sister and senior sister with amazing rapidity, and she was not quite thirty, but Ruth knew that she would never let professional advancement stand in the way of marriage.

If Ruth had automatically expected Noel to marry Sara one day, she had kept that to herself, too, and her brother's confidences had certainly never run to the subject of marriage, with Sara or anyone else.

Ruth waited for him in the dining-room and she saw him come towards her across the hall with the same thoughtful expression that had been in his eyes when he had first come in.

"Ruth," he questioned, coming to the point immediately, "could you possibly cope with a patient in the house for a day or two?"

She looked beyond him to the half-open door of the sitting-room.

"You want to keep her here under constant observation?" she surmised.

He nodded.

"She can have the spare room for as long as you think fit," Ruth agreed without the slightest hesitation. "I won't mind a bit."

"It will mean a good deal of extra work for you, cooking meals and that sort of thing," he warned. "If there's any nursing to be done, of course, we can call in help from the hospital."

"Will she be able to take a normal diet?" Ruth asked as he followed her into the kitchen. "There's some soup she can have now, and the remains of the chicken we had yesterday."

"There's nothing whatever wrong with her appetite." He was standing by the window looking out, not really seeing the scene in front of him but engrossed in the fascinating study of a new case. "Amnesia—the blotting out of memory—a forgetting," he mused. "Names, identity, home, have all been swept away behind the dark curtain." He turned abruptly. "Only those who have experienced it can possibly know the terrible desolation of not being able to remember," he said quietly.

"How will she react?" Ruth asked. "Now, I mean, while her mind still remains a blank?"

He looked up quickly.

"Don't make the mistake of imagining that this girl isn't capable of understanding in the ordinary way," he said. "To my mind, that is the tragedy of it all. The amnesiac looks completely normal, and he keeps his ordinary faculties. It's just that one particular part of his brain is sealed off—for a day, perhaps for a week or even for months. Sometimes operation is necessary. Traumatic amnesia is caused by a blow on the head and until the pressure is lifted surgically nothing will give back the memory of what went before."

"Months, you said?" Ruth asked sharply. "Perhaps even years. Do you think that——"

"I can't afford to think," he said almost as sharply. "Medicine is largely a process of elimination. We try this and that, rejecting where we have no success, trying some other way. Amnesia is quite often a shield behind which certain minds seek to avoid the unpleasant in life."

"Somehow I think this is different," Ruth said, "and so do you. That girl in there isn't an ordinary type. Her clothes are good and her hands and her hair are well cared for. She speaks nicely, too. There's something behind all

19

this, something deeply tragic, perhaps. I wish we could discover what."

The girl was sitting up on the settee, propped by cushions, her face slightly flushed, her eyes painfully questioning as they searched first Noel's and then his sister's.

"The police?" she asked huskily. "Have they found anything?"

Noel put down the tray and Ruth noticed that the handkerchief and powder compact were missing from the table. The purse was missing, too—all the girl's pitiful little possessions. Noel seated himself on the edge of the settee and watched her eat.

"Take your time," he commanded. "We're keeping you here with us for a day or two until we can establish your identity."

"Here?" There was relief in the blue eyes raised to his. "But I shouldn't impose myself on you like this. You don't know who I am. I don't even know my own name!"

"We are going to try to find that out," Noel said gently, but with a firmness Ruth knew of old. "I'm wondering about this," he added when she had finished the soup. "Will you need it? It belongs to you."

He produced the handkerchief and powder compact, and the girl put out her hand to take them, her brow still puckered as she examined the scrap of linen with the embroidered name uppermost.

"Anna," Noel said, and waited.

There was no doubt that the name struck a chord somewhere, but it failed to bring the full response he had optimistically hoped for, and he left it for the present.

"Anna will do as well as any other name just now," he said. "It has been accepted as a matter of course," he explained to Ruth as he stood up, "so that it quite possibly does belong to the past. It is not violent enough, however, to shock the senses completely and produce a stronger reaction. You might follow up the embroidery line, by the way. Tomorrow will do. See if she did that sort of thing, either as a hobby or as an actual means of earning a living."

He turned to his patient again, feeling her pulse and nodding his approval, and when he had gone from the room Ruth went forward to the settee.

"You remember me?" she asked, and was relieved beyond measure when the girl smiled quite naturally.

"Of course! You were the lady who helped me on the moor."

"My brother is doing all he can to help, too," Ruth said. "He understands this thing so well."

"Yes," the girl said, her eyes lowered to the tray she held across her knees, "he is very kind."

"We're going to call you Anna," Ruth said. "It's the name worked on your handkerchief, so we feel that it must be yours."

"Yes, it is my name," the girl said with a conviction which sounded helpful. "I feel that it is something I know, something I've been used to all my life."

"Every little thing helps, all those little details adding up to a whole," Ruth encouraged cheerfully. "Do you think you can manage the remainder of your dinner alone, and I will go and help my brother to his?"

She found Noel standing by the table in the dining-room with a pre-occupied look in his eyes.

"She is quite prepared to accept the name Anna," she said. "It must be her own, because she feels that she has lived with it all her life."

"She's married, by the looks of things," said Noll. "There's a ring on the third finger of her left hand. I wonder," he added suddenly, "if that might help."

"By the markings, you mean? I dare say it might."

"She seems so young," she reflected aloud. "Too young to be married and have come to this because of it."

"That may not be the idea at all," her brother pointed out restlessly. "We're only surmising at present, and I hope to heaven we're wrong in that respect. I've seen far too much of that sort of misery in my time."

His answer had been emphatic, and she knew that he could not find it in his heart to blame Anna beforehand for a marriage that had come unstuck.

CHAPTER TWO

EVEN IN THE corridors of the hospital, where accident and death walked hand-in-hand with every day, the story of the mysterious stranger held the attention of doctors and nursing staff alike. Anna's past was still a mystery after twenty-four hours of country-wide investigation had passed.

She sat up in bed, pressing her hands closely over her face.

"If I could only *think*!" she said aloud. "But I can! I can think, and that's the most dreadful part! The truth is that I can't *remember*!"

She turned at a slight sound near the door, to find Ruth standing there with a concerned look in her eyes.

"If you feel well enough," she said, "my brother thinks you might get up. It's a lovely day, and we could go into the garden."

Anna slipped down between the sheets, drawing the bed-clothes up under her chin.

"Does he want me to see the police?" she asked.

Ruth crossed to the bed, sitting down on the edge of it.

"Anna," she said gently, "whatever my brother asks you to do will be for the best. Please try to believe that and trust him. He does not intend to hand you over to the police unless they insist. In a small place like Glynmareth we work very much together and you are still in need of a certain amount of medical attention. Even if the police had picked you up yesterday you would probably have been brought to the hospital for my brother's verdict."

"But not here—to you." There was deep gratitude in the girl's voice now. "I should have been taken to the hospital and treated like any other patient instead of being cared for like this in your home. Don't think I am not grateful for that, and for all your other kindnesses. I know that I shall never be able to repay you."

"That's all right," Ruth assured her, smiling down into her eyes. "If we can give you your memory back it will be sufficient reward for anything we might be doing now."

"People in your profession give a great deal to their work," Anna remarked haltingly. "And you are all so kind. Nurse Craven, for instance, and your brother. They seem to understand so well how I feel, the emptiness, the terrible sense of frustration that all the concentration in the world can't wipe out."

"You mustn't worry too much about that side of it just now," Ruth advised kindly. "There are apparently so many things to be done in a case like yours that there's very little room for despair. My brother would like you to meet a colleague of his," she went on carefully, introducing the subject almost casually and trying to control the sensitive flush which invariably rose to her twin cheeks whenever Dennis Tranby's name was mentioned. "Dennis Tranby is his name and he's our local G.P. Noel and he are very good friends and quite often they work out their cases together."

Half an hour later she came downstairs, her hair brushed to a shining red-gold mane, her face lightly dusted with powder. She looked so vastly different from the bedraggled creature of the day before that Ruth stared at her for a moment in surprise, and then she realized the tremendous effort the girl was making, the desperate striving for normality which produced a courage all its own.

"I'm going to take our tray out on to the lawn," she intimated. "There's a nice sheltered spot over by the rose trellis where we can have a meal in comfort, and you can watch me pick the gooseberries afterwards!"

A vivid smile lit the girl's eyes.

"I could help with the gooseberries, couldn't I?" she suggested. "I—I must have done that sort of thing before ——"

"I'll make a tart with the first picking," Ruth decided quickly. "There won't be enough, just at first, to make jam."

"Yes," Anna agreed vaguely, groping again in the past. "It must have some connection for me—a garden like this, picking fruit in season, all the things you do as a matter of course. Perhaps I did this sort of thing once." She stood by the open door, surveying Ruth's garden with the pain of a deep longing in her eyes, the trim lawn and the neat borders, and the thick berberis hedge that closed them in and made a screen between them and the nurses' home across the way. "Will I ever know?" she breathed passionately. "Will it ever be any different for me?"

"Of course it will!" Ruth spoke lightly to banish that look "Will you carry the tray for me and I'll scrounge round for some more biscuits?"

Anna went down the short path with the tray in her hands, thinking how peaceful it was in the garden, warm and sunny and sheltered, shut off from the rest of the world and the world's problems.

23

At the end of the path she came to a narrow stream, its banks stepping down in a small rockery where purple arabis spilled its wealth of color over the stones and lay reflected in the cool water. She could imagine Ruth spending much of her day here, tending the plants or just sitting with her sewing, and perhaps Noel Melford found time to come there, too.

She thought of the doctor with a sudden intensity, aware that he was the king-pin in her problem, that his keen, analytical brain was the means by which she might return to normality, and her pulses began to beat more quickly at the thought. If anyone could help her he could. His sure, cool approach of the evening before had given her the confidence she needed to fight this thing, and she felt that he would not let go unless he believed the struggle was irretrievably lost.

"Hullo!" A shadow had fallen between her and the sun, and she turned to find him standing on the path above her, hands thrust deeply into his trouser pockets, a whimsical smile curving his handsome mouth "It's certainly an encouraging sign to find one's patient up and sun-bathing instead of lingering in bed!"

"It would have been malingering on a day like this!" she answered quickly, rising from the water's edge.

"Don't get up," he commanded. "You look—natural sitting there." His deep, almost gentle voice was in no way formal. "You like gardens, I see."

"Yours is beautiful," she said eagerly. "I've always loved flowers, and here they grow in such profusion."

"Yes?" he prompted.

"They must have grown somewhere—in a garden I knew."

Her voice had become troubled again and some of the light had gone out of her eyes.

"What sort of flowers?"

"Pinks, and fuchsia and rock roses——" She hesitated, her brow puckering with the effort she was making. "I seem to remember heather, too—great stretches of it, as purple as your arabis."

He was not looking at her directly, but he seemed to know all that was going on in her mind and he was leaving her to go on or give up as she willed.

"That's all," she said flatly. "I don't seem to get any further than that."

"You will," he told her confidently. "There's something I want to ask you, Anna," he continued after a pause, willing her to meet his eyes this time. "The ring you are wearing—your wedding ring. Will you let me take it from you for a time? You see, there may be some way of tracing the markings on it."

She drew back, fear sharpening her expression, a reluctance to part with the ring plain in her eyes. It held some meaning for her that was perhaps linked with fear.

Confusion rushed in upon her as she remembered that Noel Melford had called it her wedding ring, a veritable panic of confusion, and she could not answer him

She hesitated for barely a second, and then she held out her hand to him and he drew the wedding ring from her finger. He did not release her hand at once, however, holding it palm upwards in his to examine her finger for the tell-tale mark which a ring usually leaves on the soft flesh after a reasonable period of wear, but there was nothing to see, and his dark eyebrows went up a little in surprise. He made no comment on his findings, however, smoothing away her distress by talk of other things.

"We've had quite an event across the way this morning in the hospital maternity wing," he told her. "Quads, no less! Four girls as alike as peas in a pod and all weighing over three pounds."

"Poor Nurse Craven!" Anna smiled, forgetting her own problems. "She hoped she was going to have a quiet night!"

"Oh, Topsy wouldn't have missed it for the world! She's named them all already in her own inimitable way. One O'clock, Two O'clock, Three-five and Better-Late-Than-Never! Topsy makes us smile when sometimes we would be in despair," he declared.

"She did that for me yesterday, I think," Anna acknowledged gratefully. "I hope I shall see her again to thank her."

"I've no doubt you will," he said. "Which brings me to the second thing I want to ask."

"Yes?"

"I have a friend I should like to bring to see you."

"Doctor Tranby?"

He nodded, surprised that she should have heard of Dennis.

"Miss Melford told me this morning that you wanted me to see him," Anna said. "Is he an expert on—cases like mine?"

"Not exactly, but sometimes it is advisable to work on the theory that two minds are better than one," Noel explained. "Co-operation often produces miracles."

She raised clear, resolute eyes to his.

"Is that what we must hope for—a miracle?" she asked. "Is that what we need?"

"No." The grey eyes held hers, something in their depths demanding her absolute trust. "Miracles are not everyday things and I think we might be able to do without one in your case."

She bit her lip to stop its trembling.

"Why are you so wonderfully patient with me?" she asked. "We are perfect strangers and I may be—any sort of person."

He rose abruptly, thrusting her ring into his pocket, out of sight.

"I don't think you are—any sort of person," he said. "I'm a doctor, and I am trying to do my duty as I see it."

Ruth came out then, carrying the coffee percolator and an extra cup for her brother.

"You'll stay, Noel?" she asked. "You'll only go back to the hospital and drink inferior coffee there, anyway!"

"I'll settle for your particular brew any day!" he laughed, stretching his long length out on the grass at Anna's feet. "This may mean half an hour extra on the other end of my day, but it will have been well worth it!"

He accepted his cup from Ruth and was stirring a second spoonful of brown sugar into it when a short, thick-set young man came towards them round the gable end of the house, swinging a stethoscope in his hand.

"Anna, I want you to meet a great friend of mine, Doctor Tranby," he said, smiling down at her. "Dennis, this is Anna."

It could not have been said more naturally if they had met at a party, Anna thought, trying to conceal her nervousness because she knew that Noel demanded it, and because he had made everything so easy for her.

"You've heard our news, of course?" Tranby asked, including Ruth in his expansive smile. "Quads, no less! Of course, all the credit will go to the hospital now! We poor, long-suffering G.P.s don't come into it at all, though we do all the spade work!"

"I'll see that you get full mention in despatches this time!" Noel laughed. "You can even have your picture in the Press! They'll be on to it right away, I should think."

"Heaven forbid that I should ever adorn the pages of any newspaper!" Tranby groaned. "How would you like to have four squalling infants at once, Anna?" he asked.

"It would be something of a handful, wouldn't it," she agreed, "especially if one wasn't used to babies. But Nurse Craven will cope with them!"

"So you've already met our Topsy!" he grinned. "Wonderful girl, that, and a wonderful nurse into the bargain! Topsy isn't all fun and frolic, believe me. She can be as reliable as the next one in an emergency—probably more so than most." He turned back to Noel. "She tells me you're taking her into the theatre, old man. Good work! I'm perfectly sure she'll repay your confidence."

"Topsy's head is screwed on quite firmly," Noel returned, accepting a second cup of coffee from his sister which he drank down quickly with an eye on his watch. "One couldn't do much better than Topsy and I dare say Sara will come to appreciate the fact in time."

Sara! She would be on duty again, Ruth thought, going her rounds of the wards, ordering, checking up, seeing that everything ran smoothly and efficiently, waiting for Noel to come in to do the specials with her. Waiting for Noel . . .

Her eyes lingered on her brother's face, seeing him preoccupied with the girl she had brought into their home, and a sudden apprehension ran through her like a chill foreboding. She dismissed it instantly as foolish and theatrical in the extreme. Of course Noel would be interested in such a case as this one! It was all part of his work, a challenge to his skill, and she knew that both he and Dennis Tranby had always been deeply interested in amnesia.

Dennis was keeping the conversation going, realizing that Anna must be laboring under considerable strain at this meeting with yet another doctor, and Ruth knew that Noel would be grateful to him for his effort.

Dennis rose to his feet.

"Ah, well, this doesn't give the Press a fair chance, does it?" he demanded.

"Don't overdo it!" Ruth laughed. "Think of the proud father. No stealing all his thunder!"

"Fathers don't come into this at all!" Dennis informed her. "It's only mother and the quads who make the front page!"

The front page! Anna thought. Will they put my photograph in the newspapers, splashed all over the front page? The girl who has forgotten the past! The girl who does not know who she is!

"Don't worry," Noel Melford said, bending down to where she sat while Ruth walked towards the house with Tranby. "We won't do that to you—not if we can possibly help it. Photographs in the Press are a last resource."

Before she could thank him with any adequacy she was aware of someone coming towards them from the direction of the hospital, a tall figure in uniform who seemed to bear down upon them like some unrelenting fury.

"Noel," Sara Enman said in a peremptory voice, "there's an emergency. I had no idea you would be here. We've been looking for you everywhere. Matron thinks it is probably an acute appendix and you will want to operate immediately. Everything's ready—if you are."

It was then that she looked at Anna, her slate-grey eyes mirroring an emotion hard to define, but the other girl felt it like a rapier-thrust and looked quickly away.

Noel moved instantly and Sara smiled as professional intimacy drew them together.

"Give me five minutes to scrub up," he said. "I expect you have everything ready. I'll be back for lunch today, Ruth."

He went on ahead of Sara down the path, and Ruth came back to have a word with her.

"I had no idea Noel would be over here," Sara repeated almost on a note of reprimand. "We've got an acute waiting, but Noel can be quite sure that everything is ready to hand."

"Noel has implicit trust in Sara," Ruth said when the latter was out of earshot. "They have worked together for so long."

"Which doesn't make them two of a kind," Dennis Tranby reminded her dryly. "Women like Sara Enman have to be taken in small doses."

"I know you don't like Sara," Ruth smiled, "but she's my friend and I believe I know her quite well. She's terribly efficient——"

"Terribly is the operative word," Tranby agreed, "and no one will ever really know the Saras of this world. I'm sorry if I seem to be trying to disillusion you, my dear, but one is much better after having faced these things. People like our Sara are a law unto themselves."

"She can't possibly be as obscure as you make out," Ruth said almost testily, thinking that it seemed ridiculous to have to defend Sara like this. "She's quite open hearted, really, and so far she has been a good friend to me in time of need."

"A good friend, maybe, but no one will ever open Sara's heart," Dennis objected.

He sauntered back to where Anna still sat beside the stream, raising his cup to Ruth with light mockery in his hazel eyes, but Anna felt that these bantering exchanges veiled something much deeper between the doctor and Ruth.

"Anna," Dennis Tranby was saying, "would you like to see Glynmareth? A quick once-over, I mean. I'm going to the clinic to vaccinate some babies and you could come with me if you like."

Anna hesitated, curiously fearful of leaving Ruthr's garden and the security she had come to feel there, but there was much in Dennis Tranby's warm smile to reassure her.

"Take a coat with you," Ruth advised. "I'll expect you back for lunch at one."

"You're sure about this?" she asked when Anna had gone in search of her coat. "Taking her to the clinic, I mean?"

"Everything is in the nature of an experiment in these cases," Dennis answered seriously, adding wickedly: "I'd ask you, too, but two's company, you know! Besides, I'm sure you would refuse me in favor of gooseberry pie or some other vile concoction!"

"Since I was about to suggest that my 'vile concoctions' might be acceptable to you for lunch your remark has been decidedly ill-timed!" Ruth told him severely. "Please *don't* come back to lunch, Doctor Tranby!"

"This is too kind of you, Ruth!" he grinned. "Can you cope with four, though?" he added more seriously. "Since Anna is under observation—unobtrusively, of course—I'd like to come. The reaction I want at the moment," he went on, "is what she feels about being in a car—hence the invitation to go to the clinic with me. There might also be her reaction to children to check up on, suggesting whether she has any of her own, although we tried her out on that one with the mention of the quads—without success. Noel is going very carefully in this case. He believes that she may prove sensitive to too much direct questioning."

"I wonder who she really is, Dennis," Ruth mused. "She must be suffering all the tortures of the damned, not knowing."

Tranby led the way through the shrubbery to where his car stood parked at the end of the drive in full view of the windows of the nurses' home, and Anna saw a curtain drawn hastily aside in a room on the first floor and the flash of white apron behind it.

"Look!" Jill exclaimed as she gazed down into the doctor's garden. "There she is. She's getting into Doctor Tranby's car."

Behind her the slightly older Megan pinned her apron into place preparatory to going on duty and came to look over her friend's shoulder.

"Can't see her properly from this distance," she grumbled, "but you're certainly in for it if Matron ever finds out about that ring you put on her finger!"

Jill's face paled. Matrons moved on a different plane from Jill and upon them depends the whole chance of a girl's future career, but she was not prepared to let Megan get away with such a completely sweeping statement without attempting to defend herself.

"Why shouldn't I have put her ring on?" she demanded. "Maybe it had come off and she had put it in her pocket to keep from losing it because it was slack or something, but she ought to have had it on if she was going to die."

"Well, she didn't die," Megan retorted.

"What difference does it make? It was her ring."

"Maybe it wasn't her ring."

"You don't go round carrying a wedding ring that isn't yours!" Jill pointed out scornfully.

"Well, anyway, you had no right to put it on," her friend assured her, "though it's a bit late to go blurting out about what you did now. They'll be making inquiries about it by this time. I suppose, and if Matron knew what you'd *really* done, or Duchess Sara ever found out, you'd be for it! You'd never get any further than the probationer stage!"

With this final barbed shaft, a very new certificated nurse buckled her belt round her trim waist and rushed off downstairs, leaving a shaken and decidedly frightened probationer to digest all she had said.

And down on the tar macadam of the Melford's drive, Dennis Tranby was helping Anna into his car, well aware of the tremor which passed through her as he opened the door and she put her foot on the running-board. There was hesitation and fear in her clear eyes and her fingers gripped the top of the door as if she were trying to force something away from her.

There was little to be made of it, as far as Dennis could see at the moment, and almost instantly she pulled herself together and sat down beside him, stiffly upright, it is true, but completely composed.

Her delight when they reached the clinic was the natural reaction of someone who was genuinely fond of children in general, but it did not suggest any direct contact with a child of her own, and he drove her back to the villa at one o'clock with a decided sense of disappointment.

"Do you like travelling by car?" he asked as they neared the hospital gates.

"Not very much." She had answered him laboriously, holding her throat with one hand as if the words were being forced out and hurt her. "I could not bear to drive really fast."

"You can drive, then?"

"Oh, yes."

31

There had been no hesitation about her reply. The answer had come quite naturally to her, and suddenly she sat round in her seat to face him, saying in a strained undertone:

"Doctor Tranby, if—this can't be put right, if Doctor Melford fails to establish my identity, what am I to do? Shall I be able to work, to earn my own living? You know I can't go on accepting Miss Melford's kindness indefinitely, and I don't consider myself ill enough to be kept permanently in a hospital ward."

Her voice had trembled over the last sentence, her courage shaken a little at the thought of being dependent on medical treatments for the rest of her life.

"There's absolutely no reason why you should remain in hospital for any length of time," Tranby assured her, "but Noel wants a reasonable period to work this out. It can't be done in a hurry, and he has no hesitation about the ultimate result. Neither have I," he added as further conviction.

"And—in the meantime?"

"Wouldn't you be content just to let things go on as they are?"

"I should feel happier if I could do some sort of job."

"What can you do?" he asked casually.

Her chin quivered.

"I don't know what I am best qualified to do."

"Can you use a typewriter?"

"I'm not sure. It—seems a familiar sort of thing to me."

There was a silence as they drove up to the villa and stopped at the front door.

"Let things go just now," he advised, "and I'll have a word with Noel about the job later. He may be able to find you something to do in the hospital."

She flushed at the suggestion, not saying whether she would like the idea or not, and he got out and opened the car door for her.

Noel was crossing the hall when they went in and she murmured an excuse at sight of him, running upstairs to leave her coat.

"We've been to the clinic," Dennis explained.

"Any results?" Noel's eyes were keen, his interest sharpened immediately. "I know you hoped for something."

"There was definite reaction when she first entered the car, but she overcame it almost at once. It was quite definitely fear, though. She went through with the journey, however, and I discovered that she could drive, by the way. Will that help, do you think?"

"Everything we discover about her will help." Noel appeared preoccupied, deep in his own thoughts. "I've been in touch with the police again, but they have not had any inquiries yet about missing people. Tim Wedderburn is still away, and they've asked me to carry on in his place, so that more or less legalizes it!" He drew in a deep breath. "What a problem! I've sent the ring to London for investigation and possible identification, but it's a very old one and may have been passed on from someone else as a matter of sentiment, so we can't really expect too much from that quarter."

"Noel," Tranby said, "inevitably she's going to begin to feel her position here. A girl like that is certain to. Couldn't we, between us, find her something to do? It would be an alternative to sending her across to the wards," he added.

"No one would be unkind to her there," Noel said sharply, and Dennis thought that he might just as well have said, "No, one would *dare* be unkind to her there!"

"I know that, but does she really need to go?"

"I must keep an eye on the case. I'm responsible for her —responsible to the authorities, I suppose."

He said it distastefully, and Tranby nodded.

"I know how you feel, old man. That's why I am suggesting the job."

"What could she do?"

"You're overworked, and so am I," Dennis pointed out carefully. "We could both do with a competent secretary."

Noel considered the suggestion.

"It may be part of the solution," he agreed, at last, "to keep her employed while we grope about in this blind sort of darkness trying to discover who she is."

"I'll leave you to suggest the job to her," he said briefly. "I could do with her assistance at least two days per week."

When the meal was over Noel followed Anna out into the garden. "Anna," he said, "I'd like a short talk with you."

Her eyes met his apprehensively.

"You've found something?" she guessed.

He shook his head.

"No," he was forced to admit. "I don't expect it to come like that, Anna. I think you and I will reach the solution of this together. It may not be easy—I've never promised you that it would be," he warned, "but if you'll co-operate in every way you can I'll try to do it with the minimum of strain on your part. There's only one thing I want you to promise me," he went on gently, "and that is that you will come to me with the slightest detail of remembering. The most unimportant-seeming thing may be a key to a door in your mind that has been closed for the time being, so that we can't afford to neglect anything at all." He straightened moving a little way down the narrow path to stand staring at the shallow water at his feet as if he were about to ask some favor on his own behalf. "It would be much better if you found something to do while you are waiting," he said slowly, "something to occupy that other bright part of your mind that is perfectly normal, and—I need a secretary."

"Doctor Tranby mentioned that to you!" she exclaimed gratefully. "He has been so kind and helpful."

She paused, feeling that she would never be able to express in so many words what she felt about his own part in this tangle of her living, that she could not even begin to try, and something small and forlorn raised its head within her, something acknowledging the need for companionship and love.

"What do you want me to do?" she asked.

"A doctor has to handle a great deal of paper work these days," he explained, "and I find it downright irksome after a heavy day at the hospital. If you could get through that sort of thing for me and do the same for Doctor Tranby it would prove a tremendous saving of our time and patience! Ruth will show you what I mean," he continued. "She has been doing it for me, off and on, for almost a year, but she has so many other chores to attend to that I couldn't ask her to do it indefinitely."

"There's no reason why I shouldn't do it, why I should not try to repay you both in some way," she said eagerly, grasping at the chance to serve him. "And if I could help Miss Melford, too, while I remain here . . ."

Again she hesitated, the temporary nature of her sojourn standing between them like some kind of challenge, until he took her by the arm and said:

" 'Sufficient unto the day', Anna! Are you prepared to start work in the morning?"

She nodded eagerly.

"Whenever you like," she agreed, her eyes shining and every pulse stirring with the new experience of usefulness.

"There will be half an hour's 'third degree' before you start," he warned her lightly as they walked back to the house. "These questions we are submitting you to are absolutely necessary, Anna—you understand that? It is the only way we have of helping you."

"I understand," she said. The sun had gone beyond the black cloud of her forgetting again and her heart was darkened by misery. "I can't hope for everything to come my way—all at once," she acknowledged.

He left her with a brief smile, striding off round the end of the house to the hospital where, tomorrow morning, she would go to work, and suddenly she realized that he had taken her the first few steps towards freedom. She stood looking after him with untold gratitude in her eyes and a welling emotion in her heart which she did not attempt to name, knowing that, whatever had gone before, the memory of his kindness and understanding would always be in the future.

For a moment she could not bring herself to go back into the house even to help Ruth. The peacefulness of the garden, with its still water and the perfumes wafted on the summer breeze, claimed her, and her thoughts were still of Noel when she heard Dennis Tranby's car drive away and a gate slam somewhere close at hand.

Even then she did not turn immediately towards the house, and Sara Enman met her out there as she made her way along the shrubbery path to the villa.

There was a bright red spot of color high up on each of Sara's cheeks and her eyes were steel-grey and cold as they met the uncertain smile which Anna offered. She was very much the experienced nursing sister in her approach, however, cool, calculating and ruthlessly analytical.

"We really ought to have you over in the wards, you know," she observed. "You can't really expect Miss Melford to go on coping with stray patients like this, even if you do feel doubtful about us. Believe me, Doctor Melford has a heavy enough day's work without attending to an extra patient in his spare time."

Anna's cheeks flamed, but she tried to give Sara the credit of thinking only in terms of Noel.

"I will be coming over to the hospital," she said, conscious of a certain amount of satisfaction at being able to drop her bombshell. "But not as a patient. Doctor Melford feels that I am quite capable of holding down a job while I am under treatment and he apparently needs help with his paper work."

"The hospital has a qualified secretary to do that sort of thing, if only Noel would ask for her," Sara snapped. "Did you ask Doctor Melford to give you this job?" she asked suspiciously.

Anna hesitated.

"I asked Doctor Tranby," she confessed truthfully.

"Oh, Dennis Tranby!" Sara exclaimed scornfully. "The typical G.P.! Always interfering in things that can't possibly concern him and never getting on with his own work! He should learn to leave the hospital to those best qualified to cope with it." There was actual venom in Sara's voice now. "I suppose he passed your request on to Doctor Melford and Noel felt too sorry for you to refuse it."

Again Anna flushed.

"Doctor Melford did not say he was sorry for me."

She thought that she could not bear the idea of Noel Melford's pity, and believed that neither Ruth nor her brother had shown her anything but understanding. Pity, she felt, would have sounded the knell of hope.

"You must be rather a millstone round Noel's neck at the moment," Sara went on. "He had just got rid of a great deal of police work when Tim Wedderburn took over."

The word stung Anna, and she knew that Sara had mentioned the law deliberately, with all its subtle suggestion of something wrong in her past. She felt that she hated the older girl, but the real despair was not being able to remember, not being able to defend herself against any accusation. It came back to that a dozen times a day, really.

"I don't think either Doctor Tranby or Doctor Melford would have employed me if they hadn't needed my services or felt sure that I could do the work," she said stiffly and with a dignity she was far from feeling. "I can only do my best to justify their trust."

Sara turned on her heel with a small, articulate sound which might have meant anything, making her way into the house with a purposefulness which kept Anna where she was.

"I've just been talking to your Orphan of the Storm," she told Ruth maliciously, "and she has announced that she is taking over your job as Noel's secretary! Quick work, I should say, but I can't help wondering if Noel is entirely wise."

Ruth moved away from the window where she had been watching Anna in the garden, her hands clasped tightly in front of her, her kind mouth firm.

"Noel knows what he is doing, Sara," she said quietly.

"I sincerely hope so." Sara's lips twisted a little. "Have you noticed the absence of the wedding ring?" she went on smoothly. "That girl was wearing one yesterday, if I am not mistaken, and now she has taken it off. Could she have imagined that none of us noticed the fact?"

"I don't know." Ruth's voice rang out sharply in the quiet room. "But no matter what her reason has been for disposing of her ring, I'm quite sure it was not to deceive us."

Sara's eyebrows shot up.

"I sincerely hope your faith in her will remain justified," she murmured. "You were always much too trusting, Ruth."

"Maybe," Ruth answered easily enough, but the conversation seemed to have driven a small wedge between Sara and her, forcing them apart a little, and she was sorry. Ruth liked to keep her friends, but she also thought that she knew genuineness when she met it. Anna seemed to be genuine enough, and although the fact of the missing ring was odd, Ruth was quite sure that there would be some simple explanation of its removal.

CHAPTER THREE

THE LONG, TORTUOUS task of aiding Anna's recovery began the following morning in Noel's consulting rooms at the hospital, and in this respect he was quite ruthless. No stone was to remain unturned, no avenue unexplored. He set to work with a grim determination which surprised even Anna, who had been prepared for anything, throwing copies of half a dozen newspapers at her across his desk.

"Read through these and see if they mean anything to you," he commanded. "We may as well begin at the beginning."

While she read he worked at his desk without appearing to remember her at all, and as she turned page after page and no one item of news stood out for her to claim her interest over the others, which she supposed was what he wanted, she felt the old sense of hopelessness creeping over her and grew more nervous and restive with each passing minute.

Finaly he pushed back his chair and came towards her, his grey eyes steady on her flushed face.

"All right," he said, "don't make a labor of it. We've drawn a blank, so we're going to fold up the newspapers and go out." He turned back his cuff to look at his watch. "Slip across and borrow a hat from Ruth, and don't be any longer than you can help."

She obeyed him without question, although she could not understand why he should suddenly want her to wear a hat.

*　　*　　*　　*

Anna inspected Ruth's hat in the mirror, satisfied with what she saw apparently, because she was still smiling when she met Noel in the hall.

They drove swiftly down the tree-lined approach to the hospital and out through the south gates towards the edge of the town where a small chapel stood on a hill and several cars were already parked on the gravel sweep before the main door.

"We're getting out here," he told her as he pulled his own car in behind the others. "Don't worry about anything that may happen, Anna," he added. "'I shall be in charge and nothing can harm you."

It was strange the amount of comfort she found in that thought although she could not understand why he was taking her to a Welsh Methodist church at this time of day and on a Tuesday into the bargain. Then, as he led her swiftly down the aisle after a hurried consultation with someone at the door, she realized that they were about to witness a wedding.

Organ music filled the church, swelling to a final magnificent chord as they found a seat at the side of the aisle, in full view of the waiting bridegroom and the assembled guests, but the notes were no more than a dreadful avalanche of sound to Anna as she sat with bowed head, trying to restrain an almost overwhelming impulse to rise and run back down the aisle to the sunlit world outside. A feeling akin to claustrophobia clamped down on her senses and it seemed as if she was beating against bars in some narrow prison.

"I can't go through with it," she murmured. "I don't want to let you know, but I can't go through with it. It's not that my love has changed," she added in a breathless whisper, the words forced from her against her will and almost as if she were repeating a formula. "It's just that I don't want to be married . . ."

Noel Melford's fingers closed firmly over hers and somehow she knew that the words she had repeated were not her own. They had the hollow quality of an echo about them, an echo out of the past, but she could not nail them down to any memory. Her head was spinning round and her mind so confused by the impression she had received since entering the dim, cool chapel that she could no longer reason clearly. All she could feel was that desperate desire for escape, and then she knew that she could not escape because Noel Melford sat between her and freedom and his hand was firm and detaining on her arm.

During the ceremony, as the kindly old parson's voice suggested the full meaning of the marriage bond, Noel did not turn his head once to look at her. He appeared to be deeply engrossed by what was being said, his keen mind weighing each phrase, each turn of a sentence, to extract the fullness meaning from them, but when the happy couple followed the parson to the vestry and some of the guests made their way out to the porch with gaily colored bags of confetti, he led her out into the sunshine and straight to his waiting car.

He did not start the engine immediately, however, sitting with his arm along the steering wheel until bride and bridegroom appeared in the chapel doorway.

Anna's attention was riveted on the young couple, and Noel watched her as she sat still and erect, so still that she scarcely seemed to breathe at all. Then, slowly and painfully a single tear forced its way between her thick lashes and fell unheeded down her cheek.

As if at some given signal, he swung the car clear of the line of traffic, out beyond the chapel and onto the open moor. Anna was still staring straight ahead, eyes completely remote, seeing nothing of the road before them, until he drew up on the brow of the hill overlooking the Mareth valley and turned to look at her.

"What did you remember?" he demanded.

"The church," she gasped, and then she went on more slowly and more coherently: "When I first went in I wanted to run away."

"Why?"

"I wanted to escape, I think. I—don't think I wanted to get away from anyone in particular." She clasped her hands tightly in front of her. "Oh, it's so difficult to explain—to tell anyone——"

"It isn't difficult to tell me," he insisted. "Why did you want to leave the church?"

"I wanted to get away from something. It was like being shut up in a too-small room—closed away for life. I felt that I had been there before, that I had heard the organ playing like that before."

"For yourself?"

She passed a trembling hand over her forehead.

"I don't know. Perhaps it was personal, that feeling, but I can't be sure. I only know that I felt as if I were waiting for something dreadful to happen, that I had been there before and knew exactly what was coming, as one does in a dream."

"It often happens with the conscious mind, too." he explained, "but go on. What was it you were waiting for?"

"I can't remember that. I don't really know," she repeated. "It was like a great dark pall rolling towards me, blotting out everything—the altar, the man standing there, the music and the sunlight streaming in across the aisle. I

40

felt that I was going down the aisle and out at the church door—alone."

"What came after that?" He bent over her, willing her with all the force at his command to answer him. "Think, Anna! Think!"

"I can't!" She covered her face with her hands. "There isn't anything left now but the blackness and the emptiness."

There was a tense moment before he relaxed, leaning back against the cushioning to produce his cigarettes, his eyes narrowed in thought as they scanned the deep green valley ahead.

"Smoke?" he asked, proffering the case.

She took a cigarette clumsily, imagining her companion making a mental note of the fact that she had not smoked a great deal from the way she handled it, and suddenly she was able to relax.

"What a session!" she said unsteadily but without undue emotion. "How long before you give up altogether?"

"One doesn't 'give up' so easily as that," he assured her, inhaling deeply. "To stop trying would be to acknowledge defeat, and this effort is still in its infancy. D'you know," he added casually, "that hat is the emblem of the greatest day in my life! Ruth wore it at the graduation ceremony, and I can still see those two fantastic fully-blown roses bobbing for a vantage point in the middle of the hall. She had got herself a seat behind the fattest professor's wife imaginable who was wearing a veritable fruit-barrow on her head and evidently wouldn't give an inch!"

"What did Ruth do in the end?"

"She waved her programme so much that the fruit-barrow hat tilted forward and by sheer weight toppled into its owner's lap!"

They laughed as he started the car, and he thought with satisfaction that this was the second time in one day he had heard his patient laugh with complete spontaneity.

"I'm dropping you at the villa for lunch," he said, "and then you can go over to the hospital at two o'clock and put in a couple of hours' work to salve your conscience, if you like. You'll find a stack of filing to be stowed into that green metal cabinet next to the window in my room, and then you can take the draft of the report on my blotting-

41

pad along to the general office and have it typed. Anyone will tell you where our efficient secretary has her lair," he explained, "but don't expect her to come to the consulting room even if you ring a bell till Doomsday!"

"You're sure I won't get in the way?" Anna asked, thinking of her encounter with Sara the evening before.

"Nobody will worry about you," he assured her. "You will find you are in an isolated little world of your own in the east wing, since it is too cold for anything but the kitchens and the Superintendent's consulting rooms!"

"I'm sorry you're so badly treated!" she smiled. "Can nothing be done about it?"

"Strictly between ourselves," he grinned, "I should hate anything to be done about it! I like the idea of my splendid isolation and I rarely feel the cold."

She said quickly "Neither do I. It's warmer here, of course."

"Warmer?" he prompted. "Warmer than your home, Anna?"

She started, surprised that he should find something revealing in such an ordinary remark, and then she shook her head dismally.

"Oh, I wish I could give you some satisfaction, some kind of help when you are trying to do so much for me!" she cried.

"That will come." He looked neither disappointed nor impatient. "We must wait for it. I thought we had got somewhere in the church just now, but apparently not."

They had reached the hospital gates and he set her down on the drive, directing her to the side entrance before he left her. He was evidently not coming to the villa for lunch, and Anna hurried back to Ruth, wondering if there was anything she could do to help her. She felt so much indebtedness to both the Melfords that she imagined she would never be able to repay them, but Ruth would not even let her mention it.

"Noel is deeply interested in your case and that's the main issue," she said as they sat over their coffee. "Besides, you're evidently going to repay him in kind!"

"Doing the office work, you mean?"

"He loathes paper work," Ruth explained, "so you see if you can help him out there while he is treating you there's

42

no need to feel so very dependent on either of us. I've been doing it for him lately, but I must confess it has been rather an effort."

"He has said that I might start right away," Anna explained. "It will help keep my mind off—the other business."

"Sister Enman will be on duty when you go over to the hospital," she said instead. "If you feel strange at first, or there is anything you can't find, ask someone to take you along to her room and I'm sure she will put you right."

Anna thanked her for the suggestion, but she felt that she would not want to appeal to Sara Enman unless it was absolutely necessary. Sara had not shown any desire to be friendly even at the villa, so why should she suddenly change her attitude when they met in the hospital, which was her own particular sphere?

With a quickening pulse beat she covered the distance to the larger building, going in at the door marked "staff."

A young probationer came into view, halting on the stairs above her as if her presence there had almost shocked her into a cry of surprise.

"Could you tell me how I get to Doctor Melford's consulting rooms?" she asked, and Jill gulped and seemed to waken out of an unhappy dream.

"Upstairs, and first to your right," she directed. "That will bring you to the east wing." Jill hesitated, her cheeks flushing with a sudden impulse to confession, but all she managed was: "I helped when Miss Melford first brought you in. I hope you are better now."

Anna thanked her with one of her vivid, friendly smiles. "I think I must have been very faint with hunger and tiredness," she explained, "but I feel much better now, thank you."

"Is there anything wrong, Nurse?"

The voice was one Anna knew and she drew back, leaving the little probationer to answer Sara's question.

"No, Sister. I'm just going off duty. Is there anything you want me to do before I go?"

"Only to remember that the corridors are not the place for idle gossip!" Sara turned the bend in the staircase, silenced by what she saw, and Anna looked upwards with a small, sinking feeling in her heart. Sara looked so competent and so cruel as she stood there in her blue dress with her stiffly starched apron and cap, bristling with efficiency, and Anna knew now beyond doubt that Sara did not like her.

"You can go, Nurse," Sara told the waiting Jill without so much as looking in her direction, "but please remember that even when a nurse is off duty she is expected to behave with dignity and decorum, especially in the precincts of the hospital."

"Lecture three, page five!" Jill muttered as she scuttled away, and Anna was able to meet Sara's eyes with a smile in her own.

"It was really my fault that we were talking on the stairs," she explained. "I asked the way to Doctor Melford's consulting rooms."

Surprisingly Sara smiled back.

"Come along," she offered, "I'll take you. One mustn't be too lenient with these beginners, you know, or they will take advantage. Discipline always turns out the best nurses, just as it produces the best soldiers. I don't think Doctor Melford is in his rooms at present, but we can go along and find out."

"He won't be in until late," Anna explained to Sara's apparent chagrin. "He gave me quite a lot of work to do which will keep me busy for most of the afternoon, but I'm sure I shall be happier working."

"Possibly," Sara acknowledged with a strange inflection in her voice that was difficult to define. "But it would be much better all round, wouldn't it, if you discovered your identity? Your people must be wondering about you, to say nothing of your husband!"

The last word startled Anna, sending the hot color flooding into her cheeks. She had forgotten she was married since Noel Melford had taken her wedding ring away to send it to London in an effort to trace its origin, but now the fact was being thrust at her by Sara in no uncertain manner. The action was quite deliberate, yet she could not guess at Sara's reason for accentuating her marriage.

"It's all so—difficult to imagine," she said haltingly. "I can't remember a wedding at all. Even in church this morning, the ceremony meant nothing personal to me. Doctor

Melford thought it might, and probably that is why he insisted I should go."

"I suppose Ruth took you."

Whether it had been statement or question, Sara waited as if she expected some sort of answer.

"Doctor Melford took me himself," Anna told her. "We went in his car and sat in a side pew during the ceremony, but evidently it didn't bear fruit."

They had come to a white-painted door at the end of a long corridor and Sara paused before it, her fingers closing tightly over the handle.

"Has it never occurred to you that you might be wasting a considerable amount of Doctor Melford's time?" she asked icily. "You don't appear to be making progress or even to be making any concentrated effort at remembering, but perhaps that doesn't suit your purpose."

"How can you saw a thing like that!" Anna cried, You can go out of this hospital and know yourself to be among friends who love you and know all about you, who will go back down through the years in your company— remembering; but I can't do that. I have no past, and no friends who can remember for me, so how can you go on believing that I am not making an effort to free myself?"

"Simply because I do not think you were free before," Sara told her cruelly. "You are married. There seems little doubt about that, at least, but it may be that you were unhappily married and your subconscious finds this an excellent way out."

"How could you believe such a thing!" Anna gasped.

"It may be the truth," Sara pointed out mercilessly. "In any case, I should concentrate on that line of mental effort if I were you. It might get you somewhere."

She opened the door, ushering Anna into a trim, business-like apartment with a desk set at an angle beside one of the windows, several easy chairs and a high couch spread with a blanket under a convenient wall light.

"You'll find the office through there." Sara indicated a second door. "It will probably feel cold to work in," she warned. "I've told Noel several times that he would do better to leave his paper work to the girls downstairs who are capable of dealing with it, and I dare say he will

45

waken up to the truth when you begin to have difficulty with the medical terms," she prophesied as she swept out.

"She's not going to make life pleasant for me," Anna thought, "but if I can please Noel by the work I do I won't care."

Noel! Strange how easily the name had come to her lips, strange how inevitable it had seemed that they should be drawn together in that shadowy church on the windy hill! Could there have been someone named Noel in the past— a friend perhaps—a lover?

She found the filing he had mentioned and set to work. Everything was dovetailed to perfection, stored away for future reference—case histories, treatments, interviews, results, they were all there against the day when they might be needed again.

Working for him like this was to think of him constantly, to wonder about him and his career, but it was also to think about the man himself. How strong he was, and how patient! She would not have had the courage to come here to work for him if she had not been quite sure of his patience.

Towards five o'clock Dennis Tranby put his head round the door of the outer room while she was collecting the pencilled notes of a report from Noel's desk. He looked surprised to see her, but he said approvingly enough:

"Quick work! Noel doesn't believe in wasting time, of course. How have the first afternoon's chores gone down?"

"I've enjoyed doing them," Anna told him. She liked Dennis Tranby and he gave her confidence. "I only hope I have not made too many mistakes with the filing."

"I always thought filing was child's play until I tried it for a spell," he confessed. "It has an absolutely hypnotic effect on me. I go on doing it in my sleep!"

"So long as you do sleep."

"Don't you?"

"Not very well. But then, I had slept a lot during the afternoon."

"Noel would rather you slept naturally than give you something to put you over, but if it gets too bad you must tell him. What did you do this morning?" he asked.

"Doctor Melford took me to church. There was a wedding in the little chapel on the edge of the moors"

"I see." He stood sorting through some papers. "I've just come back from a nasty case," he informed her out of the blue. "An accident. Car overturned—glass flying everywhere and blood all over the place."

She flinched as she listened and then she covered her face with her hands and gave a little shuddering moan.

"Oh—please, no!"

He swung round the end of the desk and came to her.

"I'm sorry, but that almost seemed to ring a bell, didn't it?" He caught her elbow, propelling her towards a chair. "Sit down for a minute and try to think back," he urged kindly. "Were you in a car, Anna, and was that car involved in a smash? Did you hit another car? Can't you remember—travelling fast or something, travelling along a road and then—smash, and darkness of a sudden? Was that something like what happened, Anna? You ought to know."

"Yes," she muttered from behind her hands, "I ought to know, but I can't remember a car that crashed. I should have been hurt in that case, shouldn't I?" she added logically.

"There is superficial bruising on your thigh and your left arm, and another bruise on your head. Can you remember nothing about it?"

"Nothing."

There was such abject misery in her voice that he left it at that, and she turned towards the door as it opened and Noel Melford came in.

He looked from one to the other questioningly, and Anna passed him and went into the inner room.

"I wonder how she shaped out this afternoon by herself," he said, sitting down at his desk and moving the letters that had come by the late post to one side. "I gave her a fairly comprehensive intelligence test before I went out and she seems to have coped with it all right." He glanced down at the empty filing tray on the desk. "I had very little fear of her failing in that respect," he added, "but it's a routine check up and it is best gone through."

"What happened in church this morning?" Dennis asked.

"She told you about that, did she?" Noel smiled. "Well, there was a certian amount of reaction during the actual ceremony and the service itself seemed to mean something to her, but on the whole it was an unhappy reaction." He paused, examining the tips of his fingers with the utmost concentration for a moment. "One could deduce from it that she had been unhappily married," he added slowly. "I'm quite convinced that she is not the type who would take her marriage vows lightly, hence the suggestion of being trapped inside the marriage bond. A subconscious suggestion that, by the way."

"And five minutes ago, just before you came in just now, I had more or less got her reacting to the suggestion of an accident," Tranby said "Could it be that there was some sort of accident on the honeymoon journey resulting in the condition in which Ruth found her?"

"That could be a theory," Noel agreed, "but why no car for miles around on the moor roads? We can't rush at this too quickly, old man," he cautioned. "It's no ordinary case —or so I feel."

His friend gave him a brief, searching scrutiny.

"What now?" he asked.

"I'm not quite sure. The ring is still a possibility, of course, though I'm not expecting a great deal from it."

"What about drugs?"

"You know what I feel about sodium pentothal," Noel said abruptly. "One doesn't always get the best results that way, and nine times out of ten it leads nowhere. I fancy we'll get the truth from Anna without using too many drugs—the truth as far as she remembers it."

"And when we get that far, what then?"

"Hypnosis, perhaps. We'll see how things go first, in the course of the next few days. I always believe in giving a patient plenty of time to react normally."

"And in the meantime?"

"She stays on with Ruth, I think. I feel that she would not react over here in the hospital quite so well."

Tranby grunted.

"You know best," he agreed. "You mean to let her go on working here, though?"

"She isn't exactly in the hospital up here," Noel pointed out. "Her work will be isolated from the wards. It will also give me the opportunity of keeping an eye on her, and when she is with you you can do the same. You know what to look for."

"I hope I shall find nothing more than that," Tranby observed laconically as he turned away from the desk. "The Big White Chief's word is absolute law, of course!"

Noel laughed.

"I hope I haven't been to autocratic," he said, "and apparently my word isn't absolute law to you on occasion! I told you, I think, that little Mrs. Whittacker in Ward C was in no fit state to be left alone, but you apparently thought otherwise. She was found wandering about the grounds in her night attire at two o'clock this morning, determined to pick flowers."

"Good lord! I'm sorry, Noel," Tranby apologized swiftly. "I had no idea it was quite so bad as that, and I understood she slept like a log once she was safely tucked up for the night."

"The old lady's afraid of life just now like a little child afraid of the dark, and she seek reassurance in familiar places. I don't think that's the position with Anna, by the way," he added, as if he could not quite let the other case out of his mind. "She wants life; she's even eager to embrace it, but there's this business of the unremembered past holding her back." He paused, his brow furrowed in thought. "Anna! Anna *what?* It won't be complete, Dennis, until I know the whole story. She's helping all she can."

Tranby took out his case and offered his friend a cigarette.

"I'd relax a bit, Noel, if I were you," he advised. "You've been steadily overworking yourself these past few months, piling job on job, and here you have another tough nut to crack. Why not send the girl over here to the hospital and let Tim Wedderburn handle the whole thing when he gets back?"

"I'm hoping we'll have it cleared up before Tim gets back," Noel returned shortly. "Days—even hours—are precious time lost to anyone in Anna's condition."

"Yet," Dennis pointed out, "when it's all over and she gets her memory back she won't remember any of this. That's the way it goes, isn't it?"

"Mostly." Noel strode to the window and looked out. "A complete forgetfulness of all that happened in between," he added from that distance.

Dennis Tranby could not see his face, but he imagined a certain flatness in his friend's voice which was unusual. He did not challenge it, however, nor did he make any further reference to Anna's future.

As he observed to Ruth later in the day: "Noel seems decidedly touchy about this case, but I always thought he liked something he could get his teeth into."

"You don't think Noel might be—attracted by her?" Ruth asked uneasily. "So soon, I mean. She's hardly been here a day yet, and we know so little about her, really. I'd never forgive myself for bringing her home if that happened."

"Trust a woman to think of something like that!" Dennis chided "Good heavens, old girl, what makes you even think of such a thing at this stage? Noel is simply interested from a medical point of view, just as I am."

"I hope so," Ruth said. "But confess, Dennis, that there's something about this Anna that turns your heart over, not just with pity, either. Something that makes you want to try and try till you can free her from her bondage—something so essentially Anna that I find it difficult to put a name to!"

"The Greeks may have had a word for it!" he suggested lightly.

"I don't mean just sex attraction! It goes far deeper than that," Ruth retorted. "She's the sort of person one *cares* about, Denny, and you know it!"

"Yes," he admitted, "I think I do, but you needn't worry about Noel for all that. He'll know what to do."

"I hope so," Ruth said. "Oh, I hope so!"

CHAPTER FOUR

WHEN ANNA LOOKED back on that first week under Noel Melford's roof she could only marvel at the rapidity with which it had passed. Day followed day without any change in her condition, yet there was a normality about everything which made her almost forget that she herself was not normal. The wealth of friendship and understanding that surrounded her was more than any one person's due, she told herself, and that it should be offered so unquestionably to a stranger made her more than ever convinced of the Melford's worth.

She would have gone to the ends of the earth to serve Ruth, and although her feeling for Noel was not so easily recognizable it was equally genuine.

Dennis Tranby came in for his own share of her gratitude, as he shared everything at the villa, and she was more than thankful that she had proved useful to him. The pile of statistics on his desk had dwindled as rapidly as that which had distressed Noel, and she had extracted him from a vertitable maze of returns which he declared meant nothing to him.

The only person in her small, new world she could not like was Sara Enman, and Sara seemed determined to dog her footsteps everywhere she went. In the guise of a patronizing sort of friendship she took Anna about the town when Ruth was not available, introducing her to various social activities so that she might report to Noel on his patient's reactions to rural interests.

"Take her to the Women's Institute," Noel had advised Ruth. "Take her anywhere and see that she mixes. I think she's country bred, but one can never be quite sure, and even a casual contact at a women's meeting might bear fruit."

Ruth had agreed, but it had been Sara who had taken Anna to her first public function.

"It's going to be rather awkward introducing her," Sara had pointed out, "especially now that she's not wearing that wedding ring of hers any more. I really wonder why she took it off. I wonder what reason she had."

Noel, who had come in to snatch a hurried cup of tea, looked across the room at her with cold censure in his eyes.

"I removed Anna's ring," he said briefly. "I thought it might provide some evidence of her identity, so I sent it to London. Unfortunately it doesn't seem to be helping much at present."

Sara had flushed scarlet at his tone, but she rose to come and stand with one slim foot on the raised hearth, her arm resting along the low mantelshelf.

"Just what do you think about all this, Noel?" she asked in her most professional voice. "We're all interested in this case, you must know that, but do you really think you are

51

doing the right thing by keeping that girl here in an atmosphere which may be entirely false to her?"

He looked back at her steadily.

"I'm afraid I don't quite understand you, Sara," he said.

"It's easy enough." Her temper was only just held in check. "You and Ruth have taken her under your wing, you have been amazingly kind to her, out of pity, and any girl who had never known security before would be a fool to throw that away too quickly, even for the sake of remembering!"

"What makes you think that Anna has never known security?" he asked, willing to test her theory. "What makes you so sure?"

"Her eternal gratitude, I suppose! She is never done singing your praises and telling everyone all that Ruth has done for her." Sara drew in a quick breath and said what she had meant to say in the beginning. "She may be making a complete fool of you, Noel."

"Not necessarily." His voice was ice-cold now with the cutting quality in it which she had heard once or twice before when someone had been guilty of a grave indiscretion and had brazened out their justification in his presence. "It could mean a return to security after a period of nervous upheaval. Perhaps you haven't thought of it in that light, but the fact alone might lull the senses for a time, causing the subconscious to lie dormant and not make any effort at remembering. I'm quite sure you will agree with me, once you've thought of it."

Sara bit her lip, aware of his professional approach to her at that moment as she might have been aware of death itself. She was the nurse, the competent, trained individual who should understand the case they were discussing—nothing more! And Sara was determined to be so very much more.

"If you'll pardon my saying so," she persisted, "I think you are going quite the wrong way about things in this. Matron and I are both of the opinion that she would be much betetr in the hospital under complete supervision *all* the time, but of course we have no real right to question your decisions."

"No," he agreed frostily. "I'm rather surprised at such an attitude from Matron, as a matter of fact, when she knows the circumstances, but it really doesn't make me ready to change my mind in this instance. Anna will continue to stay here in the meantime, unless the police interfere."

A small, inarticulate sound from the door drew their attention to Anna standing there ready to go out, her pale face giving no indication that she had heard what they were saying, and Noel rose abruptly to pour himself another cup of tea, drinking it as it came, as if the physical sensation of the scalding liquid in his throat would alleviate some inner strain which could not be so easily dealt with.

"Ready?" Sara inquired, surveying Anna from head to foot and adding as they went out together: "I suppose this will be another false trail leading us nowhere. Noel insists that we explore every avenue in order to help you," she added, venting some of her pent-up anger on the object of the controversy. "It must be a great strain on him, your case lingering on like this when he expected to clear it up in an hour or two."

"I wish there was something I could do about it," Anna said unhappily. "But he refuses to let me go to the hospital as a patient, and I really believe he feels that I will react best if given my freedom."

"You know, of course, that you are not free now," Sara returned cruelly. "You can't be allowed out alone, you have to be watched everywhere you go in case of the necessary reaction. We're all forced to act gaoler in our turn."

Anna flushed sensitively.

"I don't think Miss Melford and Doctor Tranby think of it that way," she said, disliking Sara more than ever.

"And what do you think Doctor Melford feels?" Sara demanded. "Since Ruth picked you up and brought you here he's never been able to take a moment's free time, never been able to give himself a respite from work. You are his constant problem, his personal problem, since Ruth made the initial mistake of bringing you here instead of taking you to the hospital for treatment. And—forgive me for pointing this out so bluntly—but you have been trading on that, you know. You know you have their pity."

"Oh, no!" Anna looked horrified at the very thought, and then the spirit which had carried her through the ordeal of those first dreadful hours lifted its head again.

"That isn't true!" she flashed, angry at last. "I don't want anybody's pity, least of all Doctor Melford's. It's not because he is sorry for me that he has taken an interest in this case, and I know I'm just a case to him, nothing more!"

"So long as you understand that," Sara said with a thin-lipped smile. "Noel will perhaps be able to do something for you."

Anna spent a miserable evening, commiserated with by well-meaning, motherly women whom Sara let into her 'secret' and pressed on all sides to remember this or that form of procedure when nothing was even remotely familiar to her. Even the demonstrator who stood behind her rows of excellently preserved fruits began to appear like an ogre, smug and self-satisfied, in the sudden tension of suppressed nerves which was the inevitable aftermath of her scene with Sara, and at last she could not stand the strain.

"Do you mind if I don't wait for supper?" she asked. "I feel suffocated in here. It's so warm——"

"Leaving just before supper is hardly the sort of gesture that will make us popular with the catering committee," Sara observed angrily, "but I shall have to chance that."

"I don't want you to come—please!" Anna said in an undertone. "You must stay, Sara. It isn't fair of me to drag you away from your supper. Everything looks so nice." She felt as if she were speaking against time "I can quite easily find my own way home."

She was scarcely aware of what she had said, hardly conscious of having used a word which had once meant much to her and could even now tug at her heartstrings in spite of the fact that she had no real home. People were sorry for her, of course, and had offered her a temporary refuge —Ruth and Noel Melford had done that, but she had no longer the right to accept it—not when Noel considered her a burden.

She became aware of Sara hesitating, not rising immediately to her feet when she got to hers, and suddenly she knew that she was going to be allowed to go out alone.

"Please don't come," she repeated. "You must want to stay with your friends."

"It isn't really very far to the villa. Sara was watching her closely. "And it isn't so very dark yet."

Anna left her without a backward glance, feeling like some wounded animal making its escape from the killer—desperately trying to put distance between itself and a relentless enemy at all costs.

Subconsciously she quickened her pace, breathless, almost in her desire to get away. It was not only the thought of Sara that goaded her, but some inner voice urging her to free Noel Melford from the responsibility of caring for her, and she felt that it must be obeyed. To delay her escape seemed fatal, with all sorts of complications besetting her path once Noel and Ruth discovered her intention, and so she turned off the main highway through the town and made her way towards the moors.

Blindly she walked on until the last of the houses had disappeared in the valley behind her, and the world before her seemed curiously empty and cold. The sun had set in a turquoise band along the western skyline, throwing the dark shadows of the northern mountain ranges into gaunt relief, and all life seemed to be drawn down into the shelter of the valleys. The remoteness of her chosen road became suddenly frightening until a car flashed past, and then another, and she realized that she was not really far from civilization, after all. She had no idea of her ultimate destination, however, but her fingers closed over something hard in her pocket and she felt her purse stuffed with the little wad of notes which Noel had made her accept in payment for her services during that first week in his employment. It amounted to about six pounds, with what had been in her purse when Ruth had found her, and it should have spelt a certain amount of security, but she felt none. She stood quite still, feeling suddenly that she had betrayed Noel Melford after all his kindness. He had trusted her and she had gone off as soon as he had given her enough money to pay her way!

That was how it must look to the casual observer, and no amount of argument could alter the fact that she had gone off into the blue without a word of explanation or even as much as a "thank you" to Ruth. There was Noel, too, and patient tolerant Dennis Tranby whose kindly eyes had been so penetrating on occasion!

Torn between her desire to return to the warmth of their friendship and the impulse within her to go which almost amounted to the desire for self-preservation, she leaned against the stout fire fencing bordering the road, gazing across the expanse of open moor to the faintly colored clouds gathering in the western sky. It must be well after nine o'clock, she thought, yet it was not cold. She could go on walking for another hour. And then—what? Where had she thought to spend the night in her mad flight from Noel Melford's home, without possessions? She could hardly be expected to be taken in at a wayside hotel without name or reason for her journeying, a girl from nowhere!

She was forced to confess that she had not given any thought to these essential things, that blind impulse alone had motivated her actions, and a deep wave of shame swept over her at the thought. She could not go back to the villa to face Ruth and Noel and Dennis Tranby with such a story, and yet she was suddenly without the desire to go on. She felt weak and shaken and without the power to reason further when a car drew level with her and stopped, and even when Noel Melford jumped out of it she scarcely realized that he had come for her.

"Anna," he demanded fiercely, "what manner of foolishness is this?"

He took her by both shoulders, shaking her out of her apathy, turning her to face him, his mouth grim and un-relaxed and his eyes accusing.

"What made you do such a thing?" he demanded. "What in God's name, made you run away?"

"I—we weren't getting anywhere," she said weakly. "And you have other work to do."

"None that matters any more than this," he told her harshly. "Running away isn't going to help, Anna. It only puts an unnecessary strain on all of us."

"Why should you do this for me?" she cried in the utmost shame. "Why should you burden yourself with my affairs when it is all so hopeless!"

"I am a doctor," he reminded her grimly. "And until tonight you have never believed it hopeless." He was still holding her, his strong hands compelling on her arms. "What has changed you so suddenly? Why did you decide to go like that?"

"I felt that I must." What else could she tell him? What was there to say about Sara, whom Noel seemed to trust so fully? "You have all been so kind, but I have no right to stay at Glynmareth, no right to trade on your generosity like this."

"Stop talking nonsense!" He shook her gently. "There's no question of right or wrong about this, Anna," he went on. "You are my patient and I must see that you obey me, otherwise I can't go on with your case."

The hard line of his jaw made further argument seem useless, and she relaxed suddenly against him. Tears threatened to blind her, and he picked her up as he had done once before, and carried her towards the car.

Noel held her against him for a moment before he set her down in the car; then he closed the door with a snap of finality. It seemed to break a spell, and the journey back to the hospital was made in silence. Before they reached the villa, however, Anna asked nervously:

"Does Ruth know?"

"No. I met Sara on the drive coming home alone."

The news did not surprise her. She had expected Sara to return to the villa, and even though Noel had intercepted Sara on the way she was probably there now reporting the scene at the Institute to her friend.

"Do you mind if I don't—see anyone tonight?" she asked unsteadily when Noel drew up before the front door. "Perhaps you could explain to Ruth——"

He sat quite still before the wheel for a moment. She could see his chiselled profile outlined against the light from the porch, and it looked suddenly hard and unrelenting.

"I want you to go in," he said briefly. "Even if she is not alone, you must not be afraid of Ruth. She will know immediately that you are trying to avoid her if you don't."

"I feel so ashamed!" She could speak freely to him at last, confessing all that was in her heart, the bewilderment and the pain, and perhaps it was at this moment that she first realized the extent of her dependence upon him. Without him she could do nothing. Without him she was lost indeed!

"I knew, deep down, how wrong it was," she went on after a pause, "but it seemed that I was encroaching where

I had no right, butting in on your privacy and on Ruth's. I can't really hope to explain it, and I can't go on accepting your kindness without giving something in return!"

Her words dropped into a silence that could almost be felt while Noel sat rigidly beside her, staring into the gathering dusk, his hands clenched over the steering wheel. The pulse-beat of a deep and powerful emotion throbbed between them for a second, but neither stirred, caught up, it seemed, in an experience beyond words and shaken by it to the very foundations of their beings yet fighting it valiantly with all the strength at their command.

It was Anna who finally broke the spell with a small, indrawn breath like a sigh, opening the door on her side while Noel got out and came round to help her. He stood aside to let her pass into the lighted porch with a remote look in his eyes, feeling in his pocket for what she believed must be his key.

"This came today," he said, holding something out in the palm of his hand. "You will want to wear it again."

She saw her wedding ring, the pale, shining circle of eternal faith gleaming in the darkness, and took it from him with trembling fingers.

"There was nothing to report?" she asked.

"Nothing." His voice sounded flat and entirely unemotional, but he would not look at her as he turned away. "I'm sorry, Anna," he apologized, "but it's just another blank. We must expect these things."

She stood looking down at the ring, knowing it precious to her in spite of the surging ache which was welling up in her, but she did not put it on to her finger immediately. Noel had given it back to her, recognizing it as the symbol of her bondage, but it had not produced the clue he wanted. It remained only the mute evidence of the marital state, and suddenly she wanted to refute it, to know herself free as she wanted desperately to be free from the forgetfulness which imprisoned the past.

Burningly ashamed of such primitive emotion in the next instant, she turned blindly into the hall, going on into the sitting-room to find Ruth and Dennis Tranby seated on either side of the fireplace with Sara haranguing them from her perch on the corner of the mahogany centre table. She had not removed her hat or coat and looked as if she had just come in.

"After that, of course, it was no use arguing," she was saying in her clear, metallic tones. "I never have thought it wise to persuade people against their will, and the girl wanted to go."

She swung round as Anna reached the door, obviously expecting to see Noel, and Dennis Tranby got quietly to his feet as she said:

"Oh—it's you? Really, if you must wander off like this don't repeat the performance at this time of night! We need our rest, you know. We are busy people."

The patronising tone saved Anna. When she had first opened the door she had felt as if she might faint, but something about Sara's manner goaded her to stand her ground. Sara had included Noel and Ruth and even Dennis Tranby in her sweeping condemnation of her actions, but she was not going to listen to Sara now. She felt that she must be sure of Ruth's understanding, at least.

"It was wrong of me to go off like that," she admitted, facing Ruth across the room. "I can hardly expect you to forgive me for causing so much unnecessary trouble, but I think I must have done it on some mad impulse. I knew I was doing it, though. I thought it was the right thing to do when—when a week had passed and I still didn't remember who I was."

"Good heavens, a week!" Dennis exclaimed, shattering the sudden tension in the atmosphere. "What are seven days out of a lifetime? You're being far too optimistic, my girl, if you think these things are sorted out in a matter of days. Besides," he added with his easy laugh, "we want to keep you at least till the filing season is over! Didn't Noel mention that?"

Anna was forced to smile in return, although her eyes were still wide and questioning on Ruth's face.

"He may not have done," Ruth said slowly, at last, "but I certainly know I've been grateful for all your help, Anna. I've got through most of the household chores that have been mounting up because of Noel's wretched paper work and all those dreadful statistics, and I have no wish to go back to form-filling for some time to come!" She glanced at the clock in a perfectly normal way, suggesting that this

59

was no different from other evenings which they had spent together at the villa. "Which reminds me that it's well after supper time! You'll stay, Dennis, of course? I'm holding out the bait of home-grown mushrooms—the first of our new crop!"

She scarcely seemed to notice Sara standing between her and the door, but when she went towards it she added lightly: "Stay, too, Sara, if you can."

The casual invitation pierced through Sara like a knife-thurst and she said angrily:

"I'm on night-duty. I go on at eleven. In any case, I had my supper at the Institute."

Ruth waited politely for her to precede her from the room, following her out to the porch to say a brief, unlingering good night.

Anna unbuttoned her coat and went to hang it up in the hall. The light was still on in the porch and Ruth had used it to guide her to the kitchen, so that a man's figure could be seen silhouetted against the glass door as he stood hesitating outside in the small vestibule.

She knew that it was Noel standing there, and suddenly the thin glass barrier between them seemed to shatter into fragments and they were standing close, his strong arms holding her as they had done out there on the moors.

She stood without moving, shaken by an experience so tremendous that she could do nothing but stand and wait in complete acceptance until it passed, knowing it greater and more compelling than anything she had ever felt before. All things fell away before it—fear and hope and even identity, and they emerged a man and a woman in love.

How long she stood there she did not know, but not until the shadowy figure on the far side of the door melted away and she heard Noel's heavy tread crunching over the gravel as he moved out into the night again did any sense of time or place compel her, and then she turned blindly in the direction of the stairs, running swiftly up to her room to sit, cold and shaken, on the edge of her bed and ask herself, "What now?"

Ruth's voice, calling for her from the foot of the stairs, roused her.

"Supper in five minutes, Anna!"

Something in the quiet, purposeful voice steadied her, although she was far from taking Ruth's understanding for granted. That sudden revelation down in the darkened hall had explained so much. It explained her wild flight and the dull aching in her heart as she had taken the road away from Glynmareth, and it explained, too, the reluctance with which she had taken her wedding ring back from Noel.

Shame burned fiercely in her now and she pulled the ring out of her pocket and thrust it back on to the third finger of her left hand. She permitted herself a moment longer in absolute solitude before she bathed her face in the basin between the two windows and went slowly down to the others.

Noel had come in. He was standing by the fire leaning on the low mantelpiece with his pipe between his teeth, and he did not turn as she came in, but somehow Anna knew that he was conscious of her standing there behind him.

Dennis Tranby had gone through to the kitchen to help Ruth with the supper tray and for a moment they were alone.

"You know that this must never happen again," Noel said without looking up. "You must never try to go away from us for any reason but the fact that you have regained your memory, Anna. Nothing is ever gained by running away," he added, "turning one's back on a problem. We've got to fight this together." He straightened then, half turning towards her, his face ashen, his eyes harshly defiant. "I mean to fight it with every means in my power," he told her grimly, "but you've got to help. I need your help, Anna, more than anything else."

"You must tell me what to do," she said. "I am entirely in your hands."

"That's better!" Relief tinged his smile, though the bitterness of gall was already in his heart. "It's the only way we will ever get results. Tomorrow," he continued, "I propose to try an entirely new line of approach, a sort of second offensive. It will be an even more strenuous effort than this last week's, but I'm sure you can stand up to it. There's nothing wrong physically, and your co-operation will do the rest."

61

Before they had finished the meal the telephone shrilled through the hall and he rose immediately to answer it.

"It's for you, old man," he told Tranby when he came back into the room, "but I'll come with you, I think. It's that Stillwell case. I'd like to take a look at the fellow, if you don't mind? I'm still not satisfied about that tracheotomy."

"This is what being a doctor's wife can mean!" Ruth smiled as the men went out together. "A good deal of it is sacrifice, Anna, sacrifice to one's husband's profession."

"I don't think I would regard it as sacrifice," Anna said. "Noel doesn't, does he? He seems to live for his work, and I think he is content."

"Noel has seemed content enough—yes," Ruth agreed after a pause, "and I've always thought his work was enough to satisfy him in life, but now I'm not so sure."

"Has he—never thought of marrying?" Anna asked.

"There has never been anyone he cared for in that way," Ruth said quickly. "At one time I thought that Sara and he might marry, but nothing came of it. I don't think anything ever will now."

"They have their work in common," Anna pointed out with a pounding heart, wondering why she should torture herself like this by continuing to link Sara's name with Noel's.

"That doesn't add up to perfect married bliss, especially when their personalities are so divergent," Ruth answered and Anna knew a sort of crushed relief at the assurance. "I can't see happiness resulting from a marriage like that," Ruth went on, "in spite of all Sara's efforts. We have been very friendly in the past, but lately she has become very aggressive where Noel is concerned, swallowing him up, almost—a professional trait that is all too common, I regret to say. It quite often succeeds in shutting the layman out, but it also hedges in the professionals in a little tight world of their own with no other interest under the sun, which is where we began! Don't think this is possessive jealousy or anything like that," she begged. "Nothing would please me better than to see my brother happily married to someone he loved." She hesitated, looking across at Anna's flushed cheeks as if she had just seen her for the first time. "Nothing would please me better," she repeated in a slightly dazed tone, "but who are we to plan such things, to accept or reject God's pattern for our futures?"

"The future," Anna said in a stifled whisper. "At least you can hope for that."

Swiftly Ruth came close, putting a hand on her shoulder.

"And you," she said, tears welling suddenly behind her eyes. "There will be something for you, too, Anna—some recompense for all this!"

CHAPTER FIVE

NOEL MELFORD'S "SECOND offensive" brought no better result than his first effort, but he did not appear to be in any way dismayed by the fact. Rather, his determination seemed to strengthen with each new rebuff.

"We've tried everything," he said, pacing his consulting room floor while Dennis Tranby glanced through the morning papers without paying a great deal of attention to what he read. "We've had very little help from the police, either," he went on. "There's been no missing person bearing any resemblance to Anna, but one would have thought that her people would have tried to trace her by this time."

"Or her husband."

"Yes." Noel was silent for a while, striding the length of the room and back, head down, brows drawn in deepest thought. "That's what makes me hang on to the idea of an accident."

"But she couldn't just have got up and walked off—walked for miles, I mean," Dennis objected. "I'll admit that she seemed to have been on her feet for some considerable time before Ruth met her but we've scoured a radius of fifty miles and more without coming across a reported accident. There's not even the report of a car being brought into a local garage damaged or anything like that," he added.

"Cars!" Noel exclaimed. "We seem to be thinking exclusively in terms of the car. Couldn't there have been some other way? The coast, for instance. She could have walked inland form the coast for several miles before she struck the main road."

"And with all this rain about we're not going to find a great deal of evidence, supposing there has been something on the cliffs," Dennis mused. "There's been a lot of erosion, too, round about Llangarth Bay and over that way. A whole section of the cliff crumbled away there recently and the road has been closed."

"Could that have been it?" Noel halted in his tracks, gazing at his friend across the room with something like excitement in his eyes. "We've got to try everything, Dennis. These past few days I've felt that Anna has become increasingly sensitive about her inability to remember even the roads about Glynmareth, and she's shied away from me on more than one occasion, almost as if she might be afraid of what was to come. I can't account for it. I only know it makes things decidedly more difficult," he concluded.

"You wouldn't rather pass the case on to Tim Wedderburn when he comes back next week?" Tranby asked watching him through a haze of cigarette smoke.

Noel shook his head.

"I don't think so, old man," he said. "I feel that this is my cup of tea now."

"Well, then, what's our next line?" Dennis asked. "I'm in this with you, of course."

"Thanks, Dennis," Noel stopped to lay an affectionate hand on his friend's shoulder. "I'm not particularly keen on drugs, as you know, so I suppose the alternative is hypnotism."

"Shall we see what your coastal theory brings before we go that far?" Tranby asked.

"That might be an idea." Noel hesitated, conscious of tension as he had been increasingly aware of it in his association with Anna for some days now. "Do you honestly think hypnotism might yield something?"

"We can but try," Dennis said lightly. "If it doesn't, it is only another effort to go into the bag marked 'failures'."

"I—won't be any use, of course," Noel said, almost as if he had not heard that last remark. "I don't think I would get results in this instance."

"You want me to take over?" Dennis hid his surprise with an effort. "I'm willing, of course, if you think it will help."

"I'm sure of it," Noel said, not explaining why he would not attempt the experiment himself. "And meanwhile I'll arrange the trip to the coast. I think it would come off best disguised as something else, by the way—made to look like an ordinary outing. One of Ruth's picnics would be the drill, I think, and I should like you to be there, Dennis. Two minds are always better than one on this kind of job."

Especially when one's mind is so entirely biased! Tranby thought as he said good-bye, but he still maintained faith in his friend's ability to effect a complete cure.

What the final revelation would mean to Noel he could not guess, but even at this early stage in their investigation he was convinced that his friend was more than a little in love with his patient. Their afternoon together at Llangareth Bay convinced him of the fact beyond the slightest shadow of doubt.

It was a wonderful day, full of bright sunshine, with the Berwyn Mountains etched clearly against a cloudless sky to the west and Cader Idris rising above them, three thousand feet of light and shade standing supremely remote with the fertile valleys at his feet.

"We really should have gone to Lake Bala on a day like this," Ruth said, knowing nothing of their reason for choosing the coast. "You would love it up there among the hills, Anna, but Noel seems determined to make it Llangareth. The sea has always held a tremendous attraction for him, and he swims like a fish. I've packed a swim suit for you, by the way, if you want to go in," she added. "It's one I grew out of years ago, but it should just be about right for you. You're much slimmer than I am."

There was no envy in Ruth, Anna thought, none of the bitterness that spoiled Sara Enman. She was the most straightforward and honest person imaginable, willing to go out of her way to make others happy, but blunt, too, when she came up against the need for expressing her feelings in straight-from-the-shoulder terms.

"We could have done without Sara today, couldn't we?" Dennis observed as he joined the preoccupied Ruth downstairs while Anna ran up for her coat and handbag, one she had bought with her second week's wages. "I see she's managed to butt in."

"It was too difficult," Ruth told him with a frown. "Just you try fobbing Sara off with an excuse when she's made up her mind to do anything! Wild horses wouldn't move her, and I suppose we *have* taken her everywhere with us in the past!"

"She's *gone* everywhere with you in the past, you mean," he corrected. "How long before you see just what the Saras of this world are really like, Ruth? They'd take advantage of their own grandmother if it was going to further the desire of the moment, believe me!"

"You're much too hard on Sara," Ruth protested, "possibly because you have never really liked her. We all have our faults, and Sara just can't help organizing everyone!"

"It wasn't exactly her organizing abilities I was thinking about," Dennis returned dryly. "Her *dis*organizing propensities would be nearer the mark!"

"No wonder you two can never agree!" Ruth laughed, strapping the picnic hamper for him to carry out to the car. "Why is Noel so keen to go to the coast, by the way? He was positively emphatic about Llangaréth when I suggested Lake Bala as an alternative."

"He probably thought it would be cooler at the bay," Dennis prevaricated. "Besides, we haven't had our first swim of the season yet, which is disgustingly late for Noel, at least!"

"That was Sara's main reason for wanting to come," Ruth said. "She's a powerful swimmer, isn't she?"

"Powerful in a good many ways," he murmured, picking up crumbs from the breadboard "Almost overpowering, in fact!"

Ruth rapped his knuckles with the back of the bread-knife.

"If I had known you were all that hungry I could have made you a meal before you started!" she laughed, whereupon he swung her round to face him, his hands on her arms, holding her prisoner.

"Ruth, haven't I waited long enough?" he demanded passionately. "Haven't you any other answer for me than that eternal 'No'?"

She relaxed against him for a moment, looking younger than her years and curiously vulnerable as he kissed her.

"Not yet, Dennis," she said, pushing him gently away. "Perhaps not ever. I've told you so often that you should look for someone else!"

"That's no answer," he told her sternly. "Noel is old enough to look after himself and he would have several kinds of fit if he knew your reason for not marrying."

"I made a promise," she said. "How can I do other than keep it?"

"Those promises!" he said savagely. "They've spoiled more lives than enough! I can never understand why a woman binds her daughter to look after her son till some other woman comes along to marry him!"

Ruth silenced him with a look.

"Noel would be the last person to accept a sacrifice," she said, "but I did promise my mother to wait."

"Then you do realize that you are giving more than you need give," he said grimly. "That's always something!"

She put a hand on his arm.

"Please try to understand, Dennis," she pleaded.

"About your loyalty and faithfulness?" He smiled ruefully. "I guess that's why I've waited so long, Ruthey! I believe I understand you better even than Noel does."

"Yes, I think you do." Ruth turned from him with a brief smile. "That is why I am able to ask you to go on understanding for a little while longer, my dear."

Tranby turned away, conscious of impatience for the first time in all his long contact with this woman he loved, aware, too, of a deeper sense of frustration, a suggestion almost of ultimate loss. He had never let himself think that way about their relationship before. Sooner or later, he had reasoned, Noel would marry and it would be only a matter of time before he could claim Ruth after that. Now, however, the certainty of his friend marrying had grown curiously remote, as if some definite barrier had been raised between him and the way to happiness.

Dennis scratched his head reflectively as he contemplated the future for all three of them, and then he knew that, deep in his heart, he had added a fourth name to their company, conscious that it was not only Anna who was going to be involved in the ultimate revelation of her identity.

She began to wonder if the picnic had been arranged for her own benefit, to try to break up the ever-present strain of trying to find the way back to the past, and it would, indeed, have done so if Sara had not been there with her coldly supercilious smile. She was no more than a case to them, but Sara's unfortunate manner seemed to rub it in.

They went in Noel's car because it was bigger than Tranby's and would hold them all comfortably, and Sara managed to install herself in front with Noel while Anna sat behind between Ruth and Doctor Tranby.

Soon Anna had forgotten everything but the beauty of the road over which they travelled. Hills surrounded them on three sides, the high mountains of Snowdonia wreathed in sunlight with the lesser hills chequered in light and shade as the cloud shadows sailed across them. The breath of the sea was in the wind, and presently the sea itself came into view, the great stretch of Cardigan Bay glittering as if a million diamonds had been tossed down upon it from the cliffs above.

Anna drew a deeply appreciative breath, and then she was thinking that she had seen all this before. The color receded from her cheeks as she sought to remember, and it seemed that wind and rain had been driven down against those cliffs when she had last been there. It had turned the bay into a slate-grey mælstrom of tossing water and running tide and she had turned from it and run as if she were being pursued.

Conscious of Dennis Tranby watching her, she did her best not to show her sudden distress, but she was glad when they reached a little, secret bay that was their destination and she could get out and help Ruth with the baskets.

"What are we going to do first?" Ruth demanded. "Bathe or just laze about for a while?"

"That sea's far too good to stay out of for a minute longer than is absolutely necessary!" her brother declared. "How do you feel about it, Anna?" he asked. "Are you fond of the sea? Do you swim?"

"Yes." There had been not the slightest hesitation about her reply, but when she came to look at the sea again she found herself shrinking from the thought of diving into that vast expanse of water, of swimming far out and drowning in it, perhaps! "I'm not sure if I am a strong swimmer," she added uncertainly, "but I can try."

"You needn't worry about not being rescued," Tranby assured her, noting the firm determination in her tone at the end of that difficult little speech. "We're all fairly capable in that respect, especially Noel!"

Sara stood up, saying nothing, but she was the first to reappear from behind the group of rocks which the girls had claimed as a changing room, conscious of her figure's perfection in the brief black suit which was such a splendid foil for her fair coloring.

Ruth emerged with her towelling wrap hugged round her.

"One feels so pale and anæmic at the beginning of the season!" she complained. "I really must find time to sun-bathe. I freckle so badly, though, that I sometimes wonder which is worse!"

Anna, in the bright scarlet suit she had borrowed, stood leaning against the rocks looking out to sea. She felt cold and terribly distressed for some unknown reason, yet the sun was shining down more brightly than before and the sand was warm under her bare feet. It was as if a cold hand had been placed over her heart so that outside warmth could no longer reach it.

She thrust the thought aside, thinking that she must not spoil Ruth's party in this way. The men were already wad-ing into the water, and she looked round the glittering semi-circle of the bay, conscious of its beauty for the first time. The yellow curve of sand lay like a sickle between two jutting promontories, flat grey rocks stepping down to the sea and looking warmly inviting in the sunshine, but Ruth explained that they would picnic in the lee of the cliff.

"It's more sheltered here," she said, "and there are pock-ets of quicksand over by the rocks. It's not always safe in that direction, especially if a wind springs up. The waves sweep right in over the rocks in a full tide with the wind behind it."

Sara moved down to the water's edge, but she walked beside it until she reached the rocks so that she might dive into deeper water.

"It's different for Sara," Ruth said. "She's a marvellous swimmer and can afford to take a few risks."

Anna waded into the water until it was over her knees, feeling it keenly cold against her skin as it rose higher, and then, holding her breath, she plunged down through an oncoming wave. With a gasp she emerged again, the invigorating thrill of it tingling through her veins as she struck out for deeper water and heard Ruth's howl of alarm at the first shock of cold water over her heart.

"Help! It's much colder than I thought—!"

Sara had forged ahead, following Noel out into the bay, but Anna swam across it, going on alone and conscious of a sensation that was not new, the deeply penetrating satisfaction of breasting the waves with confidence and power behind each stroke. She knew that Dennis Tranby had been watching her speculatively as she took that first plunge, but he was not worrying about her now.

She swam with a growing sense of confidence, putting distance between herself and the shore now, the water washing soothingly against her chin, alone in a blue world of sky and sea with so sound in her ears but the lift of waves and the occasional call of a gull high above her head. She turned on to her back with her face up to the sun, floating leisurely with thought just escaping her. It was a glorious day, and she was in a magic world of her own, with far-off sounds lulled by the whispering of waves and nothing but the sea beneath her.

A sudden, overwhelming consciousness of great depths pierced into her mind and fear was clutching at her heart almost in the next second, a fear out of the past reducing her to inexplicable panic. The surge of water in her ears became a roar, the roar of rain and the angry pounding of waves against a rock-bound coast. The mad desire in her to cry for help—for Noel's help—was only silenced by instinctive action as she turned to strike out for the shore and safety, heedless of direction or of anything save that panic desire to feel solid earth under her feet.

She had come much farther than she had thought; her strength began to flag long before she had reached the shallower water where the bay shelved to the sea bed, and she could feel her limbs beginning to ache with a strange, numb pain until they appeared to be dragging her down.

Strong as her will to live undoubtedly was, she could feel that first hopeless flagging of the spirit which sees only a vast expanse of water stretching away to infinity on every side, and something whispered treacherously that she would never make the shore.

"I must! I must!" Her lips formed the words, but the dead weight of her limbs would not lift. The quick, decisive strokes slowed almost to nothing and then she heard Noel's voice from somewhere behind her.

"All right now, Anna! Turn on your back and leave the rest to me."

She could not believe that she was safe, that Noel was really there, but she obeyed him instinctively, and in two long powerful strokes he had pulled ahead of her and was towing her slowly towards the rocks.

Even when they reached them she knew that their ordeal was far from over. There was a strong current running round the headland and it swept them steadily northwards. If they were carried beyond that point there was no knowing what might happen, she thought, and this was all her fault . . .

With an amazing effort she began to exert her numbed limbs, helping to fight the current, but they were carried helplessly away twice before a stupendous struggle on Noel's part placed them beyond the flowing tide and they were in calm water at last.

The buffeting they had undergone had taken its toll of her strength, yet she was aware that something less easy to define had awakened most of the terror in her heart. It was the same fear that had precipitated her into that mad dash for safety, that crashing, rumbling roar of an angry sea and a relentless wind tangled up with memory trying to break through the barrier erected in her subconscious mind. It was the past pounding on the door of the present, the years that had gone demanding their share of the future and her own allegiance.

The swift temptation to let things go, to drift forever in this calm sea beyond the fury of the waves, assailed her for amoment, but she made the final effort and clambered on to the rocks without support, to collapse almost immediately at Noel Melford's feet.

"Anna——!" He knelt down, taking her wet, limp body in his arms and began to massage life into her numbed limbs. "We've made it, my dear! There's nothing to fear now."

"No." She could just see his dark head, the hair plastered against his brow, and the slope of his strong shoulders

71

gleaming in the sun. "I'm all right. You—must think me an everlasting fool, but I was suddenly afraid out there— not afraid of the sea but of something the sea had done. It's so difficult to explain——"

"Don't try now," he said briefly, the old gentleness back in his voice. "All that matters is that you are safe."

For a second his arms tightened about her and all time hung suspended in that brief embrace until Sara's voice reached them from the water below.

"Are you all right, Noel?" She was gasping with the effort she had made against wind and tide. "Oh! thank God you're safe——"

She hoisted herself on to the rocks beside them, her slim shoulders gleaming wetly in the sun, and Noel bent to help her.

"We're all right, Sara," he said in that same quiet voice. "How about you?"

"I made it," she said with a small gasp.

Noel stood up, looking towards the sand dunes.

"Will you look after Anna while I go and find her a wrap of some sort?" he asked. "I don't think the others have realized what has been happening."

Sara did not answer. She stool, tall and straight, on the slab of grey rock, watching him as he picked his way across the quicksands, her eyes stormy, her lips trembling with un- leashed passion, and when he had gone beyond hearing she turned on Anna, who sat hunched up in the sun at her feet.

"You spectacular little fool!" she hissed. "Do you realize that a valuable life might have been lost just now trying to save you?"

Anna stared up at her, too shocked to reply for a mom- ent, and then she said unsteadily:

"I know what Noel risked, and I have told him how sorry I am."

Sara laughed outright.

"A charming gesture, and one I am sure Doctor Melford will understand! Believe me, he is no fool."

Amazed at such an outburst, Anna took refuge in silence. She was far too worried about Noel to quarrel with Sara, and she watched as he made his way from patch to patch of safe sand, breathing deeply with relief when he finally reached the shadow of the cliffs.

"If we could make our own way back," she suggested then, "it would save him all that return journey."

"And give you the opportunity of presenting yourself as the heroine of the piece!" Sara scoffed. "Very well, if you must, but don't expect me to drag you out of the quicksands next!"

The childish malevolence of the remark took much of the sting out of it. Sara would undoubtedly be heartily ashamed of her outburst once she could view it in its true light, Anna thought, but jealous anger had already reduced Sara to the point where she was incapable of seeing clearly at all.

She marched ahead, following Noel's trail across the wet sand, keeping close to the line of boulders which marked the safe way, and when they reached the strip of dry beach she left Anna behind without a backward glance.

Ruth and Dennis were coming up from the sea and Dennis gave Anna a brief, searching look as they met.

"I don't think you three should have gone over to the other side of the bay even if you *are* wonderful swimmers," Ruth said as she came panting towards them. "The tide comes round the headland at a terrific pace and there are dangerous currents all along this strip of coast."

It was clear that she had no idea what had happened, and Noel glanced from Anna to Sara, silencing the latter with a quick frown.

"We could do with something hot to drink after our effort," he said casually. "Anna made it and no more, I'm afraid. We didn't warn her sufficiently about the currents."

Ruth suggested a walk after tea and they strolled up over the headland on to the narrow pathway along the coast, but before they had gone more than a mile Anna was conscious of that strange, unnerving sensation of having walked here before.

She turned to Dennis Tranby, who was walking by her side, to find him studying her intently.

"What is it, Anna?" he asked. "There's something troubling you."

" Out there," she confessed, "while I was swimming, I began to think of the depth of water beneath me and I was suddenly terrified—not for now—not for that moment out there in the sun, but for something that had gone before. I had the impression of a raging sea and rain pouring down and—and someone drowning, I think, whom I could not help. I felt cowardly and unworthy—saving myself."

By the tenseness of the silence which followed her halting confession, she knew that Dennis Tranby was more than a little interested in what she had just told him. Ruth had walked on with Noel and Sara and they were alone for a moment, the others out of sight on the undulating pathway ahead.

"Do you wish to go on?" Dennis asked. "Is there anything else you can tell me? All this is vital, Anna," he added steadily. "We may be getting somewhere, at last."

"There's only this—walking along here, high above the sea. I feel that I must have been here before,e but that's impossible." She drew in a deep breath. "Noel says it is quite a common experience, feeling that present happenings are only a repetition of what one already knows."

"This may be different," he said. "Anna," he added after a pause, "would you, as a more or less final effort, submit to an experiment?"

She stood quite still, her hands clasped tightly before her, her eyes filled with sudden pain.

"I'd submit to anything," she told him. "Anything that would end all this, that would tell me who I really am and free you all from this dreadful burden of caring for me."

"Never mind about that," he commanded. "It's all part of the job, you know."

"What do you want me to do about this new experiment?"

"Co-operate with everything you've got! Hypnotism has worked wonders in cases like yours and an intelligent approach to it often works miracles. I've discussed this step with Noel, by the way," he added to give her confidence, "and he agrees that we might try it. We can do nothing, of course, without your absolute co-operation."

"If you both think it necessary," Anna said, "I'll help all I can."

"I'll be on the job," Dennis told her, "so you needn't wory about taking up too much of Noel's time."

Put like that, he wondered if he deceived her, but Anna felt that she would probably get better results with Dennis. There would be no complications, no fear of her betraying under the hypnotic influence the secret of her love which she believed she had managed to keep, but even if it should be betrayed in that moment of mental submission to another's will she knew that Dennis Tranby would keep it as a matter of trust.

It might only be hours now before they discovered the truth, before she would be forced to accept a new way of life, leaving all this behind.

She gazed about her, conscious of a deep reluctance, of happiness stretching over these past few weeks that she could never replace even with the unremembered past.

"How is it that I know so surely that I was never so happy as I am now?" she asked, and Tranby felt it difficult to answer because he knew, with a sudden sense of misgiving, that he had realized the truth for days.

"Happiness—true happiness comes to us unbidden. I think," he said instead, "and we hang on to it instinctively while we can, fearful, almost, that it is bound to elude us because of the very wonder of it and the knowledge of how little we deserve it, I suppose."

He had spoken automatically while he grappled with the knowledge of Anna's love for his friend, his pity called into being by her simple admission of happiness. But what of the past? What of the marriage symbolized by the ring she wore? The thought left him frowning and he still looked preoccupied when the others turned to join them.

Ruth explained that they had turned back where the path ended in a dangerous landslide a hundred yards farther on.

"These recent gales have done a lot of damage," Noel observed. "Your favorite walk has been completely cut off, Dennis!"

Tranby did not answer immediately. He was thinking of something else, and the suggestion had taken complete possession of his active mind by the time they finally returned to Glynmareth.

"A word with you, Noel, if you can spare me the time," he asked when Ruth and Anna went to unpack the picnic baskets. "Ten minutes will do."

Noel glanced at him and nodded.

"In you go," he said, opening the study door. "I'll be with you in a couple of seconds."

When he followed his friend into the small, book-lined room he looked gravely thoughtful and Dennis came to the point at once.

"It's about Anna," he explained. "We had a talk up there on the cliffs this afternoon and she confessed that the sea had some sort of terror for her. Could it be that she lost her husband in that way?" he suggested tentatively. "By drowning."

Noel took a full minute to answer. Recently any direct reference to Anna's marriage had produced this constrained silence in him, as if he resented even the mention of it, but there was no real way of avoiding the fact that she was married.

"You know as well as I do that we can't build anything up in this case by jumping to conclusions," he said sharply. "The fact that her husband is dead can only be a wild guess at most." He moistened lips that had suddenly gone dry. "It will be hard enough for her facing a complete loss of memory without our making suggestions of that kind before we can be absolutely sure."

"But what about her obvious distress every time the marriage is mentioned?" Dennis objected. "That seems to me to point to unhappiness in the ordinary way, and linked with her horror this afternoon when she found herself at the mercy of the sea it looks very like a clue to me."

"But not necessarily a clue to her husband's decease," Noel reminded him. "We'll follow it up, of course, we'll follow everything up even if it leads us nowhere. All these things which apparently mean nothing can make a whole, in time. Even now, we've got several facts to go on. We know that she dreads the power of the sea, and that she felt there was something familiar on the cliff road this morning, and we also know that any reference to her marriage distresses her. Not a lot to go on, I'll admit, but better than nothing," he mused. "Tomorrow," he added thoughtfully, "you can see what the subconscious has to offer. You have your own methods, I dare say, and in the meantime I think we'll say nothing to Ruth about this afternoon's performance."

"The swimming accident?"

"Yes. I don't think Ruth realized just how serious it was."

"Nor did I. You carried it all off most commendably, and I must hand it to Sara for keeping so calm and paddling to your rescue."

Apparently Noel had not thought about Sara's part in the afternoon's adventure.

"Of course," he said. "Sara! She's always like that in an emergency."

"Supper is nearly ready, you two!" Ruth called as she passed the study door on her way to the dining-room. "I should have thought all that fresh air this afternoon would have made you ravenous!"

Sara had been invited to stay to the meal, and in spite of the fact that she was on call for duty during the night she had accepted. It was almost as if she could not bear to let Noel out of her sight until she was sure that he would have very little time to spend with Anna.

They were scarcely seated round the table when she looked over to where Anna sat and said bitingly:

"Have you really lost your ring, or have you just removed it again?"

Anna stared down at her left hand and her breath caught in a small gasp of alarm.

"Oh!" she cried, "I've lost it! It's gone———"

"Are you quite sure you had it with you?" Ruth asked. "You didn't take it off and put it in one of your pockets while you were swimming?"

"No. I'm sure I had it on when I went into the water. I haven't taken it off since—since Doctor Melford gave it back to me."

She gazed at Ruth in obvious distress and Noel was about to speak when Sara said:

"You can always get another one. They're not terribly valuable, are they?"

The cold, infuriating voice did something to Anna. She felt as if she could have reached across the table and smacked that smiling mask of a face, wiping the stupid jibe from Sara's lips, but all she did was to rise to her feet and say with a dignity which made Sara bite her lip in angry annoyance:

"One can't replace such things. The ring was—given to me by someone I loved. I feel quite sure about that now, and I shall never forgive myself for losing it in this careless way. But—marriages aren't destroyed by the loss of a ring. It is only a symbol, but its meaning goes deep enough for me to appreciate it, even if I have forgotten all about the past." She turned towards Noel, looking straight into his distressed eyes for one blinding instant, and then she moved away from the table. "Forgive me if I can't eat anything, Ruth," she apologized as she passed Ruth's chair, "I feel so utterly tired."

Before she had reached the door Noel had scraped his chair back and jumped to his feet, his eyes fiery in anger. He surveyed the table and the three people still sitting round it, and when he turned to look at Anna she had gone. He moved to the door, as if to follow her, and then he wheeled round to confront them again in cold fury.

"If anyone ever mentions this wretched marriage again I shall find some way of dealing with them," he said harshly. "For heaven's sake give her a chance to pull out of the natural fear of not knowing who she is or to whom she is bound! It will all come right in the end, but I won't have her chivvied into remembering!"

He glared at them collectively but it was to Sara that his words were really addressed, and although Dennis Tranby managed to smooth the situation a little they were an uneasy foursome until Sara made her excuses and went away.

Noel rose five minutes later, when he had given her time to reach the hospital.

"I'm going out," he said gruffily. "don't wait up."

Ruth looked across the room at Dennis in bewilderment.

"What a party!" she exclaimed. "Do you think he's gone to tell Sara what he thinks?"

"He's already done that," Dennis answered dryly. "My guess is that he has gone to work it off over in that isolated eyrie of his in the east wing."

"So long as he doesn't prowl," Ruth said.

Noel was "prowling," however. He felt that the confines of the villa were suffocating him and only action, keen and vigorous action, would work off the mood which possessed him.

He had almost forgotten what had provoked the scene at the supper-table, and Sara's part in it seemed infinitesimal now. All he could remember was Anna's pleading look and her pinched, white face and pain-darkened eyes asking for his understanding. Her words, too, kept ringing in his ears. *Marriages aren't destroyed by the loss of a ring. It is only a symbol, but its meaning goes deep enough for me to appreciate it, even if I have forgotten all about the past.*

It had been a heart cry, driven from her by Sara's cruelty, but it was meant for him, too. He plunged on through the shrubbery and out at a side gate leading to the hill, and soon he had reached the moor road with all the hounds of despair and self-denunciation barking at his heels.

The fiercely primitive urge dormant in all men had sought, time and time again, to discount the possibility of her marriage because he had wanted her for himself.

CHAPTER SIX

IF LOVE BE blind in some respects, it is almost painfully quick-sighted in others; and there was no doubt that Sara was in love with Noel. She had always been in love with him, ever since the day he had come to Glynmareth as resident surgeon. Sara, ever a fighter, had succeeded by sheer determination and application in her chosen career, succeeded beyond her wildest dreams, and here was something new upon which to fasten her ever-upward gaze. It was not long before ambition crystalized into a ruthless determination softened momentarily by a very real affection, the first worth-while emotion of her life.

Sara was so well aware of her own physical attractions that she had believed for years that it was only a matter of time until Noel would propose to her and she would move across to the villa as the Superintendent's wife. And after that the road would be broad and clear before them! Noel would progress from success to success with her by his side, specializing and making a great name for himself. There was nobody who could help him more than she could with her undoubted poise and her knowledge of the profession. A shared life and a shared interest! The ideal foundation for a successful marriage.

And now, in a day, in a matter of hours, her firmly held convictions had been severely shaken. She had come face to face with a girl who was several years her junior, a name-less creature with a frail, ethereal prettiness about her, and she had seen a look in Noel Melford's eyes that had threat-ened to topple the fairy castles she had built. It might almost have convinced her that Noel was already in love with Ruth's waif, but, self-preservation being the strongest instinct, she clung to the hope that she was wrong. She had all but convinced herself of the fact until she met Noel the following day.

Nothing could have changed a man in so short a time but some overwhelming experience, an emotion stronger than any he had ever known, and nothing could have stamped that strained, white look on Noel's face but the necessity for complete renunciation.

Sara wondered if her best approach might be sympathetic understanding, and there was great consolation for her in the fact that the girl was already married. She saw in the fact a subtle weapon near to her hand, and it was not long before she began to use it.

Her position at the hospital gave her free access to the notes on Anna's case, which were filed in Noel's consulting room, and she read what both he and Dennis Tranby added to them from time to time. Anna's reaction to any discus-sion of her marriage was still one of distress, and therefore, Sara deduced, there must have been something discreditable in her past.

Discussing it with Eluned Warth, the Matron at the hospital, she was met with a certain amount of sympathy, for Miss Warth deeply resented any sort of slight, real or imaginary, on her position, and regarded Noel's continuing refusal to bring Anna into the wards under her charge as a personal reflection of the grossest kind.

"I can't think what Doctor Melford hopes to accom-plish across at the villa that we cannot do here," she observ-ed in an aggrieved tone when Sara came in with her re-ports. "He is being most unreasonable about this case. It's one for Doctor Wedderburn, but even now that Tim is back there's no sign of the girl's being handed over to him."

"You know Tim won't say a thing while Noel has the case in hand," Sara frowned. "He's so terribly easy-going and it will suit him admirably so long as Noel gives him the odd report for his records! It strikes me," she added, watching the older woman's face for her reaction to the suggestion, "that this is essentially a police case."

"My dear, isn't that rather strong?" Miss Warth exclaimed. "I mean, you don't think that the girl has done anything *wrong?*"

"What do we really know about her?" Sara demanded. "Intelligent—yes, and a good worker, apparently from a decent-class home by the way she speaks and the clothes she was wearing when Ruth brought her, but that's all! On the other side of the balance you have the wedding ring that she deliberately disposes of—no one will convince me that it was accidentally lost out there in the bay!—and the fact that any reference to her marriage upsets her. She is also afraid of the sea and nervous of a car accident."

"Do you think that proves anything actually wrong?" Miss Warth asked doubtfully, not wishing to displease Sara by confuting her statements altogether. "She may have been in a car accident at one time."

"There were no accidents for miles round on the night she was found," Sara summed up, speaking almost as if to herself, and standing up to her full height, her lips compressed into a cruel line. "No. There's something far from right about Miss Anna's past and I mean to find out what it is if it takes me a lifetime!"

In spite of her undoubted admiration for Sara, Eluned Warth was decidedly taken aback by both words and manner, and the forceful vindictiveness of the statement made her wonder if she had ever really known Sister Enman. She had seen quite a lot of Anna these past few days, too, and had liked what she saw. The girl had seemed pleasant and willing to help in any way she could and there was nothing abnormal in her behaviour except for the lack of memory, which was a common enough thing these days. In the large city hospital where she had worked before being appointed to Glynmareth Miss Warth had seen as many as three amnesia cases brought in during one week, and all had been successfully cleared up after treatment, so that she could not really share Sister Enman's gloomy view that this was a special case.

"I think," she ventured wisely, "that we should have nothing to do with it unless we are asked."

"You may think so, but I am not going to stand aside and see my friends being exploited! Ruth and Noel are only being made a convenience of by this girl and the sooner they realize it the better!"

"H-mm," Miss Warth murmured. "That's as may be. What about your holiday, Sister?" she asked, changing the subject. "You are due ten days in a couple of weeks' time, but if you could take them before that I should be obliged. There's the inspection next month, and the fete at the end of this one. Everything seems to come at once!"

Sara considered the prospect of leaving Glynmareth with tightly-compressed lips, opened them as if to refuse, and then thought better of it. *Even if I don't go away anywhere it would give me freedom to get about here—round the district,* she considered. "All right, Matron, you can put me down for a week from today. I'll go on Thursday off night duty."

Miss Warth made a note of the date on her calendar and Sara rose with a mental note to track down Anna's past if it took her every day of her forthcoming leave even to procure one single clue.

With this intention firmly fixed in her mind she went in search of Dennis Tranby, only to find Noel's consulting room occupied by a staff nurse whom she disliked.

"Doctor Tranby is having a hypno. session," the girl told her briefly. "The 'Keep Out' notices are up, red light showing and all the rest of it!"

Sara moistened her lips. She had been about to reprimand the girl for flippancy, but she thought better of it.

"These things don't apply to me," she said tartly. "Who is in there? What patient?"

"That awfully pretty girl who lost her memory," she was informed readily. "The one who helps Doctor Melford."

"Is Doctor Melford with Doctor Tranby?" Sara asked sharply.

"Oh, no! I heard him say he wouldn't go in, and after Doctor Tranby started, Doctor Melford paced up and down in here for a bit and then went out. He looked upset."

Sara glanced at her watch.

"It's tea time," she said with unexpected thoughtfulness. "Off you go and have yours. I'll relieve you here for half an hour."

"It really doesn't matter, Sister——"

"Off you go, Nurse! I'm quite interested in this case, and I've had my tea," Sara lied. "I shall wait till Doctor Tranby is finished."

She sat down at the desk, lifting one of Noel's pencils from the silver tray and tapping it with monotonous regularity against the blotter. It made a small muffled sound, the hidden beat of a determination that grew as she waited. What was going on in there? Had Dennis Tranby succeeded in lifting the veil from a past which seemed to concern them all in some subtle, almost menacing fashion, or were they still to remain confronted by that blank wall of forgetfulness which would keep Anna in Noel's care indefinitely.

Sara bit her lip. That was one thing that must not happen! She would see to it that it did not happen with all the means in her power!

Once or twice she glanced towards the closed door between the two rooms, experiencing an almost overwhelming desire to go to it and burst it open, but years of training were stronger even than a primitive jealousy, and she continued to wait.

It was ten minutes to five when the door finally opened and Dennis Tranby stood there with perspiration beading his forehead and his whole body curiously limp and exhausted.

"Hullo, Sara," he said. "I left Nurse Crabtree on guard." He crossed to the basin to fill himself a glass of water. "Will you do what you can for Anna in there? She's feeling the strain, of course, so make her rest for a while."

"Any luck?" Sara asked almost casually.

"In a way, yes." Tranby's brows were drawn together in a frown, his dark eyes remotely thoughtful as he reviewed the impressions of the past half-hour. "I think I have definitely established the fact that she comes from farther north than this—from the north-east coast, perhaps. She was familiar with moorland country and she thought that there had always been animals about the house."

"A farmer's daughter?"

"Maybe. There was no hesitation about her acceptance of a sister, but a brother puzzled her, and the mention of her mother made her sad."

Sara realized that he was making a mental résumé of the interview rather than speaking to her directly, but she continued to listen intently.

"There was no suggestion of any definite place?" she queried, waiting for his answer with an impression of climax.

"I couldn't strike a responsive note anywhere in that respect," he confessed, "so either my geography is bad or I have been barking up the wrong tree! We'll see what Noel thinks when he comes in."

That "we" pleased Sara. It made her feel included and from a professional angle it was flattering. It could, of course, mean nothing or everything, and she remembered that Noel had not asked help with the case so far. He had made it a personal concern, but perhaps that "we" of Dennis Tranby's was tantamount to an admission of defeat. Noel might have decided to turn the girl over to the hospital. The sense of satisfaction derived even from the possibility was exhilarating and Sara went about the task of preparing a cup of hot, strong tea with a feeling of relief in her heart.

She carried it in to Anna, who was sitting in the chair beside the window where Dennis had left her, still profoundly shaken by her recent experience, yet aware by the look on Tranby's face that it had not proved entirely fruitless.

"I'm really all right," she said when Sara asked her how she was.

"Of course you're all right!" Sara said briskly, her voice professionally encouraging. "There's nothing physically wrong with you, and you will benefit immediately as soon as you are back in your native north country."

She watched her patient carefully for the expected reaction, but a heavy sense of loss was all that Anna could feel. It was as if Sara's encouraging words had opened up a vista of future pain for her instead of the happiness which she knew she should have experienced at the thought of going home where she belonged. It was as if she did not want to remember the past at all!

"Most cases of your kind clear up quite suddenly," Sara went on, "and the curious part is that the in-between time, the things that happened in the forgetful period, are themselves forgotten."

"But that mustn't happen!" Anna cried, distressed at the very thought. "I mustn't forget about Ruth and Noel and all they have done for me!"

"My dear girl," Sara returned cuttingly, "don't imagine for one moment that Ruth or Noel, or even Dennis Tranby for that matter, are doing this from any feeling of personal affection. I've told you before that we regard your sort of case as a special duty. Quite frankly, we find amnesia a most interesting study. No two amnesists are the same and each case must be judged on its own merits."

"You make it all sound so—cold-blooded when you put it that way," Anna cried, hurt beyond measure by the intended cruelty behind the words, "but it doesn't alter the fact that everyone has been so kind."

"Of course, we try to be kind," Sara answered patiently, "but quite often kindness is taken advantage of and we feel that we have to be blunt."

"That's not true!" Anna flashed. "And I know Ruth would never think such a thing. She has told me over and over again, that I am not in the way at the villa, that I am 'working my passage.' That was the way she put it and I choose to believe her."

"Ruth," Sara reminded her crushingly, "is unfailingly generous. Ever since I have known her she has been helping one kind of lame duck or another, but they've generally had the grace to realize when they have outstayed their welcome."

Anna got unsteadily to her feet.

"You needn't worry, Sister Enman," she said frigidly. "I shall leave Glynmareth as soon as I feel the slightest suggestion of having outstayed my welcome."

"Now, then," Dennis Tranby asked, coming to the door, "how do we feel after the cuppa?"

Anna looked up at him with a grateful smile.

"Quite ourselves!" she laughed. "What did I give away?"

"You'd be surprised!" he grinned. "The facts were bad enough, never mind the details! But off you go into the fresh air for a while. Better slip across to Ruth and sit in the garden for an hour, preferably out of the sun."

He wheeled round at a movement in the room behind him, and beyond his broad shoulders Anna saw Noel's drawn face with the color all gone out of it and his eyes darkly shadowed as he searched Tranby's for the truth.

"We've had a partial success," Dennis told him briefly, and Noel pushed his way past him to come to Anna's side.

"Are you all right?" His anxiety was in no way professional as he caught both her hands in his, holding them in a grip that hurt. "Anna, are you all right?"

"Yes." Her voice was no more than a whisper. "Yes, Noel, I'm all right."

"Thank God!"

He sat down in the chair she had vacated and passed an unsteady hand over his hair.

"I was never much in favor of this sort of thing," he said roughly.

"But even though it has only been partially successful," Anna said haltingly, "you once said that every detail counted, that you couldn't afford to pass over the slightest clue."

"That's true enough," he said, rousing himself. "Everything counts—everything!"

His voice had regained some of its old mastery, but his eyes still held the pain of remembering and Sara Enman turned away, hurrying out at the far door without so much as an excuse, black hatred in her heart and a fierce, bold purpose in her mind.

"I've told Anna to go across to Ruth for an hour," Tranby explained. "You won't need her, will you?"

"No." Noel was still gazing at Anna, but his mouth had taken on a more determined line and his eyes were steel-grey and hard, his lips twisting a little as he repeated Tranby's words. "No, I won't need her."

"I can easily stay," Anna offered, "if there's anything important to do. I don't feel in the least tired and I haven't really done any work this afternoon."

Noel looked down at her, smiling a little.

"Go across to Ruth," he said gently. "Dennis and I will come across later."

She hurried away from the cool efficiency of the hospital, from its remoteness, to the warmth and kindliness which the villa garden had always represented for her.

"Anna," Ruth asked, coming down the path behind her. "why have you come back home? Was this afternoon not successful? Have they drawn another blank?"

Ruth came and sat on the flat stone beside her and Anna answered without turning round.

"I still don't know who I am, but Dennis seems to think the effort was not entirely wasted."

"It has tired you," Ruth suggested. "Would you like to go in and lie down for a while?"

"No—no, thank you, Ruth. It wasn't a dreadful experience at all." She tried to pull herself together, rounding up her scattered thoughts. "More like—dropping off to sleep than anything else—a sort of overwhelming weariness, but no strain and hardly any fear."

"Dennis was confident," Ruth said thoughtfully. "He has much greater faith in hypnotism than Noel has."

The mention of her brother's name seemed to flicker between them like fire. Anna sat very still, her hands clenched in her lap, her eyes on the brown, silent water at their feet, and then she said:

"Ruth, I must go over to the hospital—permanently, I mean. Really, I must. I—I suppose I should have been under the police doctor all this time."

Her words dropped into a deep silence and then Ruth said:

"It's not because you have lost faith in Noel—it can't be that!"

"No—never!" Anna turned to face her, feeling that her heart must burst. "Ruth," she said, "I've got to go."

Months afterwards Ruth Melford confessed to Dennis Tranby that her first instinctive reaction had been to say "go" for Noel's sake, but the quality in Anna which had so endeared her to them had never been so strong as at that moment, and she could not inflict added hurt where hurt had already been accepted so gallantly. Besides, she did not consider that Anna's transfer to the hospital would solve their problem in any way, and she said so at once.

"You may as well be here as at the hospital. That's no solution, Anna, my dear. You'd see Noel almost every day, anyway."

Startled, Anna raised pain-filled eyes to hers.

"There would be Doctor Wedderburn——"

"And Noel," Ruth said quietly. "They work together, and Noel would never agree to give up your case now. Besides," she added, "if you did insist, he would wonder why."

"Oh, Ruth!" Anna cried passionately, knowing that Ruth must have guessed her secret long ago, "why had I ever to come into your lives at all! I've been nothing but a problem to you from the moment you picked me up that day on the moor!"

"We're not meant to select our own problems," Ruth said quietly, "nor to question them when they are sent, I think." She bent over and put a hand on the younger girl's knee. "We'll pull out of this, Anna—together."

Anna held on to her fingers tightly for a few minutes before she squared her shoulders in a determined effort to face this particular problem bravely.

"I'll never forget all you've done for me, Ruth—never!" she said. "And I'll find some way of repaying you—some day."

"Friendship," Ruth mused, "is a form of repayment. We all give to it unstintedly and we give to love, too, only love is the more demanding. Don't hesitate to come to me, Anna, if things go wrong for you. There may be something in my experience that you need. I am much older than you are."

Anna could not find words to thank her again. She felt as if Ruth had already poured much of her store of loving into her lap, generously, almost eagerly, and she could not do other than accept the largesse of it in the spirit in which it had been offered. Ruth knew now that she was in love with Noel, and somehow it had taken some of the bitterness out of that loving. Ruth had never believed in running away from life. She could have done so easily by breaking her promise and marrying Dennis Tranby, but that was not Ruth's way. Her own right to happiness depended upon her brother's, and she would abide by that decision.

They went quietly over the experiences of the afternoon discussing them rationally until Noel came to stand behind them on the grass. He had crossed the lawn silently, and when his long shadow fell on the stones at their feet Anna started up as if she had seen a ghost.

"Something has come out of this afternoon's session that we think should be cleared up right away, Anna," he said, taking her completely into his confidence as he had done from the beginning so that she had never quite felt the "case" that Sara had gone out of her way to assure her she was and nothing more. "It will entail a walk across the moor," he went on. "To-morrow's Saturday. Do you think you could manage it if we left early and took the car as far as Llangareth?"

"If you wish it," Anna responded instantly. "Surely, oh, surely, this will bring us to something! What did Doctor Tranby think about this afternoon?"

"We're keeping that a most deadly secret for the present," he told her lightly. "We think it may link up with something else tomorrow, but we don't want you to know beforehand in case it might confuse you." He put a hand on her shoulder as he turned away towards the house. "Chin up, Anna!" he commanded. "We'll beat this thing yet—between us!"

Ruth had agreed to go with them when Noel had assured her that her help might be valuable to them.

"Make it all seem as natural as possible," he advised the following afternoon. "Anna has the heart of a lion, ready to face the unknown with tremendous spirit, but it's still bound to be something of a strain."

"She's such a little bit of a thing!" Ruth said. "But she's even stronger than you think."

He did not answer that, and she went out to the car where Anna was waiting.

"We're going to pick up Dennis on the way," Noel announced. "He's taking the day off."

Ruth flashed him an inquiring glance, but he did not seem inclined to add anything further and she left it at that. She got into the back seat where Anna had already settled, determined, it seemed, not to thrust herself too much upon Noel even when circumstances made it inevitable that they should be together.

Dennis kept them waiting almost half an hour while he finished an overflowing surgery, insisting that they should wait indoors, and Anna followed Ruth into the spacious Georgian house, glancing about her with frank interest.

The home which Dennis Tranby had been asking Ruth to share with him for years was indeed worthy of her, a gracious, lovely old house leading directly from the pavement, but with a walled garden behind it where apple trees bent low over mossy grass and almost every flower that grew made a brilliant splash of color along the borders. Peach and nectarine and pear rambled along the walls, the fruit already thick on the branches, and a weeping willow drooped over a rustic seat beside a tile-bordered pool.

The house was furnished in perfect taste, too, the lovely period pieces carefully polished by Dennis' elderly housekeeper, who brought them coffee in the dining-room. She set the silver tray down on the end of the oval table where it lay reflected as in a mirror, and left Ruth to pour out.

Anna watched Ruth with a stabbing envy in her heart, realizing how much she longed for the peace and security of a home such as this, and then she realized that Ruth must long for it too, that it was here for her to take but for a promise made long ago when Noel was very young. There was no sign of impatience in Ruth's gentle, immobile face, however. She had achieved the quiet of perfect inward peace and it was reflected in her eyes for all to see.

When Dennis finally joined them he accepted his cup from Ruth with a smile, their fingers just touching under the delicate china, and Anna saw the unconscious longing behind that smile and knew that she was not alone in the bitterness of her renunciation.

"What do you think about these?" Dennis asked, turning abruptly to the sideboard and drawing their attention to a pair of beautifully-chased candelabra standing there, still with their sale tickets attached. "I picked them up in Bristol."

He carried them across to the light for Ruth's inspection, waiting for her verdict.

"They're beautiful!" she said at last. "I don't think I've ever seen anything so lovely, Dennis."

"They're yours," he said, "if you will accept them. I'm quite sure I had you in mind when I bid for them."

"I couldn't," Ruth said, setting them down at either end of the table where their reflection lay in the rich red mahogany as if in glass. "They belong here, Dennis."

He did not contradict her, and Anna thought that he would keep them there until Ruth came to the White House as a bride.

Looking up suddenly, she found Noel's eyes fixed on her across the room with such a look of intensity that they might have been there together alone, yet somehow he seemed to be looking beyond her, too, seeing down into the future, perhaps, and finding no hope there.

"Shall we go?" he asked almost harshly. "It's after eleven, and we did plan to get as far as Llangareth before lunch."

They motored quickly along the high road with the green panorama of the hills all about them, and then Noel turned the car towards the sea and Anna felt that she recognized the road.

"Wasn't it here you picked me up that day?" she asked Ruth unsteadily. "I'm sure I recognize it—the big, humped mountain over there and all the lower hills dipping down to the sea."

"Can you remember the exact spot?" Noel asked from the front seat. "Was there any special landmark?"

"There was a milestone and a clump of mountain ash on the far side of the road. Ruth pulled up under the trees."

She found no difficulty in remembering now and Noel nodded encouragingly, though he did not comment until she was deep in conversation with his sister about the exact location of the trees, and then he turned to Tranby to remark:

"You see, Dennis, the memory is quite unimpaired otherwise. Her brain is naturally quisk, her impressions incisive. That's what gives me so much confidence when otherwise we seem to come up against one blank after another."

They came to the trees and he pulled the car in off the road, parking it in their shade.

"We'll sample your coffee and sandwiches now, Ruth," he suggested, "and then we can walk light." He glanced round of them. "Everyone agreeable?"

Anna nodded, trying not to let him see her utter nervousness because now that she was covering old ground the past seemed to come rushing up to mock her, the part of the past she could recall. Thus far and no farther! it seemed to say. For all your eagerness you still can't remember clearly enough!

She set her teeth and bent to help Ruth with the hamper. She *would* remember! She must. She *must*!

While they sat under the shade of the trees she tried to force memory with a concentration which showed only too plainly on her pale face.

"Don't make too great a labor of it, Anna," Noel advised in an undertone, coming to sit beside her while he filled his pipe. "Just allow yourself to come to it naturally. Treat today like any ordinary day—like what it is, a planned picnic between friends."

The kindness of his words stung tears into her eyes, but she battled against them and would not let him see how much his thought for her could reduce her heart.

"If I fail in this you must let me go," she said in a stifled whisper. "I know I'm not reacting nearly as quickly as you had hoped and—and——"

"And what, Anna?"

"It isn't fair to you—all the time you are spending on my case."

"If you were only a 'case'," he said quietly, "I should still go on persevering until I had freed you from this dreadful bondage." He felt in his pocket and produced a small, gleaming object which lay in the palm of his hand as he held it out to her. "I thought you would like to have this," he said.

She gazed down at the thin gold circlet of the new wedding ring and her heart contracted with all the old agony of uncertainty.

"Put it on," he commanded. "It may make you feel more secure. You can pay me back when you feel you can afford it."

This matter-of-fact reference to the purchase of a new ring did much to steady her, and she took it from him, but she did not put it on immediately, knotting it into the corner of her handkerchief instead and putting it safely away in her pocket.

Noel made no comment as he watched. He was paler than usual and his mouth was perhaps a trifle grim as he rose to help her to her feet, but that was all.

They set out to cross the moor in the direction of the sea and he fell naturally into step beside her, with Dennis bringing up the rear in Ruth's company.

"We'll cut up over Bransby Beacon," he suggested after the first mile. "It's a stiffish climb, but it cuts off all that winding bit of road between here and the coast."

"Think you can manage it?" Dennis asked Ruth. "We can leave you serene and resting in the shade if you like."

"I'm not quite that age!" Ruth laughed back. "No! I'm coming with you even if you have to carry me back!"

"Heaven forbid!" Dennis grinned, holding out his hand to her as they began to climb. "Come on! I'll give you a tow!"

The keen mountain air went down into their lungs like a tonic, and Anna drew in deep breaths of it, climbing steadily by Noel's side. It was as if they were on a journey to a new world, and she thrust everything behind her—the desperation of these past few weeks, and the fear and the loneliness, determined to live this one day to the full.

They reached the top of the Beacon long before Ruth and Dennis, and stood there together with the whole panorama of the coastline spread out before them; not saying very much, but conscious of fulfilment that was not altogether to do with reaching the top of a hill.

Anna gazed down, shivering suddenly.

"I don't want to go down there," she said. "I feel as if —all this will be swept away if I do—all the beauty and the freedom——"

The last word baffled her and she stood wondering why she should have used it, she who was so deeply in bondage to the past, and then Noel moved, turning toward her and drawing her hands within his strong, warm grasp.

"We've got to go down, Anna," he said. "Whatever lies down yonder, whatever comes of your remembering for both of us, nothing would ever be gained by turning away."

She clung to his hands for one breathless, unhappy moment, longing to deny what he had just said but knowing that she could not, because it was the only way for them to go.

"How far is it?" she asked stiltedly.

"Not very far," he said. "You'll make it, my dear."

If his voice had trembled slightly on these last two words he gave no other sign of emotion whatever, and when Dennis and Ruth joined them five minutes later, he was pointing out Bardsey Island to Anna and the vague grey outline of Braich-y-Pwll shrouded in the mist of distance away to the north.

He offered Anna his hand as they went down towards the coast, and Ruth, following with Dennis Tranby's supporting arm about her, said almost bitterly.

"There goes the perfect partnership sacrificed to a whim of fate!"

"I'm afraid so," Dennis answered unhappily. "Pity there's nothing we can do about it. I've known Noel was in love with her for a very long time."

"It can't be more than days," Ruth corrected. "She hasn't been with us for a very long time."

"It doesn't take a man much longer than a few days to know when he's met the one woman who will ever mean anything in his life," he retorted. "I knew about you, for instance, within hours!"

"And we all have years before us yet!" Ruth said unguardedly, and on a note of despondency which was very unlike her.

CHAPTER SEVEN

WHEN ANNA HAD accepted the fact of her love for Noel, the complication of his returning that love had never occurred to her, but she could not have stood alone with him on that high hill-top and looked up into his eyes without knowing that life had played them one of its shabbier tricks, and given them a love which could never know fulfilment. That one flawless, ecstatic moment when she had realized herself beloved was all she might possess. For the rest they must walk their separate ways, apart, divided by the very token he had just given her, the slim, golden emblem of her own bondage.

The wind was whipping the sea up into little white horses, galloping in across the bay, but the waves were small and there was no pounding at the base of the cliff as she had half expected.

Expected? Her heart appeared to stand still as she halted on the narrow path and looked down. Expected or remembered? It was all the same. She had thought to find a raging sea here in this wind-swept place, and a sky dark and devoid of stars.

"Noel!" she said. "Noel, it happened here—in a place like this."

The surge of water rushed in upon her mind, but over and above it she could hear Noel's voice, strong and encouraging, urging her on.

"It had been raining, Anna, and there were high seas," he suggested. "You were in a car, driving along a cliff road."

She drew back with terror in her eyes for a moment.

"Yes," she whispered. "Yes!"

"With the man you loved," he continued inexorably.

"I don't know! I don't know about that." She turned away from him, to hide what was in her eyes. "It's all so dark. Just the car rushing through the night and the sound of the wind and the rain blotting out everything else. I can't remember anything else, Noel! I still can't remember."

The cry came straight from her heart and it struck through him with the force of a knife-thrust, but he dared not give up now.

"You were being driven at great speed along this road, Anna," he repeated. "And the man you were with was your husband. Think back. Think, Anna! *You've got to think.* You were travelling through the night with your husband in a car which he was driving at a high speed. Can you tell me why?"

He had switched the subject deliberately away from the heart-searching question of her marriage and her response was instantaneous.

"It was so late. We had to get back to my hotel." Her voice faltered, but she was concentrating on his last question. "Ned always drove fast."

"Ned?" He passed the name back to her carefully, not over-emphasising it. "How long had you known Ned?"

"All my life. He was always there."

"And—you were in love with him?"

He asked the question with no change of expression, only a small pulse beating suddenly fast high in his tanned cheek was witness to any emotion as he waited for her answer, but the feeling in his heart was one of emptiness and void, as a man might feel at the foot of the gallows who still hopes for a reprieve.

"No," she said slowly. "No."

He knew that she took that for granted and the admission did nothing to ease the tension under which he was forced to work. A name had come to her out of the past, but the searing revelation for which he waited had not followed it. A lifetime of friendship apparently lay behind the name of Ned, but it had not been strong enough to shatter the amnesia.

Without showing his disappointment, he waited for Ruth and Dennis to come up with them, suggesting immediately that they should rest there for a while before they turned back.

Anna sank down thankfully on the coarse grass and Ruth launched forth into a tale of rum-running which had been current along the lonely coast south of where they sat for some time, feeling that her companions' pre-occupied silence demanded just such an effort on her part.

Noel looked across at his friend. "Would you find it too much of an effort to take a look at the cliffs above Long-reach Rocks? I believe the road has been closed along that section, and it was a favorite path of ours at one time, remember?"

He had kept insistence to a minimum, but Tranby detected something in his voice which he recognized from long experience, and rose immediately.

"I'll concede a mile each way," he agreed lazily, "but no more!"

The look which her brother gave her kept Ruth seated on the cliff top as the two men walked away. They walked in silence for a while, drawing on their pipes, their hands thrust deeply into their trouser pockets.

"Well," Dennis demanded at last, "what now?"

"The car angle was the right one," Noel said with conviction. "There *was* a car, and it was being driven far too fast, or at least fast enough to cause Anna a considerable amount of nervousness. Then — something happened. What," he went on, "we can only guess at just now, but there's one thing we can be more or less sure about. The

COMPLETE THIS QUESTIONNAIRE AND WE WILL MAIL YOUR FREE COPY OF LUCIFER'S ANGEL BY VIOLET WINSPEAR

1. When was the last time you read part of or all of a **romance** paperback book? (Circle the number next to the answer that best applies).

   1 ☐ Within past week.
   2 ☐ More than one week ago & up to a month ago.
   3 ☐ More than a month ago & up
   4 ☐ More than 3 months ago & up to a year ago.
   5 ☐ Over a year ago.
   6 ☐ Don't remember.

2. What type of romance paperback book was that? (Please describe type below).

   1 ☐ Romantic suspense.
   2 ☐ Historical romance.
   3 ☐ Gothic romance.
   4 ☐ Romance (Other than suspense, historical or Gothic romance).
   5 ☐ Other.

3. How long have you been reading Harlequin books?

   1 ☐ Less than a month.
   2 ☐ Between 1 and 3 months.
   3 ☐ Longer than 3 months but less than a year.
   4 ☐ Over a year but less than 5 years.
   5 ☐ Over five years.

4. Within the last month, how many Harlequin books have you read? (WRITE IN NUMBER) _____ (If "none" write in "0").

5. Who is (are) your favourite Harlequin author(s)?

   1) _____

   2) _____

   3) _____

6. Approximately, how much did you spend on paperback books in the past 6 months.

   1 ☐ Less than $20.   2 ☐ Between $20. and $50.   3. ☐ more than $50.

☐ Mrs. ☐ Miss

_____
Name   (Please Print)

_____
Address

_____
City   State/Prov.   Zip/Post. Code

COMPLETE AND MAIL TODAY WE PAY THE POSTAGE!

PRINTED IN USA

J80 ☐   ☐

car was being driven by a man Anna knew well, someone called Ned, whom she had known all her life."

Dennis looked puzzled.

"The name brought no revelation, no complete remembering?" he asked.

"Nothing at all definite."

"This Ned person?" Dennis asked. "You feel that he might be the husband?"

"Probably."

The short, clipped admission left Noel's lips as if it had been driven from him against his will, and he strode on without speaking for another hundred yards or so until Tranby said:

"We've established the car and the husband. It was being driven at a high speed and Anna was afraid. Supposing," he added quietly, "the car went over the cliff?"

"And she jumped clear just in time?" Noel's lips tightened. "No, Dennis, it won't do. These things just don't happen."

"There was considerable bruising, consistent with a fall," Tranby reminded him.

"And no car found afterwards!"

Tranby drew him towards the edge of the cliff.

"Look down there."

Beneath them the water churned and boiled against the base of the cliff, breaking on a ridge of cruel-looking rocks several yards out from the shore, and even on this comparatively calm afternoon the scene was one of wrath leashed only for the moment, of power unlimited surging in towards the land. Noel watched the waves breaking far beneath them and cascading back again to be lost in the great roll of the bay, with a sickening doubt growing in his heart.

"What *can* we know!" he exclaimed "What sort of evidence can we really piece together with certainty? Anna came near enough to the truth just now, but the scene isn't the one that is dominating her subconscious to the exclusion of everything else. Her own safety was not the overwhelming thought in her mind on that night." His strong voice underlined the words and he bent to knock the contents of his pipe out against a boulder as if it no longer gave him any satisfaction. "Until we can find what was," he added, "we'll continue to come up against these disappointments, the blanks in this story that are constantly confronting us."

Tranby followed him farther along the cliff top with his brows drawn together in a deep frown, and even when they came to the first warnings of erosion he did not speak. The cliff edge had been cordoned off, and they halted simultaneously where the road had been closed to traffic, looking along the winding way ahead, their eyes speculative as they measured the distance between road and cliff.

"Anyone coming round that bend at speed on a darkish night could quite easily go over, especially if he wasn't paying a great deal of attention to the road," Tranby suggested. "Right over, Noel, without so much as a sign."

"And no track marks?"

"Let's walk on."

Tranby led the way, and less than a couple of hundred yards ahead a whole section of the cliff was cut off where part of it had crumbled into the sea.

Noel went through the ropes and strode across the narrow grass margin to the edge of the cliff, standing there for a long time in deepest thought before he turned and came slowly back to his friend.

"It could have happened here," he agreed, "and there would be no sign of tire marks or anything else. The whole cliff face could have given way not long after the weight of—say a car —had bumped across it." He was staring down at the grass, frowning, reluctant to accept the evidence of surmise. "These are only calculations built on the slightest evidence, of course. We can't afford to jump too hastily to conclusions."

"But we're pretty certain about the car, old man," Tranby pointed out. "If Anna came anywhere near here she could not very well have walked."

"She walked back to the main road."

"Granted. But why would she come to such an isolated spot as this in the first place, unless she came by car?"

"People walk considerable distances for pleasure."

"But not in the sort of clothes Anna was found in—a light frock and a thin coat and high-heeled shoes, and not in the early hours of the morning, unless something decidedly unusual has happened!"

Noel straightened, still looking out towards the sea.

"I've been through all that," he admitted, "over and over again, and all I can honestly accept is the fact that she drove late at night—or even through the night—with someone called Ned."

"Whom we presume to be her husband."

Noel turned with a look in his eyes that was as turbulent as the sea itself.

"On that assumption," he said slowly, "we are believing him dead."

"If we can prove that a car went over there at any time during the past few weeks I believe that will be the answer," Tranby said, not looking at him.

Noel turned away

"I didn't come here to prove that," he muttered harshly. "Our first duty to Anna is to break the amnesia, to give her back her identity."

They continued to search the cliff top for half a mile, all along the area of erosion, but there was nothing to be seen. The heavy rain on the night of the accident had been repeated on three days during the week which followed; the by-road was permanently rutted and there was no sign of tracks running away from it.

"What we have left out of our calculations," Tranby said, "is the fact that all this could have happened before the rain started. We had three weeks of dry weather before that deluge, if you remember, and the ground up here would be baked hard. It would take an hour or two, even of that kind of rain, to soften it up enough to take an impression."

Noel nodded, but he did not seem to be thinking about a possible accident now. His eyes were remote and troubled and the determination of his mouth and squared, set jaw was greater than ever.

"I've got to take Anna back over this ground, step by step," he said. "It's the only way. If there was an accident, I believe it was the climax to something else and that's why we're not getting any further on this particular track. You got the evidence, under hypnotism, that she lived 'among many animals' and she appears to be happy and familiar with a country background. She has also filled in a good many Ministry forms without hesitation for us both, which might suggest that her people were farming somewhere at one time."

"Could be," Tranby agreed. "So where do we go from there?"

"Home, I think," Noel said surprisingly. "I want to have a look at a map."

"There's the A.A. map in the car."

"I want something more comprehensive than that. A physical map from an old atlas would do," Noel decided, and Tranby led the way back to the road without questioning him further.

"There's been a fairly big landslide back there," he told Ruth as they rejoined the two girls on the cliff top. "Quite a fall, in fact. Half the cliff has gone over and the road has been closed."

Anna stood very still, listening, her face pale and tense, and for a moment Noel Melford found himself hesitating, wondering whether he should force her to go back with him along the cliff then and there or wait to carry out the plan he had already prepared in his mind.

He decided on the latter course, driving back to Glynmareth when the eventually reached the main road with a firmness of purpose that even Anna did not miss.

"Leave me with her for half an hour," he commanded Ruth. "You can take Dennis into the garden and make yourself useful picking weeds!"

Anna had gone upstairs to take off her coat, and when she came down Noel was alone in the hall, waiting for her.

"Will you try something with me?" he asked. "It's an experiment that I think might work."

"I'll do anything," she promised, "that you think will help."

He led the way into his study, drawing a chair forward to the desk for her to sit down, and after a brief search in one of the drawers he found a relief map of the British Isles which he kept open before him while he talked

"We're going back over some old ground first," he explained, "and I would like you to write down any impressions you get as we go along. Don't mind about me. Just write what you feel—what you know about."

Slowly, and with a subtle domination she did not even feel, he began to tell her about his own youth, about the long school holidays which he and Ruth had spent with friends in the north and the excursions of his student days.

100

At first Anna was far too interested in what he had to tell her of his own early background to think deeply about herself, but soon she began to compare the range and scope of his travels with something limited in her own life. There was much in what he told her which was familiar, however, and gradually she found herself responding more readily to the picture he was building up. The moorland scene became vivid until she could almost feel the rush of wind against her cheeks and the sting of rain with the bite of snow behind it blowing in from the sea.

She took up the pencil he had laid near her hand and began to play idly with it on the sheet of notepaper which he thrust across the desk towards her, but it was some considerable time before she began to write. Her thoughts had been too busy following his to swing away on their own, and suddenly he stood up, looking intently at her across the desk.

"You know about that sort of thing, Anna," he said. "Now write what you know."

He turned his back to her, gazing out into the garden while she sat at the desk without moving, and then, as if obeying some impluse which she dared not refuse, she began to write, slowly at first and then more quickly until she had covered both sides of the sheet of paper.

By the time she had reached the bottom of the second page the effort had exhausted itself and she pushed both pencil and paper from her, staring down at what she had written as if it had been taken from her almost against her will.

Noel gathered it up without comment and put it in his pocket. He came round the end of the desk and put his arm about her shoulders, and the brief, friendly embrace all but reduced her to tears.

"Don't give up," he said steadily. "I really believe we may be getting somewhere, at last."

She smiled at him, her heart recoiling in cowardly fashion at the thought of what must inevitably come of their success—parting and heartache and loss such as she had never experienced before. She knew that instinctively, but if Noel thought of it in that way there was no evidence of such thoughts in his expression as he walked with her into the garden where Ruth and Dennis Tranby had started to mow the lawn.

When they had had their evening meal they sat for an hour in the gathering dusk, chatting idly, until Noel rose to do his customary late round of the wards. Tranby went out with him, crossing the shrubbery to the hospital in his wake, though neither of them spoke until they had reached Noel's consulting rooms. Then Noel took the sheet of notepaper out of his pocket and passed it to him without comment.

Tranby read what Anna had written.

"Do you think she would have gone on writing if she had not come to the end of this?" he asked, flicking the paper with his thumb. "There's quite a lot here, but most of it is inconclusive."

"I think the effort exhausted her at that stage," Noel returned. "She's terribly sensitive about all this, Dennis, and I can't take the risk of forcing her too far. What we've got there is interesting enough, and I believe I shall be able to work on alone for a time with the information on the paper."

"There's not a great lot," Tranby mused. "Just this very beautifully expressed love of the countryside and a rather disjointed description of an old house standing on the moors."

"'An old grey farmhouse within sight and sound of the North Sea'," Noel quoted. "And after that she has written the letters ALN—almost as if she were groping for a name."

"They could be part of a word," Tranby agreed, pacing up and down the room with the sheet of notepaper in his hand. "The name of a town or perhaps a village. Maybe it might be the name of the house itself," he suggested, wheeling round to see how his friend took to the idea. "It's pretty flimsy evidence to start a search with, I know, but it's better than nothing at all."

"I believe Anna came from the north of England," Noel mused doggedly. "We have the mention of the North Sea to go on, which means it would be somewhere on the east, and then there's the moorland country she remembers and describes so well. That would give us a stretch of the north-east coast from Yorkshire to Berwick to search, which is rather a tall order, especially since the police seem unable to help us with their list of persons missing. No," he added with renewed vigour, "we can't wait for the police. We've got to tackle this on our own, and the three letters are our first real clue. ALN! I wonder what they mean?"

"After this case is cleared up to your satisfaction I'm joining the Sleuths Department of Scotland Yard!" Tranby grinned. "Let's leave it for tonight, old man. It will keep. Anna is happy enough where she is."

But not completely happy, Noel thought as he put the paper in a drawer and reached for his white coat. Not completely happy. That's something I may be able to do for her in time, though, and I've got to do it unselfishly. I even may have it in my power to give her the happiness she needs—indirectly.

He found Sara on duty when he reached the wards and she went round with him.

"I'm going on holiday next week," she told him as she re-arranged the screens round the last bed. "I've ten days to take and Matron would like me to get them in right away. We're not too busy and the weather is good at the moment."

"Where do you intend to go?" he asked idly, consulting her report on the patient they had just left. "Abroad again?"

"You know I told you that I hadn't booked up in time!" Sara felt like shaking him out of his obvious indifference. "I couldn't fix anything definitely at the time of the epidemic, and after that it was rather late. I don't really mind," she added conscientiously. "I couldn't have left Matron in a flat spin at the time with all that extra work on her hands, and sometimes I wonder if we don't miss quite a lot of the beauty of our own country by rushing off to the Continent whenever we have a few days to spare!"

"True enough," Noel agreed. "I've met people in London whose knowledge of Paris and Geneva was far greater than any conception of their own country north of the Home Counties! Where had you thought of going?"

"Oh—possibly north," she answered evasively. "I've never been to the Lake District—or to Scotland. By the way, Noel, I wonder if I might borrow that new book of yours on the streptomycin theory to take with me. I could read it through while I was away."

"All work and no play makes Jill a dull girl!" he laughed, "but have it by all means, if you must!"

He thinks that my work means everything to me! Sara mused bitterly, forgetting that the impression was one which she had gone out of her way to foster in the past, largely for his benefit so that she might emphasize her own suitability as wife and helpmate to a busy doctor.

"I can't see any hope of reading it through otherwise," she said.

"You'll find it in my consulting-room," he told her. "In the right-hand drawer of my desk, I think. By the way," he added, referring to the report he still held, "I'd like a word with Greaves about this X-ray tomorrow. Arrange it for me, will you?"

"I'm going off duty now, but I'll put in a note, and I'll collect the book on my way." She smiled at him as they parted. "Thank you, Noel!"

When she reached Noel's room she looked about her as she usually did, with a kind of hunger in her eyes, and then she straightened her shoulders and pulled open the nearest drawer. A sheet of blue notepaper lay on top of the book she sought and she picked it up, staring at it curiously. Part of it appeared to be covered by what she could only describe as 'doodling' a mass of strange-looking hieroglyphics and half-formed sentences jotted down at random, while underneath was what read like a school girl's essay on a day in the country.

Her face flushed dully as she read on, turning the page with a quick flick of her wrist so that her starched cuff crackled with the abrupt movement. She had even forgotten where she stood and that she was reading someone's private papers, and the stiff front of her apron rose and fell as her breath came more heavily between her parted lips.

When she had read to the end of the second page she laid the paper back in the drawer and turned towards the door with the book she had come to borrow clutched against her breast.

She had found a weapon near to her hand, at last, and she meant to use it with what speed she could.

"Ten days!" she murmured, "I could do it in less than that time, with any luck!"

Two days later she told Ruth that she was going off on a rambling holiday.

"Don't expect more than the odd postcard," she laughed. "I don't intend to stay more than a day in any one place!"

"But surely," Ruth objected, "you have some sort of objective, some definite end in view?"

Sara smiled thinly.

"I dare say, but quite truthfully I don't really know what it is—not yet!"

Ruth considered her doubtfully. She had half expected Sara to suggest that they should go together, as she had done once before, but the invitation had not been forthcoming and, somehow, she had felt glad. One reason was that she did not want to leave Anna at this crucial stage in her journey back to memory, and the other was all tangled up with this new and distressing feeling of being entirely out of tune with Sara.

Their friendship had been one of long standing and Ruth regretted any hint of a rift in the lute, but there had been occasions lately when Sara had been most difficult to understand. Her attitude towards Anna, for instance, had been almost vindictive, and she had been moody and taciturn quite often when she had shared a meal with them.

"You don't mind going alone?" she asked, and Sara was swift to refute any suggestion of loneliness.

"Not in the least. I never did worry about being left in my own company," she declared. "I can always find something to do."

"Of course," Ruth said, "if you're going to move about . . ."

"I intend to start at York and go north from there," Sara said. "Old walled cities have always had a fascination for me."

Ruth could not quite shake off the conviction that Sara was not telling the truth, although they had gone often enough to Chester together, and there was probably some fascination in linking up those old, walled cities and travelling down into the past. Sara had made her decision about that sort of holiday so quickly, however, that it seemed she might have another motive for journeying north so determinedly, and when she left Glynmareth at the end of the week she had a look in her eyes which did not seem to reflect the holiday spirit at all. But very soon Ruth had forgotten about Sara in her concern for her brother.

Noel was lookig positively unhappy these days, she thought, with that tense, strained expression about his face and the remoteness deepening in his eyes. He ate so little, too, that she began to worry about his physical needs, but nothing she could say by way of protest called forth more than a deprecating smile.

"You know I never did eat a lot," he would point out. "You're becoming a Mother Hen!"

"I'm not the type who fusses unnecessarily," she retorted sharply on one occasion. "You eat next to nothing and you work far too hard. What you need is a holiday."

Surprisingly, he agreed with her.

"I've arranged with Tranby to take over for a few days," he said.

"A few days isn't going to do much good," Ruth declared belligerently. "You're entitled to a month. Why don't you take it and get a real rest?"

Some inner sense, some urge to protect that which she loved, had prompted the suggestion, but suddenly they were both thinking of Anna and looking at one another with the knowledge of her dependence on them in their eyes.

"I'd take care of her," Ruth promised. "You needn't fear. There would be Dennis, too."

He turned from her and strode to the window.

"I won't be away for more than a week—perhaps not even that," he said. "I'm going north, Ruth, to work on a clue we've picked up. Both Dennis and I believe that Anna came from somewhere in the north country—the north-east coast or the North Riding of Yorkshire."

"Yorkshire?" Ruth stood questioningly before the word. "Does Sara know about this?" she asked bluntly.

"Sara? I shouldn't think so. What makes you ask? She's on holiday, isn't she?"

"Yes," Ruth said slowly, "she's on holiday. I wondered, though, if she knew before she left."

"There's no reason why she should have been told," Noel answered indifferently. "It isn't a hospital case."

Ruth would not burden him with her thoughts at the moment, and so she switched the conversation back to Anna.

"I wouldn't say she had a Yorkshire accent," she demurred. "In fact, she hasn't much of an accent at all."

"We're not going by an accent," he told her. "It's something far more definite than than. Anna wrote some impressions for me and the letters ALN appeared through them, suggesting that it was a familiar name out of the past, and both Dennis and I feel that we could help her if we could find this place. Of course, the greatest achievement would be to trace her relatives through it."

"So that's why you've been poring over all those old atlases," Ruth guessed. "I wondered. It still seems an amazing thing to me that her people have not claimed her," she added.

"It's about the most callous thing I've ever known," he returned, scowling "Dennis established pretty firmly that she has both father and sister, during that hypnotic session last week, but he thinks her mother may be dead. Anna showed a quiet acceptance of that sorrow consistent with death in these circumstances. There was nothing like the distress registered when her marriage was mentioned, for instance."

He spoke about Anna's marriage so rarely now, but Ruth knew that the thought of it was constantly in his mind, as it was in her own. They could not get away from it, nor could she blind herself any longer to the fact that her brother was deeply in love with the girl she had brought home.

Remorse quite often pursued Ruth with a relentlessness which she could not turn aside, and yet, on the other hand, she could not regret having helped someone so much in need of her kindness and understanding as Anna had proved to be.

That the amnesia would be finally broken she had no doubt, her fears were for her brother in the process.

It was Anna herself who seemed to see farther than any of them, however.

The day after Sara had gone off on holiday she came across from the hospital at five o'clock, following Ruth into the sitting-room instead of going upstairs with her coat, as usual.

"Ruth," she asked, "could you spare me a minute or two?"

107

"Ten, if you want them!" Ruth turned from the window to smile at her. "I don't suppose Noel will be in much before six. He's gone to Bristol about that new appointment."

"I—hope he'll get it," Anna said. "But you'll hate leaving here, Ruth."

"Yes," Ruth answered with absolute candour, "but I can't stand in his way."

"Making sacrifices is part of life," Anna said in a strained undertone which completely changed her voice. "Ruth, I want to go away."

Ruth glanced at her sharply.

"We've been over all this before," she pointed out.

"I know, but—I feel it will be best to go. I've thought it all over. Sister Enman said once that a fresh mind on a case was sometimes nine-tenths of the way towards a solution, that—that a doctor could be too near to a case to see it objectively." She paused, clenching her hands nervously by her side in an effort to still their trembling. "I wonder if Noel would put me in touch with the specialist he told me about in Bristol? He mentioned him the other day when —when we hadn't got very far with the tests we were doing, and I thought I could—go into hospital there." She raised dark, unhappy eyes to Ruth's, as if pleading with her to understand. "Don't think I don't appreciate all Noel has done," she begged, "or that I think he has failed. It's just—just that I feel someone else might be—the best decision."

Ruth came across the room to stand facing her on the hearthrug.

"Anna, my dear, that isn't your true reason for wanting to go is it?" she asked gently.

"How can I stay!" The cry came straight from Anna's heart, wrung from her against her will. "How can I go on accepting your kindness and doing nothing in return! Ruth, I must go. I must!"

Ruth's eyes lifted suddenly to the door to see her brother unexpectedly standing there with a look in his eyes that seared straight across her heart.

"Anna, what nonsense is this?" he demanded, striding across the room. "You know you have no right to talk like this—no right to leave us. You know I can keep you here by compulsion, if I wish!"

Softly Ruth tiptoed out of the room, drawing the door behind her, leaving them face to face with the most hopeless situation she had ever been a party to, her pity reaching out to them, yet conscious that there was nothing further she could do. It remained to Noel, now, to resolve their problem.

"If you wish!" Anna echoed Noel's last words with a kind of hopelessness which he had never heard in her voice before. "But you must not force me to stay. You know I must go. You know it is the only thing to do now."

She looked at him, trying to keep the agony of her love from welling to her eyes, but he saw it and came to her in one long stride.

"Anna—my little love!" Roughly he took her into his arms, holding her close, his lips against her hair. "How can I bear to lose you? How can I let you go!"

She lay in his arms, conscious of peace abounding, of the world and its problems suddenly shut out. Only the caressing movement of his hand against her hair seemed real in that moment when his love stood confessed in all its tenderness and passion. And then, swiftly, he pressed her head against him in an agony of longing reflected poignantly in her own heart, and put her gently but firmly from him. She saw the compressed lines about his mouth and the hardness of his eyes as he said harshly:

"This is no solution. But I beg of you not to run away. I'm giving myself another week to solve all this. After that I shall be forced to take you to someone else."

"You are going away?" she asked unsteadily.

"Yes. If you stay here quietly with Ruth you'll be helping all you can."

If you stay quietly with Ruth! Did he know how much he was offering her, how much she longed to stay forever in this lovely backwater where life's rush and turmoil was muted, and kindness, and love surrounded her on all sides?

"I'll stay," she promised at last, "if Ruth will have me."

"I don't think there's any fear of that," he told her as he turned towards the door. "Ruth has accepted you, Anna, and that means a great deal."

He told his sister his plans when Anna had gone to bed and they were alone, and Ruth found herself frowning over them.

"You're quite sure about this?" she asked. "You think it is sure to bring results?"

"I'm hoping it will—hoping against hope."

"At whatever cost to yourself?" Her eyes were steady on his. The time had passed for pretence between thm.

"At whatver cost," he repeated firmly.

"Then go," she said, "and God bless you, my dear!"

CHAPTER EIGHT

NOEL LEFT GLYNMARETH early on the following Monday morning, travelling across country until he reached the Great North Road, which he followed as far as Boroughbridge. Here he decided to spend the night, putting up at The Three Arrows, where he dined well and slept comfortably, setting out early again for his real objective.

Over breakfast in the hotel's spacious dining-room he had studied a road map of the district, and instead of continuing on the main highway he branched off and was soon winding along narrow by-ways, through little villages as old as time itself, flanked by the broad acres of Yorkshire he had heard so much about but had never visited until now, the rich agricultural belt of waving corn and heavy-eared wheat that lies close under the knees of the Hambleton Hills.

He had made up his mind to follow every clue, no matter how slight, and the vilage of Alne lay somewhere ahead of him.

Once, when he stopped to ask his way, he realized how little he really had to go on. He was searching for a girl called Anna in a possible half-dozen villages or small towns over a wide area of the north-east coast, and he had nothing but a snapshot to help him with his explanations.

The most likely person, he considered, would be the local vicar, and when he had steered the car through a beautiful avenue of trees, like a cool green tunnel in the summer sunshine, he came upon the village church with its gaunt, many-gabled old vicarage facing it across the road.

The door of the vicarage stood hospitably open on this warm July day and the vicar himself came in answer to his summons. He was evidently a man who knew his flock, and it was obvious after only a few minutes' consultation that he could do nothing to help.

"It's an unusual name for these parts," he pointed out, adjusting his horn-rimmed spectacles to study Noel more closely. "I should have remembered it even if the girl had left here many years ago."

Another blank, Noel thought as he offered the older man his thanks and his sincere apologies for wasting his time. Was it always going to be like this? Was he never going to be able to give Anna back that blank period in her life, the only way in which she was not completely normal?

His destination now was Northumberland, and he drove straight on for the next three hours, forgetful of food or fatigue as he felt instinctively that he was coming nearer to his goal. Here he came closer to the sea, that grey North Sea of Anna's remembering, and here, too, were the very moors and the grey old houses she had described so accurately!

Coming upon them for the first time, he marvelled at the fund of detail she had managed to convey in this respect, and took new hope from it. He had come thus far and the way seemed suddenly clear.

His first objective was Alnwick, but he did not waste much time there. He was now more than ever convinced that the letters ALN were incorporated in the name of this northern town, but he felt that he would have to search outside the town itself for her actual home.

Then, almost by accident, he came upon a signpost on a road going towards the sea with a word printed on it which made every nerve in his body vibrate with excitement. Here, perhaps, was journey's end!

A sudden, ungovernable sense of loss and disappointment assailed him for a moment as his love crushed all other considerations out of his mind, and he saw himself handing Anna over to someone who had a greater right to comfort her than he would ever have.

Fierce, primitive jealousy blinded him, but he knew that he must not waver. What he was doing was his own part in her return to life, all he could give her for the future, and he must give it willingly. What he was about to lose had never really been his to take. Some other man would gain because he had the prior right, and Anna would eventually forget him.

He had said it himself. "When all this is over you will remember the past but you will have forgotten all that came between" He tortured himself with the repetition of the thought, wondering if there had ever been a case history to prove differently, searching his mind for the hope, and then he acknowledged that it was one of the mercies for which man could not account and that he should not wish it otherwise. A merciful blacking out, that was all!

Alnmouth! The name on the signpost danced before his eyes in the sunlight, mocking him, and then he let in his clutch and drove on.

Far ahead he could see the red-tiled roofs and the church spire of a fairy-tale village rising clear against the blue of sea and distant horizon, a cluster of tiny houses built on a spit of land with a shining curve of silver river girdling it round. It looked so much out of this world that he was almost tempted to take it for a mirage until he remembered the down-to-earth signpost which had said ALNMOUTH—4 miles.

The road wound with every hundred yards and he lost sight of the village from time to time, coming upon it again at a new angle of beauty and feeling more than ever convinced that here was his destination. His pulses quickened as he drove through the narrow main street between old sandstone cottages and the little village shops, and before he thought of looking for an hotel he drove straight on to the sea front.

It seemed, when he reached it, that he had come to the edge of the world, and he thought that perhaps the end of his search would mean just that for him. When he had acknowledged his love for Anna it had not been intentional, but now he let the full force of it flow over him like a great tide, sweeping away all reserve. His hands clenched on the wheel he held, and his eyes were darkly passionate as he searched the wide horizon as if, out there in the void, he might find an answer to all this. When it is all over, he thought, I can go to sea. Ruth must be convinced that she should marry Dennis and settle down, and not wear herself out as my handmaiden for the rest of her life. And I must find the strength from somewhere to go on afterwards —alone.

In spite of the heat of the sun a cold wind seemed to blow in from the sea, and he turned the car round and drove back a little way along the cobbled street to a picturesque little inn he had noticed.

The proprietor of "The Schooner" could just manage to find him a single room, although it was in the height of the season, and when he had washed and changed he wandered down to the lounge. He had quite forgotten that he had not eaten all day and was turning his next move over in his mind when he heard his name from the other side of the room.

"Noel! Noel Melford, by all that's wonderful!"

His surprise was no greater than Sara's appeared to be, and he went towards her with a sense of companionship stirring in him which he had never felt in Sara's company before, and which was probably the aftermath of that chill loneliness of spirit he had experienced out there on the sea front. Here was someone who would understand, someone who knew all about his present problem and would be willing to help, viewing it with him from the professional angle, at least. The emotional one was not a thing to be shared even by an old acquaintance like Sara.

"How good to see you!" he declared with far more warmth than he had ever used at their meetings in the past "Like a breath of home in a foreign land, in fact," he added, laughing.

"May one ask what made you choose this particular 'foreign land'?" Sara smiled, sitting down again.

She wore fine blue tweeds with a grey knitted jumper and, out of uniform, she looked softer and altogether more feminine, somehow. Noel realized that he had never thought of Sara much—out of uniform. She was the perfect nurse, and she was Ruth's friend. Apart from that, he had never really studied Sara's attributes, only knowing that she had irritated him at times in a vague, inexplicable way but she was both efficient and indispensable at the hospital, so that he accepted her in his home both as Ruth's friend and an interesting colleague.

"You may!" he returned, adding more seriously: "This appears to be something of a coincidence, Sara, you and I

113

being here together. I know, of course, that you're on holiday and I ought not to thrust hospital affairs at you like this, but perhaps Anna's isn't quite an ordinary case."

"Was it ever a hospital case?" Sara asked somewhat sharply. "You were more than a little interested in it right from the start."

"Yes," he agreed with a frankness which struck like a knife, "and I am hoping that I may come to the end of my quest here."

Sara gazed down at her neat brogues. They were stained with seawater and sand and suggested that she might have walked some considerable distance along the shore.

"Have you — found anything?" she asked.

"I arrived less than an hour ago," he explained, "but I must start my inquiries right away. In a small place like this it ought to be easy."

She looked out of the window for a moment, not answering him, and then she took out one of her own cigarettes and tapped it thoughtfully against her case.

"Noel," she said, "doesn't it occur to you that you might be wasting your time?"

He looked at her in frank surprise.

"In what way?" he asked coldly.

"Do you really think this girl *wants* her memory back? You've tried everything and failed."

She saw a pulse beat quickly in his cheek as he struggled with some emotion or other, but it did not daunt her. Sara was far too sure of herself to be easily intimidated.

"Failure is something I shall never admit," he said harshly. "One can't bear to go on seeing the shadow of fear in a woman's eyes like that and do nothing about it. Besides, it is my duty to my profession to go on trying."

"Not exactly." Her voice came clipped and cool as he held his lighter for her. "We all considered that she should have been handed over to Tim Wedderburn long ago, you know!"

His mouth hardened and he snapped the flame out with a quick flick of his wrist.

" 'Handing people over' isn't as easy as that, Sara," he said. "To a sensitive nature like Anna's the thought of being in the hands of the police is never conducive to a rapid solution of the problem."

Sara bit her lip. She had not intended to antagonize him, and she did not trust herself to answer. She felt that she could have swept Anna and her eternal problem into final oblivion without a qualm, but here she was with Noel, alone with him at last in a veritable paradise that had stirred even her unresponsive heart, and already the girl he had championed had thrust herself between thm! She saw Anna as a pale ghost which she was determined to lay forever as soon as the opportunity came her way, and she had believed that opportunity near enough before Noel had suddenly appeared on the scene. She recognized that she must move warily now, that Noel would not be dictated to nor would he deviate from his chosen path until he was certain that it was leading him nowhere.

Let him stay, then, she decided, and draw one more blank to dishearten him finally, perhaps! She had spent two days in Alnwick making the same sort of inquiries as he was about to make here, and she was convinced that he girl had not lived there, yet a tenacity which had always been evident in her work had kept her where she was. She would not help Noel. She knew that he could not afford to be away from Glynmareth for any great length of time, but she still had eight days in which to sift this mystery to its dregs and she was determined that she would be first to come upon the truth.

There was no doubt in her mind that Anna had a secret, and for her own peace of mind she preferred to think of it as a shameful secret. The subconscious distress shown by the girl whenever her marriage was mentioned pointed to such a state of affairs, and Sara had heard it said that she had been greatly upset that day when Noel had taken her into the church.

Noel, Sara concluded, was being far too conscientious over this case, and here he was prepared to spend several days of previous leave following up a slender clue!

Something that she could not understand herself made her determined that she, and not Noel, should be first to discover Anna's background, a primitively cruel streak in her make-up which sought for a weapon to destroy her enemy. For Anna had taken on that guise in Sara's mind ever since the evening at the villa when Noel had defended her, telling them passionately that the marriage must never

115

be mentioned again. Sara had been quick to grasp the fundamental reason for Noel's outburst, but she was far too much of an egotist to believe that he had already passed the stage of just beginning to care for the younger girl.

The situation became enlarged in her mind out of all proportions, until she almost believed that Noel had been her accepted lover before Anna had come upon the scene, and she was determined to rid herself of her rival at any cost. It was for this reason that she felt so disgruntled with Ruth, whom she believed to have failed her abominably over the affair, and so she refrained rather pointedly from asking Noel about his sister.

She could not keep her mind from Anna, however, and when they had gone into dinner together she felt that she must get to know Noel's plans.

"Of course you know I'll help you all I can, Noel," she told him with an intimate smile. "This won't be the first time we've worked on a difficult case together, quite apart from the hospital, and I dare say it won't be the last. Do you remember the old gardener who used to pester Ruth for her autograph because he imagined she was Ellen Terry?"

Noel smiled.

"He was a harmless old soul, and I'm glad he died in harness rather than in an institution. I think he would have liked the idea of going out as he did—just falling asleep among his flowers. I should have hated to have to certify him."

She studied him with her elbows on the table, propping her chin, her head on one side.

"Sometimes, when I'm permitted these intimate glimpses of you," she said softly, "I think you're far too sensitive to have become a good doctor. People recognize that sort of thing, you know, and take advantage of it."

He laughed.

"My dear Sara, I assure you I don't often open my heart, and certainly not to my patients! A doctor, like everyone else, is the better for a certain amount of sympathy in his make-up. Otherwise, he becomes merely a healing machine."

"It's sympathy then, that has brought you up here on such a slender clue?" she asked quickly.

"You can call it that," he said. "Sympathy and determination to solve this problem in the shortest possible time."

"How long can you give yourself?"

"Unfortunately, only a few days. Four at the most."

"Noel," she said suddenly, "why not leave it to me? Suppose we draw up a plan of action? Two minds are always better than one, and it will probably save time in the end."

Noel hesitated.

"Truthfully, Sara," he confessed, "I don't think I have a plan yet. I rushed off here more or less on an impulse when I had what I considered to be a good enough clue to be going on with. I started out by going to a place in Yorkshire, but I drew a blank there. I did discover, though, that people are eager enough to help in a case like this, and I am hoping I shall meet with the same sort of co-operation here. There's no earthly reason, though, for you to spoil your holiday."

"Why shouldn't I help?" she argued. "You appear to be willing to give up part of yours."

"It's different in my case," he said briefly.

"I can't see why," she told him calmly. "Unless, of course, you're in love with your patient."

The suggestion had been forced from her on a mounting wave of jealousy which swept discretion and all else before it, and she saw the smile fade out of his eyes and his handsome mouth, harden as he answered her.

"You know that Anna is already married," he said stiffly. "There can be no question of love—or anything else between us."

"How simple that sounds, Noel!" she said. "Sometimes you remind me of an adolescent schoolboy for all your achievements!"

"The ideals of an adolescent are often enviable," he returned quietly. "And now, if you'll excuse me, I think I'll take a walk on the sea front. I've been driving all day and it has left me cramped."

Fool; Sara called herself. Fool, to have chanced so much!

Angry at herself for the way in which she had taunted Noel, and angrier still that he had avoided her company for the remainder of the evening by going off to walk by the sea alone, she decided not to be in the lounge when he arrived back. It really didn't do to let a man see you were running after him, she mused, although she had virtually pursued Noel for years.

From the window of her bedroom she saw him come back up the narrow main street shortly before ten o'clock with the boatman who ran the ferry across the mouth of the river, and she could scarcely contain her curiosity until the following morning to know whether or not he had gained any information from that source.

The effort was made, however, and the consequent feeling of virtue added to her self-esteem as she waited for him to put in an appearance in the breakfast room about nine o'clock.

He came in from the direction of the main door, windblown and hatless, obviously straight from the shore, and he came directly across to where she sat.

"I've been out along the links," he explained. "There's a howling gale blowing and the sand's flying about as if it were the Sahara, but I've thoroughly enjoyed it."

"Any progress?" she asked casually, as their breakfast was brought in. "I wondered if you had made any contacts last night, but I was too tired to wait up and see."

"I had a long talk with one or two of the locals, but it didn't get me very far, I'm afraid. I mean to get in touch with the vicar this morning," he added, "and then I might try the registrar in Alnwick. It's a long shot, but Anna may even have been born hereabouts, and I am determined not to leave one stone unturned."

"She may even have been married in the parish church," Sara suggested with intent to hurt. She was quite unable to keep herself from reverting to the one topic whereon hung Anna's marriage. "That would be a useful line to take, I should think."

"Yes." He buttered his toast abstractedly "I wish you would do something for me, Sara."

"You have only to name it."

"See what you can make of things in the local shops. Buy the odd tube of tooth-paste here and there and pick up any sort of information you consider might help. We believe that Anna has a sister and that her father is alive. Dennis Tranby got that much from the hypnotic effort last week. And then there's 'Ned', of course."

118

"The husband?"

"We presume so."

"How else would you explain it?" she asked icily.

"It's dangerous to start 'explaining' each small detail in a case like this," he reminded her. "Ned could quite easily have very little significance, you know."

He was hoping for that, she thought jealously, but he could not write off Anna's marriage simply because he had fallen in love with her himself; Besides, Sara comforted herself, Noel wasn't the type to take the marriage vow lightly nor seek to cast it aside, even if his own heart was grievously involved.

She poured herself a second cup of coffee with growing confidence and agreed to sound the local shopkeepers while he went to pay his call on the vicar.

As soon as she saw him again she knew that he had been disappointed. Anyone who knew Noel Melford realized that the tightness about his mouth was determination in the face of setback, and she had worked with him for years.

"Well," she said slowly, "no luck?"

"Absolutely none. The vicar was on holiday and I saw his locum, a charming fellow who said he would do what he could for me but didn't think he would be half so useful as the man on the spot."

Sara said: "Bad luck!" but was secretly glad, although she had not done much better herself.

"I went the rounds and bought myself enough toothpaste to last me a lifetime!" she laughed, "but the name Anna just didn't ring a bell anywhere in the village, and these people generally know the locals for miles around."

"I've made up my mind to try Alnwick this afternoon," Noel said, his disappointment sticking in his throat like all bitterness. "I thought I was going to get somewhere down here. In fact, I could have sworn it!"

Sara put a warm, friendly hand over his where it lay on the table.

"Must you go on with this, Noel?" she asked gently. "You're wearing yourself out. I know how galling it is to have to admit defeat, but really you've done everything in your power to solve this problem. Why not turn the whole thing over to the proper quarter when you go back, and have done with it?"

"You mean, of course, the police?" He was looking at her as though he hardly saw her. "That is the last thing I shall do," he said stubbornly. "Don't ask me about it again, Sara."

She flushed scarlet.

"Very well! If you wish to go on being made a fool of I shall certainly not interefer again, but I shall still try to help, if it is only to prove to you how wrong you are about this girl!"

It was a speech so completely typical of Sara that Noel did not even consider it odd. He smiled at her strange offer and went on with his meal, smoking two cigarettes in rapid succession when he had finished, sure sign that he was thrashing out some major problem in his mind.

"Excuse me, sir," the hall porter said at his elbow as he stubbed the second end into the ash-tray. "You're wanted on the telephone. A long-distance call, sir. Would you take it in the office?"

Noel rose at once, pushing back his chair, and Sara met his eyes inquiringly.

"Sounds as if it might be Glynmareth," he satisfied her. "I phoned Ruth last night to ask about Anna."

Anna! Always Anna, Sara thought savagely. He *was* in love with the girl! Any fool could see that now!

Tense and angry, she waited his return, and saw immediately that something had upset his plans. He was frowning and there was a slight flush on his tanned cheeks as he strode back to their table.

"It was Ruth," he said. "There's been an urgent call for me from Bristol."

"Noel, your appointment!" The color ran up into her pale cheeks, and ambition deepened the lustre in her wide-set eyes. "It means that you've got it! They would never send for you like that otherwise."

He smiled faintly.

"You have more confidence in my ability than I have, Sara!"

"You're far too modest, my dear!"

"Perhaps I am conscious of my own limitations."

"Noel," she demanded sharply, "you're not contemplating turning this Bristol offer down, are you?"

He shook his head.

"I would be several kinds of fool to do that, but I haven't got the job yet."

"This can mean nothing else." She swept his objections aside with her usual imperiousness. "It's yours for the taking."

"I'm not so sure. It could mean that the Board just wanted to take another look at me!"

"I've told you you're being far too modest!" She rose to her feet, smiling down at him. "I really think this calls for a celebration, you know!"

"Sorry, Sara," he apologized, "but there just won't be time. I've got to be in Bristol by tomorrow evening."

She bit her lip in exasperation, but the thought of his new appointment was compensation of a kind. If he accepted the post, if he moved to Bristol to this job he had always coveted, he would be forced to leave Anna behind!

That she would also be left behind in Glynmareth did not affect Sara in the same way. There were such things as transfers, and she was not without her own personal ambition, although she would have been ready to sacrifice her career at Noel's bidding any day.

"I won't be able to wait to hear the result!" she declared truthfully. "We will miss you at Glynmareth, of course — terribly. It's certainly a plum of a job, Noel. You've been very lucky."

He smiled crookedly at the left-handed compliment but did not say anything, and half an hour later, having paid his bill and packed his one small suitcase, he was waving Sara farewell and driving swiftly off down the narrow main street.

With his back to the sea and that winding road before him he seemed to be leaving hope and a high endeavour behind, yet he was not so foolish as to turn down the substance for the shadow. He could come back to Northumberland after the business in Bristol was settled.

It was over three months since he had sent in his application for the appointment and he had almost given up thinking about it, presuming that the position was already filled; then the summons of last week had come out of the blue and he had gone to Bristol as one of a short list of eight doctors and been interviewed by a row of elderly gentlemen with varying qualifications, and told that he would hear from them "in due course."

This further interview surprised him, but he was far too ambitious to think of turning it down, even in the present circumstances. He decided that he could write to Alnwick for the information he sought, although the personal contact would have been more satisfying.

There was, of course, Sara! He thought about Sara for a long time on his way south, considering her good qualities and her strange idiosyncrasies which, manlike, he could still smile at and call harmless. Sara would rout out anything there was to find, and she would probably look upon it as a sort of crusade now that he had been forced to come away with his own task unfinished.

Sara's idea of a crusade was hardly the same as Noel's, however. It was a grim search, a desperate seeking for the power to destroy, and she lost no time in setting about her plan.

It was quite by accident that she made her first contact. The weather, which had been fine for weeks, suddenly began to show signs of deteriorating. A dull grey haze lay over the sea, creeping in from the east, and the blue gradually faded from the sky. There was no definite cloud formation; just the universal greyness and a heaviness of approaching storm in the atmosphere which she should have accepted as a warning.

She was too keen on her objective, however, too wrapped up in her own purpose to notice the vagaries of an English summer, and early the following morning she set forth on foot along the coast, travelling northwards and slightly inland with a packed lunch in her green canvass satchel and her mackintosh strapped across it as a precaution. Her shoes were sensible but light, and she had scorned a hat.

She set out in comparatively warm sunshine at ten o'clock and walked until one, and by that time the first sign of rain had drawn a hazy finger along the sky. She wondered if she should turn back along the coast or walk on, trying to find a main road, in the hope of getting a bus back to Alnmouth, and finally decided on the former. About a mile

122

back she had passed a farm house, and ahead of her there seemed to be nothing but a wild stretch of open country.

The first splashes of rain fell on the dusty road before her as she came in sight of the gaunt old house standing high up against the skyline, and she hurried towards it as the only means of protection she could see for miles.

The farm, when she reached it, wet through and curiously aggrieved at the failure of her light mackintosh to keep out the deluge, was a square, unpretentious place built of native stone, grey against a grey landscape, with low out-buildings on either side of it and a Dutch barn sheltering it at the rear. It looked austere and cold with its closely-curtained windows, as if its inhabitants had no desire for contact with the outside world, and she was somewhat surprised when a young girl opened the door to her.

"We saw you coming up the path," the girl said in a sullen tone which did not exactly suggest a ready hospitality. "You'll be wanting to shelter from the storm?"

"If you wouldn't mind," Sara said.

Reluctantly, it seemed, the door was opened a few inches farther and the rain spattered in on a stone-flagged passageway scrubbed scrupulously clean and laid with home-woven rugs.

Sara passed the morose-looking custodian of the door to find herself confronted by several closely shut inner doors, all looking about as uninviting as the outside of the house itself.

"I brought a mac," she said, "but I was right up on the moor when the storm broke and I had no idea how fierce your northern rain can be! A light raincoat is apparently of very little use in these circumstances."

The girl eyed her bright scarlet coat with silent contempt while she closed and bolted the door. She said nothing, and Sara had time to notice that she might have been attractive in a dark, northern way but for her glum expression and the look of resentment in her eyes, before her guide flung open another door and motioned her into a room which looked and smelled as if it had not been used for months.

Strangely enough, it was a most attractive room and might even have been termed comfortable but for that deserted, unused look it had acquired. The green carpet was shabby but good, and the three-piece suite was of green velvet muted almost to grey, which seemed to prove that the room had known the joy of sunshine streaming in through its narrow windows at one time and had not always been shrouded in the gloom of the heavy curtains hanging there now.

The lack of flowers about the place was strange, too, since the garden surrounded by its grey stone wall was full of flowers, riotous but unattended bloom which she had noticed even in the rain. Perhaps someone had died recently, Sara thought. The whole place had the air of death about it.

The girl left her without a word, returning in a few minutes with a burly Northumberland farmer whose hard eyes looked Sara over from head to foot before he spoke.

"Caught in the storm, eh?" he asked, adding with a surprising change of tone when he saw her plight: "By gox, but you're wet, hinney! Best come in an' dry yoursel' at the kitchen fire, where it's warm, an' my lass will get ye something to drink."

"I'd be grateful for a cup of tea," Sara admitted, ignoring the girl's dark scowl. "There's nothing like being soaked through for making you feel cold!"

"Ye look fair chilled tae the marrow," the farmer commented. "Run on wi' ye, Jess," he added to his daughter, "an' bring a sup o' milk. Maybe there's a bowlful o' soup left in the pot, too."

"You mustn't trouble, really," Sara protested, although the hot soup would have been welcome. "I'm quite sure you've had your lunch by this time and I have some sandwiches with me to eat. If I might just have the warm milk, that will do, and perhaps the rain will have cleared away by the time I've finished."

"You could get a lift back from the egg van."

It was the first time the girl had spoken since they had come back into the room and the low, cultured tone was strangely out of keeping with her slightly untidy clothes and the darkly scowling brows. Sara looked at her again as she followed her into a low-raftered kitchen, scrupulously clean as the passage outside and warm with the smell of newly-baked bread. She was a strange creature, this Jess, curiously like the old man in looks, dark and sturdy, with a full bosom and broad hips, a typical product of the moors, and somewhere beneath it all slumbered a fierce antagonism. She looked out upon the world with resentment, as if it had done her a grievous wrong. Like a hunted animal, Sara thought, wounded and resentful, and waiting its opportunity to strike back.

"Your job will be looking after the hens, I suppose?" she asked conversationally.

"Everything about this place in my job now," the girl told her sullenly. "I do everything in the house."

She went through to the stone-flagged dairy, banging the door behind her, and Sara took off her wet mackintosh to hang it over a chair away from the fire.

"Don't pay any attention to her," the farmer said, looking after his daughter. "She gets into these black moods at times and there's no getting her out o' them save just to bide your time."

"Doesn't she like the work on a farm?" Sara asked idly.

"She likes the outside work, but the inside was never her job—not till recently." His own brows had drawn together in a swift scowl. "Somebody else did it, but things have changed since then, and I can't get a woman to stay in this place for love nor money. It's ower far from the bus routes an' the pictures, I warren!"

"It is isolated," Sara agreed, "but I expect it has its compensations. It is really beautiful countryside, and I should imagine that one could see the sea from here on a clear day."

"Ay! Up on Clifton Bank ye can see the whole of the coast from Coquet to the Farnes! And behind ye there's the Cheviot an' a' the hills o' the Borders!"

His tone implied that human heart could scarcely want more, but Sara felt a sneaking sympathy for the moroselooking Jess, if, indeed, the loneliness of her remote home was the reason for her darkened outlook on life.

"Your daughter seems to find it lonely," she suggested. "Are there no other young people near at hand?"

"Plenty o' them!" the farmer declared. "She could have company if she sought it. There's the Young Farmers an' a' the village entertainments to amuse her, but she'll have none o' them these days." He looked away from Sara, seeming to add almost against his will, "Maybe she's missing her sister."

"You have another daughter?" Sara asked politely.

"I *had* another daughter." The dark brows were more closely drawn now, the eyes beneath them stormy as the sky behind the window-frame. "We don't talk about her. I've disowned her," he added bluntly.

Sara looked up in alarmed surprise.

"Oh," she said lamely, "I'm sorry!"

"You needn't be," he answered. "None of us are here."

That, Sara thought, was just not true, for behind the hardness of those flint-like eyes even she could discover a longing that wrestled with pride and anger, waiting to come uppermost at the slightest provocation.

The girl, Jess, brought in a pan of milk which she set on the hob to warm while she ladled soup from an iron pot and set it before Sara in the same resentful manner. She appeared to be living within herself, trusting no one but her father, and she regarded Sara almost with suspicion.

Sara finished the soup and ate her sandwiches while her shoes dried out before the fire. The farmer had muttered an excuse and gone out to the byres, but the unsmiling Jess remained as guardian of her kitchen, standing foursquare in the doorway waiting for Sara to finish her meal and go.

"You must miss your sister," Sara ventured when the silence grew oppressive, but she was scarcely prepared for the girl's reaction to her sympathy.

The dark eyes flamed into hatred at the mention of her sister's name and Jess moved into the shadows beside the dresser in the corner, busying her hands with some task which took her beyond Sara's line of vision.

"Really," Sara said, "you're anything but communicative, Jess. You are bound to miss someone who lived in the house with you for years and shared your work."

"She did everything in the house," Jess fairly spat out. "I worked on the land with my father."

So, that was it! Sara thought. Resentment because she was now bound indoors when her heart and her whole talent lay elsewhere.

"Did your sister go away to be married?" she asked casually, in spite of a pointed reluctance on the girl's part to go on discussing the past.

"Maybe she got married. We don't know."

The voice, coming out of the shadows, sounded hollow, disembodied, somehow, and Sara realized that she would only be making herself more unpopular by pressing for an answer to her questions.

"What is your other name, Jess?" she asked.

"Marrick."

"It's a nice name. Is it a common one round these parts?"

"No."

Sara sighed. That was evidently as far as she was going to get. Jess Marrick was not going to be drawn about the past, and something perverse in Sara wondered why. Curiosity about these people, living their dull lives away up here on the moors, was the last thing that should have stirred her, yet she did feel curious.

When the farmer came back he brought the news that the rain had slackened a little and the egg collector's van was on its way up the hill.

"You can't go back to Alnmouth in this wet clout," he said, lifting the sodden mackintosh. "Jess'll lend you one o' hers. You can send it back with the van since we know where you're staying."

"That's extremely kind of you," Sara acknowledged. "And most trusting. I'll see that Jess gets her coat back as soon as possible."

"Get the coat, lass," the farmer urged, seeing his daughter's reluctance to do his bidding. "And see to the eggs. How many have we this week?"

"Thirty dozen." The girl stood staring back at him in the middle of the floor. "What coat will I fetch?" she asked.

"You've got an old coat, surely!" her father exclaimed almost roughly. "Go get it, and don't let us have so much talk about it!"

Sara almost laughed outright at the irony of that last remark, but she felt that laughter was a thing that had died suddenly in his house and that her own mirth would be out of place. She waited for the van to draw up at the back door and heard it with a sense of relief.

After several minutes, in which she made the acquaintance of the egg collector and was assured of the necessary lift back to the main highway, Jess Marrick reappeared with a fawn burberry which had seen better days but was probably still useful and waterproof, and Sara accepted it gratefully.

"It's too short," Jess assured her with gloomy satisfaction. "You're far taller than I am."

"All the same," Sara told her in her best hospital manner, "I shall be grateful for it, Jess. Thank you very much."

She slipped the coat over her suit and thanked the farmer in his turn as they went out to the van.

"You're welcome," he told her without much enthusiasm, and the van slid away down the incline and out through the white-painted yard gate.

"I don't think I should like to live in a lonely place like that permanently," Sara remarked to the driver. "It seems to have stamped its remoteness on the Marricks and no mistake!"

"Oh, the Marricks are all right," he replied. "The girl acts a bit oddly at times, but it's best to take no notice of that. Moody, she is, but kind enough in her way, like old Abraham himself."

"Abraham Marrick!" Sara mused, turning the name over in her mind. "What a grand sound that has!" She glanced back at the gaunt old house before it was lost to view over a dip in the hilly road. "Do you come here often?"

"Once a fortnight. It's enough for me! I take spells with another chap."

He was talkative, and Sara learned much that she did not want to know about egg collecting for the Ministry before she was set down at a convenient bus stop on the main road.

The sky had cleared and the rain had almost ceased, falling now in a thin drizzle, which was not unpleasant, and she decided to wait in the shelter of some nearby trees until the bus arrived.

"By the way," she asked idly before she dismissed her valuable companion, "what is the name of the Marricks' farm? I may decide just to post the coat back to Miss Marrick."

"Alnborough," he told her, as he let in his clutch. "Just Alnborough. That'll find them all right."

It left Sara with a feeling of unreality, of the impossible happening, of success, perhaps, after long failure.

"*Aln*borough," she repeated to herself. "*Just Alnborough!*"

She thrust her hands deep into the pockets of the borrowed raincoat and her fingers closed over a scrap of linen left there, no doubt, by its owner. Idly, not even thinking of what she was doing, she pulled out the handkerchief and examined it, and in an instant her preoccupation with the house she had just left was transferred to this very ordinary, everyday object in her hand.

Smoothing it out with fingers that shook a little, she found it had to credit the evidence of her own eyes, for across one corner, embroidered in exactly the same way as on the handkerchief which had given Anna her name, was the one word "Jess."

In that instant the temptation in her was to run back to the farm at Alnborough, so sure was she that this was journey's end as far as her search went, but the bus that would take her back to Alnmouth was already rounding the bend in the road, and she was astute enough to remember that a problem was best considered with a calm mind and apart from excitement.

Even when the bus had drawn level, however, there was still a certain amount of hesitation in her mind, but the facts that there would not be another bus for two hours and that she had no excuse for returning to the farm so quickly, made her board it when it finally stopped.

Her heart was beating rapidly and her eyes gleamed with a strange satisfaction as she was carried rapidly towards the town, for she was sure now that she had stumbled upon at least part of Anna's secret. There was, in fact, no doubt in Sara's mind that Anna and the daughter whom Abraham Marrick—that grand old man, as Sara now described him to herself—had disowned were one and the same person, and in the shortest possible time she meant to learn the whole truth.

Jess Marrick, in spite of her moods and her scowls, would, she considered, be easier to intimidate than the old man himself, although she was quite willing to admit that even Jess might prove difficult when it came to discussing the past.

"But how can I fail?" she murmured. "How can I?"

All that evening she went about the hotel humming to herself, and she even put a phone call through to Ruth, leaving a message for Noel to say that she thought she would have news for him soon.

CHAPTER NINE

NOEL RECEIVED SARA'S message three days later when he returned from Bristol, with mixed feelings, having heard there that his appointment to a large new hospital on the outskirts of the city was more or less a certainty.

As Sara had observed, it was a decided feather in his cap, a stride rather than a mere step forward in his career, but the parting with all that Glynmareth had come to mean to him was doubly hard now when he considered the problem of Anna's identity.

Torn by hopeless desire on the one hand and an unwavering sense of duty on the other, he knew that he should now hand her case over to Tim Wedderburn, but he shrank from that step as sensitively as Anna did herself. To pass her on to the police seemed like sentencing her to death in the most cold-blooded way possible, yet he would be almost sure to come up against authority in one form or another if he obeyed the dictates of his heart, of every surging pulse-beat in his body, and took her with him.

She had proved an efficient and helpful secretary and he knew that he could count on Ruth to understand, but gradually the truth had been borne in upon him and could not be denied. It was not as a secretary that he wanted Anna. She was the love of his life, and he knew that she would remain that no matter where he went or how long he lived, but he had no right to tell her these things.

There was, on the other hand, the alternative of refusing the Bristol appointment, but deep in his heart he knew that he had very little choice. Whether he went to Bristol or not, Anna would one day recover her memory and from that day onward she would be lost to him. A clean break and the almost certain assurance of forgetfulness lay ahead for her, while for him only the tortures of the damned seemed to present themselves. He could never hope for forgetfulness, nor could he justifiably convince himself that there might be any other way out of this hopeless situation.

He was determined, however, that Anna would not be handed over to police care while he had the slightest say in the matter, and from that point he evolved a plan which he hoped to persuade Ruth to carry out.

Like every other city, Bristol must have its housing shortages, and he knew that he could obtain bachelor quarters in the hospital annex until he had found suitable accommodation elsewhere. This might take time, and the Glynmareth authorities would want the villa for their new superintendent as soon as possible, so that there was very little hope of Ruth's remaining at the villa for any length of time after his departure.

A week or two, however, might serve to solve Anna's problem, and to leave her with Ruth and in Dennis Tranby's care would be the next best thing to taking her with him. There would be week-ends when he would be free and could travel back to Glynmareth to confer with Dennis, a prospect as bitter-sweet as any he had ever known, yet one he would be called upon to accept as the only small measure of compensation he could permit himself.

With these problems ever-present in his mind, he did not even think of Sara until he received her message, and not even then could he have imagined her activities in Northumberland after he had left.

Losing no time, Sara returned to Alnborough the morning after she had found the handkerchief in the pocket of Jess Marrick's raincoat, ostensibly to return the coat but in reality to sound Jess about her sister. Sara thought of it more as prising out a secret, and a latent streak of cruelty in her nature afforded her a certain vindictive satisfaction at the thought of imposing her admittedly strong will upon the other girl. Jess was not really formidable, she reasoned, and the moroseness must be the result of some recent bitter experience. The scowling unfriendliness could quite easily be the defence of a sensitive nature erected against further hurt.

When she reached the farm it was deserted, but she caught a glimpse of a bright headscarf and a swinging skirt far up on the hillside, and knew that Jess Marrick had gone up there with the dogs.

Slowly she walked to the gate, hoping now that she would not meet the farmer on her way, but she passed unmolested on to the rough moorland and stood waiting for Jess in the shelter of a disused hut half-way up the hill.

The girl started in surprise at sight of her, calling off the dogs who stood growling in her path.

"I came to return your coat, Jess," Sara said. "And this."

Coolly she held out the square of white linen embroidered with the other girl's name, and just as coolly she stood waiting for Jess Marrick's reaction.

She was not to be disappointed. Indeed, it was far more primitive than she had expected.

"She did that!" Jess cried, snatching the handkerchief out of her hand as if she would tear it to shreds and stamp it underfoot. "I should never have kept it! I should have destroyed it long ago!"

"Come now, Jess," Sara coaxed in her most engaging manner, "surely things were not as bad as all that between you and your sister? D'you know," she added confidentially, "I always think one feels a lot better for having discussed this sort of thing, if not with an intimate friend, at least with someone who might understand." She paused for a moment before continuing directly: "Tell me about her, Jess. I'm quite sure it will help."

"Nothing will help anything—not now," Jess Marrick maintained, determined to keep her tight-lipped silence even in the face of such protestations of sympathy and understanding "She's gone, and we're well rid of her. That's what everybody says."

"Everybody, Jess?"

"All those who know."

"Your friends?"

Jess glared at her.

"I have no friends. She was the only one."

"But surely there's someone special, some boy friend, perhaps?"

"There's no one," Jess repeated with absolute finality.

"Was there someone—once?"

The painful color which flooded into the dark face was answer enough for Sara, and she bent closer to the other girl to suggest:

"And your sister married him. Was that it, Jess?"

The girl's look became fierce to the point of hatred, and it was hatred against her present inquisitor as much as against her absent sister. It was a wild, ungovernable fury against the whole world because she had been treated badly by someone she had loved and respected. Her anger had the bleak quality of despair about it, although rancour had also gone deep.

She was reluctant to confide in anyone, however, least of all Sara, whom she could not like.

"I don't want your sympathy," she said with a curious dignity that shut the other girl out, and Sara's anger immediately sought another weapon.

"Your sister's name was Anna," she suggested tensely. "Did you believe her dead?"

"No."

Sara noticed that the dark eyes had registered pain at her use of the familiar name and her heart lifted with satisfaction. At least, she was on the right track!

No amount of further questioning, however, would induce Jess Marrick to discuss her sister or the past, and she even walked a little way ahead of Sara until they joined old Abraham at the front gate.

He was leaning against the wall, talking to a younger man in worn riding-breeches and leggings which were stained with the mark of moss and bog water, and the two seemed on the most friendly terms. Neighbors, no doubt, Sara concluded, noticing the younger man's work-roughened hands and weather-beaten complexion, which stamped him as a typical product of those wild northern fells. He had a warm, friendly smile that embraced everything about him and included Sara as she drew level with Jess, but it was the younger girl at whom he looked longest, and he greeted her with a shy awkwardness which suggested attraction.

"Hullo, Jess," he said. "I came over to see if you would be going into Alnmouth to do the marketing."

"Not me!" Jess flushed and tossed her head. "Happen I want to go to Alnmouth I can go with the bus from the crossroads."

The rebuff was another form of defence, Sara thought, feeling sorry for the young farmer who recoiled visibly before it.

"This is Bill Cranston, a neighbor o' ours," Abraham Marrick explained, obviously angry at his daughter's treatment of the young man. "This young lady will be going back to Alnmouth, Bill," he added, as if one passenger would be compensation for the loss of another. "I warren she'll be more grateful to ye for a lift than yon ill-mannered daughter o' mine!"

"I would," Sara assured him engagingly. "I seem to upset Jess, Mr. Marrick," she added, turning to the farmer, "but I should like to come and see you again, if I may?"

"Come whenever it suits ye," the farmer responded. "So long as yer don't expect to be fussed over. We never keep company these days."

He said so with suggestion of regret in his voice, although the frown that accompanied his words was still forbidding, but Sara had made up her mind to return again and yet again until she had sifted this mystery to its dregs.

By accepting the lift back to Alnmouth she hoped to hear something of the Marrick's past from Bill Cranston, who was so evidently in love with the morose Jess, and she decided that the best way to obtain what she wanted was to pretend to misunderstand the younger girl.

"Is Jess Marrick ever pleasant?" she asked as they drove off down the hill. "She looks as if she might even bite the hand that fed her!"

"If that's meant to be a smart crack at Jess' expense," her companion scowled, "I don't think it very funny. She's got plenty of reason to be fed up with life."

"Because she is forced to work indoors, or because her sister ran off and married the man she wanted?" Sara demanded bluntly.

His work-roughened hands gripped the steering-wheel a shade more closely and the speedometer climbed from thirty to forty and up to fifty miles an hour before he answered through set teeth:

"Nobody could be expected to understand Jess unless they knew," he said. "She's had a rough deal, and she'll be slow to get over it, I warren."

134

"Unrequited love," Sara mused. "So many of us have felt its barbed shaft. Perhaps I could tell you more about that than you think, Bill."

"Jess' love wasn't unrequited, not in the first place," Bill Cranston said savagely. "She was engaged to a fellow who went to sea. He'd got his mate's ticket and he was doing well. They were going to be married after his next trip but one. The date was fixed. We all knew about it——"

"Yes," Sara prompted, "go on."

He shifted his position uneasily, taking his foot off the accelorator as they approached the main road.

"I don't know why I should be telling you all this," he said half-resentfully, "but I cannot abide Jess being misunderstood. We were all brought up together," he went on disjointedly, "Anna and Jessica Marrick and me, and maybe I thought I had some sort of chance with Jess before Ned Armstrong came on the scene, but I might have known that a farming bloke like me would never have a look in with a uniform in the offing. Besides," he added grimly, "Armstrong had a way with him. Maybe it was a way with women," he added, speaking bitterly for the first time. "Anyway, there was no one for Jess but him right from the first. When he was at sea she wrote to him every day, and when he had leave he was here at Alnborough and Jess brought him to all the local functions to show him off and let us see how happy they were."

His jealousy was thick in his pleasant voice, but he was in no way ashamed of it. Bill Cranston was far too natural for that, too much a son of the soil to dissemble about passions and beliefs.

"Anna had arranged a holiday in North Wales for just before the wedding," he went on doggedly now that he seemed determined to get it all off his mind by repeating it, "and the day before she set out on her holiday she got a letter, addressed to her at Alnborough. It had a Swansea postmark, and Anna was always one of the confiding sort where her family were concerned, but she would not show them that letter or tell them what was in it. She was all cut-up about it, though, and she left Alnborough the next day with a Judas kiss for Jess when she was going! I'm not saying that I know all the details, but I know that the old man took it hard, and so did Jess. It seems that she found the letter half burned in her sister's bedroom grate, and it was from Ned Armstrong."

Bill paused dramatically, and Sara felt that he must surely be able to hear the quickened beating of her own heart as she waited with held breath for him to go on with his story.

"Do you mean that—the sister and Ned went away together?" she asked when she could wait no longer. "Anna Marrick went off and married her sister's fiancé?"

"I expect so," Bill admitted miserably. "Anyway, that's what Jess believes happened, and the old man thinks so, too. They've never heard from the other two from that day to this—never wanted to hear from them, either, I should think. Old Marrick won't have Anna's name mentioned in the house any more."

"I don't suppose Jess Marrick ever told anyone what was in that letter she found," Sara suggested. "The half-burned one, I mean."

"There seems to have been a missing page," Bill Cranston admitted, rising to the carefully-placed bait. "Ned had written to Anna to say that he must see her at once. It was imperative, he said. He was no longer happy about his forthcoming marriag. Jess read all that, and when she came to the missing page, but it wasn't difficult to guess what had been on it or why Anna had taken it with her. It would be the instructions about their meeting, no doubt, and he ended the letter by saying that he couldn't go on pretending any more to Jess, and begged Anna not to fail him. He said he was keeping her to her promise, and that was the dreadful bit for Jess, I warren."

He lapsed into silence, wondering if he had already said too much to a stranger, but Sara was quick to reassure him on that point.

"Thanks for being so frank with me, Mr. Cranston," she said charmingly. "The Marricks were so very kind to me yesterday when I was caught in that thunderstorm that I feel as if I know them quite well now. By a rather strange coincidence, too," she added deliberately, "I also believe I may have run up against Anna Marrick. Bill," she said familiarly, "can you keep a secret?"

"Sure," he said. "I've kept plenty in my time. I don't know why I've talked to you like I have about the Marricks today, but I suppose it sort of had to come out."

"Yes, Bill," Sara said, "I'm sure it had. I believe Anna, Marrick is in Wales at this very moment suffering from loss of memory, but I can't be sure. No one can be sure until this girl's identity is proved beyond a shadow of a doubt," she added, "but I believe that she married Ned Armstrong and there was some sort of accident afterwards. We'll have to get together and check up on dates."

Sara's heart misgave her for a moment. Supposing—just supposing there had been no time for a wedding ceremony? That would leave Anna free! She realized that her primary interest in Anna Marrick's case hinged upon whether she had married Ned Armstrong or not, and now it would seem that a few hours might be about to defeat her.

"First of all I must get into touch with the hospital where I work," she explained to the bewildered Bill. "I'm a nurse, but perhaps you have already realized that," she added egotistically.

"No," he answered vaguely, "I guess I'm not very quick about things—placing people and the like."

"Oh, well," Sara said. "Never mind that now. The point is that I have come across a girl whom I firmly believe to be Anna Marrick, but just in case I should prove wrong, I want you to promise that you won't say a word at Alnborough until you hear from me in a day or two."

She watched her companion as she spoke and saw him struggling with his sense of loyalty to the Marricks and his own desire to do the right thing.

"Suppose this is Anna," he said, at last. "This girl, you say, has lost her memory. Does it mean that she wants to come back here—that Ned Armstrong and she have split up?"

It was obvious that he viewed the possibility of Anna's return to Alnborough from a personal angle now, wondering if Ned might yet effect a reconciliation with Jess. If so, his own hopes of finally winning her would be gone, and Bill Cranston looked the type who did not abandon hope easily. The way he lived, the constant struggle for survival against the elements in that exposed hill country, had bred in him a tenacity far above the average, yet he had seen how deep Jess Marrick's love had gone and how terribly she had been afflicted by her lover's treachery.

The fact remained, however, that Anna and Ned were married. Nothing could alter that, Sara thought, and she herself held the key to the whole situation. She even believed that she could detect a faint resemblance between Anna and Jessica Marrick.

"Were the Marrick girls very much alike?" she asked as they drew near her destination. "Jess is very much like her father—the same sturdy build and coloring, and the same eyes."

"And Anna was the exact opposite," he said. "She took after her mother. Mrs. Marrick was small and a bit frail-looking, and she had red-brown hair the same as Anna's when she was a younger woman."

He drew the car up in the middle of the broad market place, bumping to a standstill before the local saddler's, where he had several purchases to make and Sara got out.

"I mean to travel south tomorrow morning," she said. "I've been most interested in this case right from the beginning. The doctor who has it in hand is—well, a particular friend of mine."

She smiled at Bill, satisfied that he appeared to read her exact meaning into the words and conscious of a strange form of elation derived from a mere insinuation, which was as near as she dared come to claiming Noel Melford's affections at the moment.

"Maybe you'd like to take something to eat with me," Bill offered awkwardly, not really wanting to spend any more time in her company but feeling that it might be expected of him.

"I'd love to—some other time, Bill," Sara assured him pleasantly. "I may be this way again, very soon."

"Would you bring Anna back?" he asked, surprised.

"Quite conceivably," Sara answered with a look in her eyes that was almost triumphant.

She had still almost a week of her leave to take and she would offer her services to Noel in whatever capacity he cared to use them, and if he had been appointed to the job in Bristol it might very well mean that she would bring Anna north. Noel could not be expected to go dashing off across the length and breadth of the country even on so definite a clue as this appeared to be, and she could quite easily relieve him of the responsibility. In so doing she would wind up all this wretched business of Anna Marrick, and the girl could be forgotten with the utmost speed.

The prospect lent speed to Sara's plans and she travelled overnight from Newcastle-on-Tyne, arriving at Glynmareth half an hour after Noel came in from Bristol.

He was still discussing her message with Ruth when Sara came to the door, having paid off her taxi at the villa gate instead of taking it round to the nurses' home, as might have been expected.

Ruth saw her approaching through the window and her fine lips set a fraction of an inch more firmly.

"Good heavens, here's Sara herself!" she exclaimed. "I wonder what can have gone wrong?"

Noel wheeled round and went to meet Sara at the door.

"Hullo, Noel!" she greeted him with the assurance of one who holds all the trump cards, "I'm sorry to land on you like this with, I'm afraid, a great deal of trouble on my hands, but no doubt we can work it out from here together."

He stood aside to let her pass into the room where Ruth was waiting, making no comment, but Sara was not to be intimidated by silence. She greeted Ruth effusively.

"My dear," she declared "I really have missed you these past few days! I've got so much to tell you both, too, that I didn't wait to go over to the Home first."

"Have you found ou anything about Anna?" Noel asked almost coldly.

"Anything!" Sara permitted herself a thin smile. "My dear Noel, I hope I have found out *everything*!"

"Perhaps you would like some tea," Ruth suggested. "I had it ready for Noel."

"I'm gasping for a cup," Sara declared, so much on the old friendly footing again that Ruth wondered if she had misjudged her.

"Sara," Noel said irritably, "what have you to tell us?" She gave him a long, direct look, full of subtle meaning.

"Nothing very pleasant, I'm afraid Where is she, by the way? Not gone?"

"She's still working at the hospital—helping Dennis," Ruth said. "But the sooner we can relieve her of this dreadful bondage of forgetfulness the better. What have you found, Sara? Is it really important?"

"It's not a particularly pretty tale," Sara warned as she sat down at the tea table which Ruth had set just inside the french window. "It began some time ago, apparently, when a girl called Jess Marrick became engaged to her sea-going boy friend and her sister, Anna, had designs on him, too."

Without looking directly at Noel she could see his every movement, the small pulse beating rapidly in his cheek and the color fading slowly out of his face. Of course, she realized that she must hurt him by telling him all this, but far better that he should be hurt now, she decided, than afterwards when his affections might be completely involved. No one could possibly remain in love with a girl once they had heard the story she had to tell!

"Anna Marrick!" Noel repeated, as if he had heard very little else but the name.

"Anna Marrick that was," Sara pointed out briefly. "She's been married since then. She wore a ring, remember, when she first came here. Well, apparently the sister and her fiancé had settled on a day for their wedding and everything was arranged. They were to be married after Ned Armstrong's next trip abroad and Anna Marrick had arranged an early holiday for herself so that she might remain with her father when her sister had gone off on her honeymoon."

Noel was still on his feet, standing rigidly beside the mantel-piece where he had put his untouched cup of tea and staring down into the empty grate. He was waiting for Sara to finish her story with his jaw set in a hard line and his muscles taut, and when she spoke again it was with a certain amount of misgiving.

"There's no doubt about it that we have Anna Marrick here, Noel," she continued in an effort to justify her rather dramatised version of the story. "The two girls are more or less alike," she lied easily, "and the farm where these Marricks live is called Alnborough. What more could we want? It's quite a distance from our *pied-à-terre* at Aln-mouth, but it hangs together with your first clue, doesn't it?"

Noel did not contradict her. He seemed to be seeing beyond Sara's story to a dark country of his own imagining, but she could not tell from his expression what he thought.

"Please go on," he commanded her.

"Seemingly, after her sister had gone, Jess Marrick found a letter written to Anna by Ned Armstrong and delivered at Alnborough the day before in which he begged Anna to meet him from her holiday resort in Wales! It was undoubtedly a love letter, and in it he declared that he could not go on with his marriage to Jess. Anna Marrick believed that she had burned that letter, but Jess found part of it in her sister's bedroom fireplace, charred but still readable."

Sara paused, but neither Ruth nor Noel spoke, and she was forced to continue a trifle uncertainly:

"Anna Marrick went away and did not return. Perhaps she did not even check in at the hotel where she had booked a room for a week, and as far as the Marricks are concerned she ran away with her sister's fiancé and married him. They never want to see her again or hear her name mentioned at Alnborough!"

"That, of course, needn't account for the silence on the part of this Ned Armstrong," Ruth pointed out unhappily.

"Perhaps he was too ashamed to go back to Alnborough and just went off to sea again after his marriage to Anna," Sara suggested.

Noel said suddenly: "I don't believe in this marriage!"

"Could one ask why?" Sara said after she had drawn breath.

"Simply because I don't believe there was time. If Anna had checked in at her holiday hotel her luggage would have been there and her disappearance would have been reported to the police when she didn't return."

"She may have had no intention of checking in at that particular hotel," Sara pointed out. "She could quite easily have written or telephoned to cancel her reservation."

She saw that her argument had struck home. Noel's face was now so drawn and colorless under its tan that she actually felt sorry for him, yet she could still recognize the need to drive home her advantage.

"It was rather a shock to me, too, as you can very well imagine," she told them. "One doesn't exactly expect this

141

sort of thing, but I suppose I should be hardened to odd life histories by this time. These sort of stories keep cropping up, don't they? It must have been pretty hard on Jess Marrick, though."

Noel looked at her as if he had not heard.

"The Marricks must be brought down here," he said. "A meeting with her family may revive Anna's memory in a second or two."

Sara smiled.

"You're going to have plenty of trouble convincing Abraham Marrick that he should accept his daughter again," she said.

Noel regarded her coldly.

"Whatever you believe Anna has done, Sara," he said, "you will admit that it is still our duty to see her through this and to enlist all the help that is necessary."

"I can't believe Anna would do what you say!" Ruth declared stoutly. "She wouldn't do a thing like that—she's not capable of hurting a fly!"

"You must both be quite mad!" Sara exclaimed, unable to curb her anger any longer. "How can you go on trusting a girl like that? Or are you both so completely blinded by her charm that you just won't see!"

Ruth rose to her feet.

"I don't think we are so easily blinded as all that, Sara," she said stiffly.

Sara turned in Noel's direction, ignoring the girl she had called her friend.

"What do you intend to do?" she asked

"See Anna Marrick through this—to the best of my ability," he answered as he strode past her through the open window and out into the garden.

"I wouldn't have believed Noel could have been such a fool!" Sara exclaimed, anger having the upper hand now. "He's running right into trouble by trusting that girl in the way he does!"

Ruth's hands were trembling as she began to gather up the untouched tea-things.

"It's not a question of trust, Sara," she said, keeping her voice from rising on a note of angry contempt by a tremendous effort. "Noel must look at this entirely from the medical angle now, and his one clear duty is to follow up

142

this clue of yours and restore Anna's memory by returning her to her people."

"Noel can try to bring old Marrick down here if he likes," Sara sneered, "but he'll be a master of persuasion if he succeeds! From what I saw of him he was a man who would not easily be swayed once his mind had been made up, and he certainly had no use for his younger daughter. If Anna proves to be that daughter—and I fail to see how even the most baised mind could have believed otherwise now!—she will have a good deal of explaining to do all round."

"We can hardly sit in judgment," Ruth said briefly. "Somehow, Sara, I still have the utmost confidence in that girl."

Nonplussed by this unexpected attitude, Sara turned angrily away, finding nothing to say in the face of Ruth's continuing trust, but trying to console herself with the belief that they would emerge doubly disappointed in the end. For every gesture of faith there would be a detail of Anna Marrick's past to counteract it, and the beginning would be Abraham Marrick's refusal to accept his daughter into his home again.

Sara went off to the nurses home in high dudgeon, although her curiousity would not allow her to stay there for long.

From one of the top windows overlooking the garden she saw Nel leave the villa twenty minutes later and go in the direction of the hospital and, her heart pounding heavily with unsuppressed jealousy, she imagined him going straight to Anna.

Noel did seek Anna out, but with far less confidence than Sara had given him credit for. Shaken by the story he had just heard, he was far from accepting it in detail, yet it held much of the elements of truth in so far as names were linked and Alnborough could well be the incompleted word of Anna's painful efforts at remembrance. With fine contempt he discounted the greater part of Sara's story as a jumble of inconsequential facts. The main point remained to establish contact between these people and the girl he loved, and to do it with the least possible hurt to Anna herself.

He found her struggling with the intricacies of the typewriter keyboard, which she had set out to master while he was away, and she jumped up in surprise at sight of him, the swift color mounting to her cheeks as their eyes met.

"You've got the job!" she said, her confidence in him as sure as Sara's had been but infitintely more pleasing to his ears. "I knew you would. Oh, Noel! I'm so glad, and Ruth will be so very pround!"

"I suppose so," he smiled. "How has Tranby been treating you while I've been away?"

The impluse to take her in his arms was almost more than he could withstand, and he fumbled for his pipe and filled it while he glanced at the accumulated letters on his desk.

"He's been very busy with you away," Anna told him, "and that means I've been kept fairly busy, too." Her eyes were raised suddenly to his, a deep anxiety of pleading in their depths. "There's been nothing else, Noel—no remembering. I'm sorry."

He took a quick turn about the room before he came to stand beside her.

"Anna," he said, "I want you to do something for me. I want you to write a letter just as I dictate it. We won't need this." He moved the typewriter aside. "I want it to be in your own handwriting. It's going to your father."

She swung round, staring at him, but she did not speak. She picked up the pen he laid on the desk, her hand trembling a little as she waited for him to begin.

"Head it 'Glynmareth Cottage Hospital, Merioneth, North Wales'," he said. "And the date."

He waited, and when she looked up a second time he drew a deep breath and started the letter itself.

"Dear Father,

You will see by the above address that I am being taken care of here as the result of an accident. I have unfortunately lost all memory of the past and my doctors believe it can only be restored by a meeting with people I once knew or a return to a familiar scene. You could help me by coming here to see me, and Doctor Melford will make all the necessary arrangements for your journey as soon as he hears from you that you are willing to come.

I am enclosing a snapshot taken in the garden here so that you will see that I am quite well otherwise.

Your affectionate daughter,

Anna Marrick."

Noel waited after he had uttered the name, tensely expectant, but Anna wrote the full signature as a matter of course and without undue emotion, drawing a firm line beneath it as if it was a task she had accomplished hundreds of times. The action convinced him beyond doubt that they were on the right track and he was conscious of sudden, tremendous elation.

"This is it, Anna!" he cried, catching her by the shoulders to look triumphantly into her questioning eyes. "We're more than half way there already!"

"You think—my father will come?"

"Of course he'll come!"

"Supposing it's wrong? Supposing we're just making another shot in the dark?"

He shook her very gently, his lips curving in a one-sided smile.

"This isn't a chance shot, Anna," he assured her. "It's the end of our quest."

She crushed down something that was far from the happiness she should have felt, seeing the inevitable end of all this rising to mock her, yet she could not let him guess that she valued her present happiness so much that she would glady have gambled the past and even the future to retain what she now held for a few brief weeks longer.

"Everything comes to an end sooner or later," she said. "This had to come. Somehow, I knew it would."

"We'll all help," Noel said, not quite trusting himself to look at her now. "Ruth and Tranby and I are all behind you in this."

She thanked him as best she could, but an emotion stronger than any she had ever known threatened to crush the words back into her throat, choking her.

"Don't cry, my dear," he said gently, his own voice roughened. "God knows, Anna, we may have a steepish hill to climb yet and we are only human. I'd put my faith in Ruth more than in anybody, though. She has never wavered in all my knowledge of her, and I don't think she'll fail us now. Even if these people don't claim you as their daughter, that isn't the end."

"If I only knew the end!" Anna cried. "If I could only see a little way ahead!"

The age-old plea, the cry for the power of God so mercifully denied!

"It isn't fair to you, Noel," she added after a moment. "All this uncertainty and worry when you are going to a new job——"

"Don't worry about me," he said. "I thrive on that sort of thing!"

He had forced a lightness into his voice that he was far from feeling and she recognized it and responded to it immediately.

"You have only a few more weeks to thrive!" she smiled, and then stood aghast at the prospect.

They remained facing each other, all their carefully prepared defences down, and with a sudden movement he had taken her into his arms and was crushing his lips against hers.

"My God, Anna, I can't let you go! I can't bear to let you go!"

"You must! We can't—ever mean anything to each other." She held on to his supporting arm even as she strove to put a world of reasoning between them. "Neither of us is really free. You owe it to your career to go on—and I must go back to—whatever was there before I came to you."

Her voice broke, and for a moment longer he held her to him as if by the intensity of his embrace he could shut out all that stood between them, and then he put her gently into the chair where he had found her and strode from the room without a backward glance.

CHAPTER TEN

THE LETTER WAS sent off to Northumberland that evening and the tension of waiting for the reply began for them. If Noel had thought to save Anna by telling her only the bare essentials, he realized quite soon that he could not shield her from her own sensitive forebodings, and he was forced to watch the mixture or eagerness and dismay with which she watched each post come and go.

Anna knew that she had not even given the letter time to reach its destination before she was looking for a reply, but the hours seemed to stretch out interminably between post and post, while she attempted to go about her normal everyday tasks as if she was not walking perpetually in the shadow of doubt and fear.

During this time she came closer than ever to Ruth, for without actual words Ruth offered her a sympathy which could only have arisen out of complete love and under-standing.

Knowing the full story, Ruth had no doubt that Anna was the daughter of Abraham Marrick, and she managed to view Sara's version of it wath an unbiased mind, coming to the conclusion that they would not be in possession of the real truth and all the details until Anna's memory was finally restored.

She realized that her brother thought so, too, but Noel had to approach the situation from the medical angle, also, and be ready to shield his patient from any sudden shock which, Dennis had explained to her some time ago, might have the reverse effect to the one they wanted.

Dennis was constantly at the villa these days, adding the assurance of his friendship to theirs, and quite often Anna's heart came near to overflowing when she sat in their company and realized what a precious gift they were offer-ing her for what she considered to be so little in return.

"Ruth, whatever happens I shall never forget these past four days," she said as they cleared the breakfast-table that Saturday morning. "You've given me such faith in human nature that whatever is to happen now, or has happened in the past, I feel that I can face it with some sort of courage, at last."

"You always had that courage." Ruth assured her. "It isn't just born in an hour, Anna. The hour may recognize it, but it is part of us—a fundamental part—or it just isn't there at all. The folk without it go to pieces in an emergency, but you showed so much courage when you first came here, fighting this thing in the beginning, that I'm quite confident for you now. I've heard Dennis and Noel speaking about it often enough, and I'm sure it has made Noel's work easier."

A faint flush rose in Anna's cheeks. Did Ruth know?

"When will he get to Bristol to take up this new appointment?" she asked.

"It's not official yet," Ruth said. "There's all the red tape to unravel yet. Probably he won't know until the end of the month."

And I shall know—when? Anna's heart began to beat suffocatingly close to her throat, and the hand she put to it was trembling. When would she be done with the agony of parting and the heartache and all the useless longing that clamored in her night and day, giving her no rest? To live here always, to keep Ruth's friendship and Noel's respect! That was all she wanted, now or ever!

She looked down at the thin gold circle on the third finger of her left hand, seeing it through a mist of tears and the searing white flame of sudden remorse. Ned! she thought. Ned, what happened to us? I couldn't have married you!

Ruth put a hand over hers, seeing the distress.

"Don't think too much about it just now," she counselled. "We have made progress and that, in itself, must be a good thing. You could never have gone on not knowing, Anna."

"No, I realize that, but—it's this dreadful feeling of helplessness that's so paralyzing. I've left everything to Noel——"

"That's in the nature of things where a doctor is concerned. A diagnosis is necessary in every case, and a cure —if possible."

And what was the cure for love? Anna could not answer that, nor could Ruth, but she got to her feet as the garden gate swung on its stiff hinges, and crossed swiftly to the window.

"Here comes the post," she said. "I'll get it, Anna, if you like"

Anna sat deathly still while Ruth was out of the room. It seemed as if she could not move, as if every muscle in her body was tense, waiting for their verdict in the letter they were expecting, and she felt as a man might while he sat waiting the return of the jury in a matter of life and death. And then Ruth came back into the room and said simply:

"It's from Northumberland, Anna, but it's addressed to Noel."

Anna rose unsteadily to her feet, gripping the back of her chair until the knuckles showed white through the flesh.

"Is it from my people, do you think?" she asked with all the old rush of unutterable loneliness sweeping over her at the thought of belonging again. "Do you think it might be an answer to the letter I wrote to my father?"

"I don't know," Ruth said, laying the envelope down on the table between them. "Take it to Noel and he will tell you."

Anna lifted the envelope and held it between her hands, the writing on the outside coming up to meet her in vague, blurred lines, advancing and receding dizzily in a meaningless jumble of letters which yet held their own strange meaning, the handwriting known to her yet just evading her power to put a name to the sender.

"Oh! if I could only think," she cried bitterly. "If I could only remember everything!"

Ruth let her go out without answering. She will remember, she thought, and that remembering will affect each one of us!

Anna did not know how she managed to reach Noel's consulting rooms, but when she did her first overwhelming reaction was relief to find that they were empty. He had not completed his rounds of the wards and she was assured of a few minutes' grace in which to pull herself together, so that she might confront him with at least a semblance of dignity and self-control.

She laid the letter on his blotting-pad and crossed to the window to wait. Whatever the envelope contained, she was determined that the burden of it must not be placed on Noel's shoulders again, and so adamant was she in this respect that she was almost tempted to open the letter and read its verdict before he came. She shrank from the impulse, however, shaken by the thought of an emotion so powerful that it could all but shatter the principles of a lifetime, and when she heard Noel's footsteps on the corridor outside she swung round from the window to face him, her cheeks devoid of color and her eyes, with a world of pain in their depts, fixed on the door through which he would come.

There was a feeling of fatality in the sound of the heavy tread she had come to know so well, a sense of events crowding in upon her over which she had no control.

Noel opened the door and stood looking at her for a mment, and then he saw the envelope lying on his desk and he moved across the room and lifted it without a word.

The letter contained two sheets of notepaper covered in neat, symmetrical handwriting, a woman's handwriting with a purposeful thickness about it on the down strokes which suggested determination and a force of will above the average.

It was headed simply "Alnborough, Thursday", and was the reply, through Noel, to Anna's appeal of almost a week before.

"Dear Doctor Melford," Noel read,

As my father is unable to reply to the recent communication he received from my sister, Anna Marrick, I am taking the liberty of answering it through you. My father took a slight stroke on receiving the letter, but I am quite sure that I understand his feelings in this matter and can advise you about them without delay.

My father and I want nothing more to do with my sister, Anna Marrick, whose photograph I am returning herewith. My sister went away with my fiancé on the eve of our marriage, so perhaps you will be able to understand my feelings about all this, and my father can never forget that he trusted Anna with her mother's wedding ring to give to the man she was about to marry, with his blessing on it for our happiness. The unforgivable will never be discussed in this house, and I can assure you that we want no more to do with Anna Marrick that once was.

Yours sincerely,

Jessica Marrick."

Noel crumpled the strangely-phrased epistle in his hand until it was a tight ball which he tossed into the waste paper basket without comment.

"Noel," Anna whispered, "was it—about me?"

"I'm not very sure." He came over to stand beside her, putting a protective arm about her slim shoulders. "We've come to rather a ticklish bit in this case history of yours," he went on with that studied medical impartiality she had heard him use in his work many times during the past few weeks. "It may involve another visit to the north of England, but this time I want you to come with me. We'll make in a family outing, if you like. It's quite time Ruth had a week-end free from the eternal domestic round."

Blessing him inwardly for that casual approach which was calculated to give her courage, Anna went in search of Ruth, and Noel sat down at his desk and lifted the telephone that would put him through to the hospital switchboard.

"Get me Doctor Tranby's home, will you, please?" he asked. "You can say it's urgent."

Dennis came to the other end of the line without delay.

"I say, old man, I'm in the middle of my surgery! Is there anything wrong?" he asked.

"I'll want you to take over here for a couple of days, Dennis," Noel told him. "I'm going north again."

"A reply to the letter?" Dennis asked, immediately interested.

"Yes, but hardly the reply I had expected."

"You can't mean that the old man has refused his help?" Dennis said aghast.

"I'm not quite sure who is refusing," Noel answered. "A letter came this morning from the sister. Oh, they're Anna's people all right. There seems to be no doubt whatever about that. They recognized her from the snapshot we sent, but there's some ugly business about a family quarrel that must be cleared up right away."

"So long as it finally gives the lie to that trumped-up yarn of Sara Enman's it may not be so bad!" Dennis said hopefully.

"That's just it." Noel's tone was clipped, hiding all emotion. "It doesn't. It appears to be the same story with a good deal of personal venom thrown in."

"Look here, old man, I've got to come over there and see you. It's no use us talking over the phone like this. I'm damnably sorry about everything——"

Noel cut him short.

151

"You needn't be. I've no intention of letting anything under the sun come between Anna and her chance of regaining her memory—not even murder."

His voice was so emphatic that Dennis would not have argued even if he had felt inclined.

"What do you propose to do?" he asked.

"I intend to make these people face facts in a realistic way. The father has apparently had a stroke of some kind—a shock to the nerves, no doubt. It may or it may not be serious, but in any case I intend to go north at once and I shall take Anna with me—Anna and Ruth."

"I wish I could offer my help in a less static role," Dennis said, "but we can't both be away from the hospital at once. Are you taking Sara back with you?"

Noel's most decisive "No!" rang across the distance between them with no suggestion of doubt about it whatever.

"Thank heaven for that!" Dennis observed. "Wherever that woman goes there's sure to be mischief!"

"She's had her say," Noel returned grimly. "I'm not concerned with Sara any more, though we certainly have her to thank for discovering Alnborough."

Which will be a most bitter pill for Sara to swallow, Dennis thought when the line had gone dead.

There was no hesitation about Ruth's decision to accompany them on that fateful journey north, and Anna could only marvel once more at the real meaning of friendship.

Noel was determined that no time should be lost and they set out immediately, their small week-end cases packed with the necessities for a few days' stay.

Sitting in the back of the car with Ruth, Anna felt utterly dependent upon them both, but she knew that neither Noel nor Ruth grudged the time they were spending on her behalf. Noel had not told her all his plans, but she knew that he would not be returning to Northumberland so quickly if he did not believe that he would find the solution to her problem there, and the nervousness she had been trying to hide ever since he had come back from the hospital increased with each northward mile.

She had not pressed him to tell her the contents of the letter he had thrown into the waste-paper basket beneath his desk, but she knew that it had started them on his journey. It was enough for her that Noel considered their presence in Northumberland necessary, and she knew that it was being made in her interests. She could bring sane and cool reasoning to bear in that respect, but it was useless to try to reason against the dictates of her heart, which saw the remaining hours of her present happiness pouring out like sand through a glass and she powerless to stay it.

At seven o'clock Noel pulled the car up at a wayside hotel.

"We're not going any further than this tonight," he said. "It will make it too much of a strain. I think I should be able to get rooms here. It's not quite on the beaten track, although it's one of the best places I know. I came here a lot during my hospital year at Sheffield."

So very often Anna had tried to picture his past, to see those years he could remember so clearly and all they had contained, envying him the power to look back and wondering, sometimes, why he had never married. She knew that he had immersed himself in his career to the exclusion of a great many other things, but she also knew from experience that love could come unawares.

In the last few weeks she had tried to remember just when she had fallen in love with Noel—she who had no right to fall in love with anyone!—but the knowledge escaped her. It had not come upon her as a sudden revelation, but the days had become suddenly fair and full of life, and she, who had known despair and had walked in dark places, had been led out into the light again, into the beauty and the full glory of life, to see it through new eyes.

Nothing could ever dim that memory for her! No, not even Sara's oft-repeated warning that returning memory of the more distant past would blot out these intervening weeks forever!

The certainty of her belief that all this must endure even if it could only be in bitter-sweet retrospect was the one sure thing in her mind, a conviction so lasting that she accepted it now without question or doubt.

An indifferent traveller at any time, Ruth reached the hotel with a raging headache which nothing would alleviate but a darkened room and a good night's rest.

"It's dinner and straight to bed for Ruth," Noel ordered when he joined them in the quaint little upstairs lounge adjoining the dining-room. "You'll feel all right in the morning, old girl!"

"This is really all my fault," Anna said, distressed by Ruth's obvious discomfort. "You would never have come on such a long journey by road if it hadn't been for me."

"I've got used to this sort of thing whenever I leave home," Ruth said imperturbably. "I come prepared, and I don't intend to become a martyr to car-sickness and never go out because of it! Noel will give me a bromide and I'll sleep as peacefully as a baby! Once the motion of the car stops going on in my head the symptoms gradually die down."

"I know you'd far rather be back in the garden at Gynmareth," Anna said, wondering suddenly if she would ever see Ruth's garden again.

Had she stood beside the laughing brook for the last time and felt the sun-warmed grey stone under her feet as a parting caress?

The angony of the thought stabbed through her, finding its relentless way to her heart. You will never return again, something seemed to be repeating within her. This is the end! The end!

"What a delightful place this is!" Ruth said. "Everything is so old-world and perfect, not in the usual pseudo-olde-worlde way one sees so much, but absolutely genuine!"

"It's not really difficult to recognize the genuine article," her brother returned quietly, his eyes just resting on Anna's burnished head where the gleam of the wall bracket behind them picked up the rich glint of red in her hair. "The real thing has a depth and beauty that all the clever shams in the world can never achieve." He pushed the drinks he had ordered across the small table between them. "It can't make the headache any worse," he told Ruth, "and it might help you to enjoy your dinner."

"It wouldn't hurt me to do without a meal," Ruth said, "but you've spoken so often about this place that I feel I really ought to see the famous dining-room before I die!"

"Is the headache as bad as that?" Anna asked with a smile in her eyes that was more tender than teasing. "I don't think I've ever had a headache, but I do sympathize."

"Not even when you were flung clear of the car that night?"

Noel's question exploded between them, cutting across their lazy conversation with the impact of an eruption, and he sat waiting intently for the effect he hoped it would produce.

Anna's hands flew to her face, as if she would protect it, and she lowered her head defensively, as if something had shattered only a few inches from where she sat, but her eyes, fixed on the polished surface of the table before her and the three half-emptied glasses, were still puzzled and full of pain.

"I can't, Noel!" she pleaded. "I know about the car—but that's all. Perhaps it will all come back gradually and I'll know why I was there and what exactly happened, but just now it's as if someone were holding back a curtain just sufficiently for me to catch one glimpse at a time."

"It will swing clear one of these days," he said, trying to crush back his disappointment. He would have liked to take Anna back to Alnborough, remembering.

They emptied their glasses and he led the way into the dining-room, a superb apartment surprising in proportion and furnishing for a hotel situated in such a remote spot, and Anna followed him down the shallow, red-carpeted steps to their table in one of the window bays with a feeling that here was their real parting.

Whatever tomorrow brought, whatever there was to face of pain or heartache in the days which would follow, this was their day. She knew that Noel had meant it to be so, that he had brought her here to share his own memories of the past, those happy, blissful days when he had first applied all he had learned in six years of study.

It was easy to picture him coming here with a small party, a younger, not quite so grave Noel standing at the head of those shallow, carpeted steps with his firm brown fingers gripping the wrought-iron rail, surveying the scene before him with that calm assurance of his until the head waiter came to show him to his table. Almost jealously she wondered about the women in his party, the girls who might have circled that shining parquet floor in his arms and laughed with him afterwards over a bottle of wine, perhaps even walked with him in the walled garden beyond the terrace where shadowy flowers shone ghost-like in the moonlight.

Thrusting jealousy out of her heart, she vowed that nothing should be allowed to spoil this respite which fate had granted her and presently, when the orchestra in the corner began to play, Noel pushed his chair back and asked her to dance.

"You're not too tired, Anna?" he said.

"What a question!" Ruth answered for her. "I couldn't listen to that music and not want to dance at Anna's age!"

"You're quite sure you won't feel lonely if we leave you, Methuselah?" Noel laughed.

"I'll watch you," Ruth said.

Anna swung out on to the floor in Noel's arms. He did not speak as they danced. The music seemed to isolate them in a world of their own, wiping out past and future, dimming everything but the love she knew returned and would accept tonight. For this one evening Noel had decreed that it would be theirs, acknowledged silently between them because the spoken word would only tarnish it, and to that end he had brought her here where he had known his greatest happiness in the past.

When the dance had ended she encouraged him to speak of those happier days, and Ruth joined in with her own recollections until she decided that she must go to bed.

"It's still amazingly light," Noel said when he had carried the sleeping-draught up to his sister's room and seen her safely settled. "We'd both feel much better for it if we walked some of that dinner off in the garden."

They walked along the water's edge in the hush when the birds had ceased their singing, the poignant beauty of it catching at Anna's heart with every step and making her doubly conscious of what she was about to lose. Tall trees fringed the stream, its surface glassy-smooth between them, like a pathway leading straight to some unknown land, but she knew that no paths were straight in life, and wondered where the unseen way ahead held for them both. She had been leaning on Noel's strength for so long that the thought of going on without him was almost unbearable, but she knew that the effort was to be demanded of her, probably within the next forty-eight hours.

They walked in the shadow of the trees along a narrow pathway edged with flowers, until the light died out of the sky and a bat flew blindly before them, causing her to draw back and shiver.

"Shall we turn in now?" Noel asked. "It's after ten, and we've come quite a way since this morning."

To turn back, when she knew that she must go on to the inevitable end! Anna felt her heart contract with the old pain of longing as they turned to face the faint glow in the west that was the aftermath of the summer sunset. The shadows neneath the trees were dark, like the shadow of death, and the persistent bat flew across their path again. The fear which Sara's careful words had driven deep rose in her again, fear that returning memory would wipe out this night forever, and subsconsciously her steps dragged as they neared the bridge and came in sight of the hotel.

Noel opened the door set in an archway under the high wall and they passed into the garden again. It lay beneath the rising sickle of a new moon, silvered with opalescent light, the faint scent of moss roses rising in the cool night's air as they passed between the bushes along the tiled pathway leading to the house.

Out here in the night she could believe that no problems awaited her, yet she knew that they lingered in the shadow cast by the house itself. The garden offered them their hour, and she grasped it hungrily, not wishing to speak, not even counting the minutes as they fled from her forever.

At the end of the pergola, where the fallen rose petals looked like snow, Noel halted and turned her to face him.

"Good night, Anna," he said, and it was as if he had said good-bye.

CHAPTER ELEVEN

THEY REACHED ALNWICK shortly after twelve o'clock the following morning, and Noel drove straight to the hotel where he had booked rooms for them by telephone before leaving Glynmareth.

"This is going to be a ticklish business just at first," he told Ruth, coming into her room while Anna unpacked in the bedroom next door.

He spoke in a low tone, as if he already sought to protect his love from what might come, and Ruth had no doubt about his reactions to the story Sara had told. He would stand by Anna now to the bitter end, and if his faith was shaken, even then he would give no sign of it.

Ruth had not taken time to wonder about her own faith in the matter. She had come on this long and, for her, difficult journey because Noel needed her, and perhaps for Anna's sake, too, realizing that the girl might be more in need of her friendship at this moment than ever before. Ruth was one of those people who offered themselves freely to whoever has need of their help, and her patience and understanding were something to be wondered at.

"I've decided to go on to Alnborough alone," Noel added as he paced to the window for the second time. "I can't take the risk of breaking the amnesia and involving Anna in a family row into the bargain. One thing will be enough at a time. I must see those people and use my judgment about how to bring about a meeting between them."

"The meeting is, of course, absolutely essential?" Ruth asked.

Absolutely. But I must be a hundred per cent sure about them first."

She considered his broad outline against the sunlit window.

"All this is most distressing for you," she said. "I shall be thankful when it's all over."

He squared his shoulders and turned to face her.

"I can take it," he said. "Do something with Anna, Ruth. If you can stand a bus journey after all the motoring of these past two days, take her for a run to the coast. Alnmouth isn't much more than four or five miles away, and you'd both love it. It's a perfect little gem of a place."

"Suppose it brings back memories for her? Could I cope?" Ruth wondered.

"Yes, I think you could. I don't expect any violent reaction on her part. She's not the type." He paused to cram tobacco into his pipe. "She'll be upset, of course, but you'd be able to deal with that. It might even be more natural coming that way," he mused, "and decidedly less of a shock to her system. I'll deal with the other end of this wretched tangle in my own way."

His mouth hardened as he contemplated the forthcoming meeting with the Marricks, and Ruth knew that he was deeply prejudiced against these people because they had made no attempt to trace Anna in the first place. Tolerantly, she tried to weigh the fact against the story Sara had told them and wondered what truth Noel would learn before the day was out.

They had lunch together in the oak-panelled dining-room of the old hotel, eating little between them, their thoughts on the events ahead, and Anna felt that she must no question Noel, that the most she could do to help at this stage was to comply unreservedly with his every wish.

Ever since they had driven into this grey old town with its battlemented castle and wide market place, a stirring of recognition had urged her to explore it further. She felt like a blind man groping along a wall for the objects he knew must come against his hands, only she was doing it with her mind, stumbling in a grey mist of uncertainty which was gradually—very gradually—clearing.

"Let her find her own way to places if she looks as if she could," Noel advised his sister before he went out to the car. "That might possibly be the answer."

He had tried to sound casual, but as he drove away his face reflected the turmoil in his heart, and he knew that his confidence had been a mask for his own protection as much as for his sister's peace of mind. He had not dared to look too long in Anna's direction and see that strained expression that very rarely left her eyes these days. He had thought to say good-bye to her last night in the quiet garden, but the agony of their parting was to be longer drawn-out than that.

Anger stirred in him at the thought of the people he was about to meet, a saving anger, draining some of the emotion out of him, yet he had no real right to judge the Marricks beforehand. Sara had described them as hard-working, honest people with a grim determination never to forgive a wrong woven into the fabric of their living, and he could not connect them with what he knew of Anna in any way.

Best, therefore, to wait till he met them, he decided, swinging the car over the Lion Bridge and out to open country.

It was good land this, green and undulating, rising to the knees of the hills with brown rivers threading their way through it to the sea, and the road over which he travelled led like a river itself between high green banks until it finally began to climb on to the rougher moorland of the north.

The last shreds of his doubts about Anna's identity vanished as the car sped onwards, for here, in the minutest detail, was the scene of that word-picture she had produced for him at Glynmareth. Here were the green uplands and the distant Border hills rising clear against the northern sky; here were the winding roads and the stunted thorns leaning away from the prevailing wind, and the sheep gazing on the open moor or cropping the finer grass by the wayside. Here, on a clear day, from any high place round about, the wide belt of the grey North Sea might be seen like a band of silver on the horizon, and here the four winds of heaven would blow free and strong and untrammelled across the hollows with the scent of heather and the tang of salt in their breath.

No wonder she had loved it! No wonder it had remained the strongest impression in her subconscious mind when all else had been momentarily blurred by paralyzing shock!

He stepped the car up to sixty, taking corners at a speed which would have surprised him in a saner frame of mind, watching the signposts for a word that had burned itself into his mind in the past few days.

ALNBOROUGH—3 miles, he read at last, slowing down as he turned into the by-road. It was hardly broad enough to take the car, and the banks on either side were high with scentless mayweed and blue with the gleam of harebells. A gatekeeper butterfly zigzagged its way before him for a moment and then was lost, and then the undulating road claimed all his attention as it wound now east, now south, a road that went up and down like a switchback but always progressed in the direction of the sea.

After a while it opened out and he was high on the moorland, still climbing, still dipping down into hollows where the green bracken swayed in the wind, and then he saw the house perched high on a rise before him. There could be no mistaking it. Anna had described it too well, and he drove straight to it and got out at the white-painted gate to walk the remainder of the way.

The quiet of a summer Sunday afternoon lay on everything about him, broken only by the distant bleating of sheep and the fall of water in a hidden ditch beside the path. He noticed subconsciously that the garden on either side of the path had been well laid out but was now overgrown for lack of attention, its paths choked with weeds and the flowers rioting everywhere, together with blown poppies and invading scabious. Two magnicient hollyhocks flanked the doorway of the house, impervious to neglect in their tall majesty, and as he knocked boldly on the green-painted door he marvelled that they should grow to such splendor in this exposed spot.

There was a long silence in which he experienced an irritating sensation of being watched, either from within the house or from some unseen vantage-point near at hand, and almost impatiently he swung round on his heel and strode over to the rough gravel and round the gable end of the house to the back.

Here he was confronted by a youth bringing in half a dozen cows from the adjoining pasture, and he addressed him abruptly:

"Is your master about?"

The boy considered him doubtfully, in the way of country folk to whom time is a plentiful commodity.

"I dunno that you can see him," he said. "He's been taken bad wi' a stroke."

"I've heard that," Noel said patiently. "As a matter of fact," he added, "I'm a doctor, and Miss Marrick has just written to me. She may be expecting me."

It was a long shot, but the innocent piece of subterfuge produced the desired result. The cows were prodded until the leader was safely inside the byre where they would waited to be milked, and the youth put his tousled head in at the door of the house and shouted something unintelligible which might have been heard at the far end of the uplands if only it could have been understood.

He turned and touched a forelock.

"Go right inside, sir," he said. "She'll be down in a minute. She's got the milkin' to do, anyway."

Noel went inside, standing in the centre of the great, raftered kitchen where a fire burned in the grate in spite of the warmth of the summer's day. He felt sure about Anna now, more sure with every minute that passed that this had been her home, and he looked about him at the scrupulously tidy room with its shining brasswork and scrubbed table and wondered about the second daughter, the sister who Sara believed had been betrayed by two people whom she loved.

Jessica Marrick came slowly down the stairs to meet him. She had not troubled to run a last-minute comb through the dark tangle of her hair and her clothes were still the rough working garments which she habitually wore. She had made no concession to a Sunday afternoon apart from putting on a clean apron to milk the cows.

"I'm Noel Melford, the doctor you wrote to in answer to your sister's letter," Noel explained as he studied her closely. "I felt it best to come and see your father rather than write again."

"What difference will it make, coming here?" she demanded, the sullen light in her eyes charged with extra resentment as she noticed how handsome he was. "It won't make us change our minds about—about things."

"What things, Jess?" he asked tolerantly. "There are some things that we must do in spite of obvious prejudices. We cannot, for instance, refuse help to those in acute physical and mental distress because we harbor some sort of resentment towards them." He kept his eyes on her sullen face, willing her to listen to what he had to say. "Frankly," he went on, "I have come here to enlist your help. Your sister was put into my care suffering from loss of memory over three weeks ago and we have only now been successful in tracing you. There would appear to have been an accident of some sort, in which she was involved, but so far we have not been able to trace anything. That is why I have come from Wales to ask for your co-operation. I have brought Anna with me."

At the sound of her sister's name Jessica Marrick drew back as if she had been dealt a physical blow and her eyes dilated with uncontrolled passion.

"She will not come here!" she cried. "She would not dare!"

Noel took a step towards her, although he would not have been surprised if she had flown at him with all the ferocity of a cornered animal.

"Now, Jess," he urged gently, "can't we talk this over without all this fuss? I'm not belittling your loss or suggesting that some injustice has not been done somewhere, but there is abosultely nothing to be gained by an attitude of hatred and non-co-operation in this instance. Anna must be helped to get her memory back, and you are the only person left who can help her. You say that your father has had a stroke, so we could not inflict such a strain on him at present. It's up to you, Jess."

He kept his eyes on her, demanding that she should consider what he said, but Jess Marrick would not waver in her decision nor give away one inch. This was a battle of hurt pride against an appeal for sympathy, Noel realized, and hurt pride could be a revengeful enemy.

"What right have you to ask me to do this?" she burst out passionately. "You don't understand what she did to me. You can't know what she is like!"

"I think I do know what she is like, Jess," he said patiently, "and that is why I have come here to appeal to you to forget the past for the sake of the present and the future."

"She stole the man I was going to marry!" Jess spat out, glad when she saw him flinch at the crude accusation, glad that she had the power to inflict hurt.

"And because of that you are going to refuse to help me, even when I tell you that I know how you have suffered, even when I say that I am in love with Anna and have no hope of ever claiming her love in return?"

The appeal silenced her and she stared at him as if he had struck her.

"You?" she said. "But—Ned Armstrong married her didn't he?"

"We can't find any trace of him," he explained. "He didn't rejoin his ship. We telephoned to the owners in Swansea, but these thing happen quite frequently, it appears. The fact remains that Ned Armstrong has not tried to trace Anna in all these weeks and—we must find him, or find out about him."

163

"He wrote to her," Jess muttered, following her own train of thoughts down into the past, "and she went off to meet him. She knew that she was going to him, and she said nothing. She left us without a word, with that Judas kiss of hers, and next day I found the letter!"

"Can you tell me about the letter, Jess?" Noel's face was pale and strained now, his mouth more tightly compressed than ever. "It may help us to discover what exactly happened to them."

Jess hesitated, looking for a moment as if she would still turn on her heel and leave him, and then she said slowly.

"It came just before she left to go on her holiday to Wales and she was—agitated about it. I know she didn't sleep much that night, for I heard her pacing about her room next to mine. But that wasn't when she burned the letter," Jess added. "I was in her room the next morning and it wasn't in the grate then."

Noel supposed that she had gone to her sister's room afterwards in search of the all-important letter, but he made no comment, and after another pause in which she remained deep in thought, Jess went on in the same resentful tone:

"They must have made it up between them—what they were going to do. He gave her an address where he was staying in Swansea and she must have replied to him there and agreed to meet him, because there was a complaint from the hotel she should have gone to at Harlech several days later. The people said that she hadn't taken up her reservation, but we had found the letter burned in her room before then."

"And you didn't reply to the hotel," Noel summed up, "or notify the police that your sister was missing?"

"We knew where she was!" she answered defiantly.

"You *thought* you knew where she was," he suggested. "Has it never occurred to you in all this time that you might have made a mistake about Anna?"

She glared at him.

"We knew what she did," she affirmed. "They went away together. They had it all planned beforehand."

"Had they? I wonder. You were very much in love with Ned, weren't you?" he asked. "Possessively in love, Jess. Was that not so? Forgive me, but I have to be blunt to get my point across to you! Have you never thought that you might have lost Ned without Anna being involved in it at all, that he might just have—changed his mind?"

The painful color of hurt and embarrassment flew into her cheeks and her stormy dark eyes looked sulkier than ever as she strove to refute his suggestion by added proof from another source.

"That Nurse Enman, or whatever she was, said that Anna had married Ned Armstrong!" she declared.

He did not argue the point because he had not found an answer to that himself, and Jess added with fine sarcasm:

"Maybe you can undo that knot, too, since you've come to prove to us how innocent she was?"

"I've come to beg you to help her," Noel answered, "that's all. And I don't see how you can possibly refuse."

He knew that she was about to turn down his appeal, that no amount of further argument would sway her, and then a voice hailed her from the floor above. It was guttural and indistinct, and Noel looked up in the general direction of the sound.

"Your father?" he asked.

She nodded.

"He won't see anyone."

"I'm a doctor," he reminded her. "Perhaps he will agree to see me. Did he know that you wrote to me in reply to Anna's letter?"

The tell-tale color climbed into her cheeks again, answering him before she said:

"Why should I bother him with her affairs? She had cut herself off from the family and he never wanted to see her again after what she did."

"So you wrote without telling him," Noel mused, "in order to keep me away?"

"I wrote what I did because I knew he didn't want her back," she defended herself. "He could never forgive her," Jess reiterated. "He could never get over her taking my mother's ring. It was meant for me, and she used it for her own purpose, to marry the man I was engaged to! My father put his blessing on that ring when he entrusted it to her, and it was to be for the first of us who got married. She took it with her when it was meant for me!"

The strangled pronouncement was so fraught with jealousy that Noel could feel genuinely sorry for her, seeing the warped outlook of an older sister deeply resentful at the idea of the younger being married first, and added to all that was the fact that Jessica Marrick firmly believed Anna to have married the man she loved.

It was the same story that Sara had repeated, only now it held poignancy as well as venom. He was acutely sympathetic with Jessica Marrick in that moment, but he could not afford to let sympathy over a love affair stand in his way.

"May I go upstairs?" he asked. "I can explain everything to your father."

"If you must."

Reluctantly she stood aside, watching him as he mounted the narrow stairs, and Noel found himself wondering what would become of her after all this was over.

The only door standing open on the upstairs landing was evidently Abraham Marrick's bedroom, and he went in to find the old man seated in an arm-chair near the window.

To a trained eye such as Noel's, it was evident that the first effect of the seizure was just wearing off, and he felt intense relief as the older man measured him with a keen scrutiny.

"Your daughter wrote to me and told me about your illness," he explained, holding out his hand to shake the gnarled one the farmer extended as he edged a chair forward with his foot.

"My name's Melford—Noel Melford, and I've had your younger daughter under my care in a Welsh hospital for the past few weeks."

Abraham Marrick stiffened in his seat.

"I want nothing to do with her," he declared harshly, but Noel was far too keen a psychologist not to detect the secret yearning in him for his favorite child.

"Mr. Marrick," he said bluntly, "there are a great many things that have to be overlooked in life, if not actually forgotten. I'm not here to ask your forgiveness on Anna's behalf, only to plead with you as her physician to help her in the desperate situation she is in now. Even though she has no true memory of the past, I am quite convinced that

166

her love for her family is one of the strongest emotions she knows. Home life and family ties have brought the greatest response in all our tests at the hospital and she has been greatly concerned about you, even though you are nothing more than a name to her at present." He leaned over and put a hand on the other man's knee. "As I see it," he said quietly, "it is your duty to see her."

"Duty?" The word seemed to stick in Abraham Marrick's throat. "My girl didn't show much sense of duty when she ran off like that, wi' nary a word!" he declared bitterly.

"That's where I need your help," Noel pointed out. "We must link up dates, and only you and Miss Marrick can give me what I want."

After the barest pause the farmer let his body relax, and sank back in his chair.

"I'll do my best," he agreed, his hands unclenching under the warm pressure of Noel's long fingers. "I never thought to see her again——"

He spoke as if he had just heard of a miracle, and Noel's lips curved in the slightest of smiles as he felt for his diary in his waistcoat pocket.

"Now, let me see," he began, fingering through the pages. "My sister brought Anna to our home in Glynmareth suffering from loss of memory, on the twentieth of last month. You are a farmer, Mr. Marrick, so you are sure to remember the gales which were sweeping our country during that particular week—rain and high winds that made it more like March than June."

The old man nodded.

"Ay, well I remember them, and I told that girl o' mine they would have blown themselves out by the end o' the week, which they did!"

"Mr. Marrick, do you remember exactly when Anna left Alnborough?"

Noel could not keep the note of tension out of his voice, nor could he pretend any longer that this was nothing but a routine check-up. It was more than that; it was a question of faith, with his own trust the target for any dart that fate might care to throw.

"She left on the Monday," the farmer said. "We went with her as far as Alnwick, because it was market day, and she caught the bus for Newcastle there. We saw her on to it. She was to travel from Newcastle by the night train, so that she should have reached North Wales early the following day. The Monday would be the eighteenth of the month, for I paid bills that day and had them receipted and dated. "Yes," he added decisively, "that was right! I looked them up, you see, just to make sure——"

"There's no need to make any more caluclations," Noel said with something in his eyes that was like liquid fire. "We've got a story here in a nutshell! Three days of it! The day Anna left here, the day when she travelled on to some unknown destination, and the day when she was found by my sister wandering on the moor near our home!"

He got to his feet and stood staring out through the window, speaking rapidly, as if time were an urgent factor even now.

"Only Anna can tell us what happened in between the eighteenth and the twentieth, but I am quite convinced now that she was the victim of an accident, something swift and terrifying which blotted out memory and all else for several hours. When she regained consciousness she was wet and cold, and she did the most sensible thing she could have done in the circumstances—began to walk. She walked till mid-day, when Ruth found her." He wheeled round to face the older man. "This amensia—this forgetting can be cleared up in two ways," he explained. "The return to a well-remembered scene and the sight of known faces could bring everything back in a flash, or, if the amnesia is traumatic—the result of a severe blow—operation on the brain is necessary. We've come to the point in Anna's case," he added bluntly, "where memory should return. I've brougth her to the door, Mr. Marrick. It is for you to open it to her."

The silence after he had finished speaking could almost be felt, but he waited confidently, sure that he had struck the right note.

"What do you want me to do?" Abraham Marrick asked at last.

"I want you to let me bring her here, in my own way."

"Tears trickled slowly down the old man's weather-beaten cheeks; tears of which he was no longer ashamed.

"Ah did wrong," he said in broad dialect. "Bring back the bairn into ma hoose."

Noel gripped his hand and wrung it warmly.

"Thank you," he said simply. "You won't regret it, Mr. Marrick."

Quietly he made his way back down the stairs to find Jess standing at the foot with her dark brows drawn in a scowl. He could not say whether she had overheard their conversation or not, and he did not care.

"Go up to your father," he commanded, "and see that he goes to bed for a while. Take him something hot to drink and don't let him talk too much. He'll want to get up in the morning." He held her sullen gaze with a steely look ."And remember, Jess, no scenes! One heated argument could cause a great deal of trouble just now. He'll have excitement enough tomorrow, but I shall be there to take charge."

"You're bringing her back!" she accused. "You've talked him into it!"

"Yes," Noel said, "I'm bringing her back."

He did not believe that Jessica Marrick would hold out against them once her father had made his decision, and he raced the car back to Alnwick with the blood hammering a mad tattoo in his veins, his whole horizon brighter for that half hour's talk with an old bewildered man whose bitterness had not really gone very deep.

It was ridiculous to feel such childish disappointment, he told himself, when he found the lounge empty and Ruth and Anna not yet returned, but reasoning has little understanding of love's impetuosity, and he looked at his watch impatiently a dozen times during the next half-hour.

"They're going to be late for dinner," he thought almost irritably when seven o'clock came round and there was still no sign of his sister. Ruth should have known better!

Between seven and half-past Ruth came into the lounge alone.

"Where's Anna?" Eagerness and dismay mingled in his voice and his eyes searched his sister's, demanding an explanation.

"We walked so far," Ruth explained, "she went straight up to her room to change her shoes. What news?" she asked.

"We're getting somewhere at last," he said, relieved that no harm had come to them. "Anna Marrick left here on the eighteenth and you picked her up at Glynmareth two days later!"

"On the twentieth," Ruth agreed. "Yes, go on!"

"Well—don't you see! One day was hardly time enough to have met this Ned Armstrong fellow, far less married him!"

Trained to composure, trained to meet the vagaries of life without undue comment, he had not been able to conceal his fundamental relief at the thought of Anna's marriage being more or less an impossibility in these circumstances, and the little human revelation of the man under the skin of the doctor endeared him to Ruth more than ever. In her own heart she knew overwhelming relief for his sake, yet she realized that she must not tell him so—not yet. From this intimate moment of revelation onwards, he would be the doctor again, intent upon his case, living for nothing else until success came his way.

"But you think she did meet him?" she asked.

"I feel almost certain of it, in face of that letter. Armstrong had made an appeal to her which, being Anna, she would not refuse, and she went to meet him as he had suggested. Whether he was in love with her or she with him I don't know, but that's immaterial at the moment."

"What about the sister?" Ruth asked with a hint of sympathy in her pleasant voice.

"She's not taking this too well, of course. She's still resentful.

"We'll have to try to understand that."

"You will when you've seen her!"

"You're sorry for her, Noel?"

"Yes, damnably sorry, but I don't intend to let her stand in my way. I've won the old man over, so we can dispense with Jess Marrick's co-operation for the present."

"Do you think she will try to make trouble?"

"I don't see how she can, but we can always take precautions."

"What has she to lose now?"

"I don't know. Since we don't believe Anna ever married Ned Armstrong—nothing."

"All this—doesn't account for the ring," Ruth pointed out doubtfully.

"I've got a theory about that," Noel said. "Can you remember who helped you that day at the villa? You told me you called to a nurse going off duty."

"It was one of the probationers—Jill, I think they call her. I thought I'd better see Matron myself, and I asked her to hold the fort while I was away."

"Can you remember what you told her to do?"

"I wouldn't give her an order," Ruth considered, "but—yes, I think I suggested she might look through Anna's pockets for some evidence of identity. When I came back she had laid out a purse and a few coppers — and the handkerchief with Anna's name on it."

"And the wedding ring was on Anna's finger?"

"Yes. I think that was when I first noticed it—when I came bock from the hospital," Ruth agreed. "Noel, do you think——?"

"These superstitious Welsh!" Surprisingly, there was an amused light in his eyes now, making them kinder. "Sentiment before duty every time!"

"You think Jill put the ring on?" Ruth asked incredulously.

"I'm almost sure of it! Rather than let the stranger die with it in her pocket, Jill would risk it. The third finger of the girl's left hand being the only place that a wedding ring should go, Jill would put it there with never a second thought. By Jove, Ruth, I think we've got it!" he exclaimed. "The answer to a good deal of anguish and heart-searching!" he added quietly.

"I hope you're right, my dear," Ruth said as Anna opened the door of the lounge and came in. "I've felt all day that she was coming right to the brink of remembering."

Anna came towards them almost shyly, her eyes questioning Noel, and he said briefly:

"We're leaving everything till tomorrow. There's not a great deal to explain at this stage, but we are getting somewhere, at last. I've met your father, Anna. He's been ill, but you will be able to see him tomorrow."

He was evading a detailed explanation of his plans, and Ruth knew that he was depending on the element of surprise to revive memory where so much else had failed. He did not want Anna to spend the next few hours counting the time to her ordeal, her nervousness and anxiety mounting until they finally defeated his object.

"Where did you go?" he asked.

"When we came off the bus at Alnmouth we had some tea," Ruth told him.

"At 'The Schooner'," Anna added eagerly. "As soon as I went in I knew I had been there before, Noel, and I thought, after that, it would all be easy——" She broke off, but her brow was no longer clouded. The groping was upwards, towards the certain light. "I knew that I had been there often in the past—happily. If it had only been a matter of place and environment," she added with amazing insight into her problem, "I'm sure everything would have cleared for me there and then, but that's not all it is. It's about people, Noel——"

"Yes," he agreed quietly. "I know. Your concern is with Ned Armstrong."

The name drew all the color into her cheeks and Ruth saw her hand clench suddenly over her handbag.

"If only I could *do* something!" she cried.

"Whatever you want to do," Noel said, "whatever you had set out to do, will all come right in the end, Anna. We —even now."

They went into dinner, and Anna noticed the difference in Noel as he ordered their meal. He looked unaccountably younger and far more sure of the situation than he had ever can't rush things. We must be prepared to wait for results been, and her pulses quickened as she let her thoughts go forward to tomorrow. A few more hours were all that might be left between her and the past. It was like walking backwards in time, re-living her life, step by step, back to that dark curtain which divided her from so much of that past that had a definite bearing on the present, too. Without the memory of the past the present was meaningless, and she knew that Noel had recognized that long ago.

Tonight, however, there was a new warmth in his voice, and his eyes were clear. It was as if he were trying to tell her that there was no need to fear, and she took fresh courage from the thought.

She even slept peacefully that night, untroubled by any dream, and when the morning came her courage was renewed. She was first down to breakfast, but Noel came in soon afterwards.

"You've been out walking!" she greeted him. "You've got a look of fresh air about you!"

"I never sleep much after six," he said, taking the chair opposite her and unfolding his table napkin. "Anna," he added suddenly, "before Ruth comes I want to tell you that, whatever today brings, you can always count on me. I love you, my dear—whatever that is worth in this hopeless situation."

He did not tell her that he was fool enough to believe that her marriage had never taken place. He did not want to confuse her unnecessarily, and she still wore the wedding ring like an amulet. The ring he had bought! He smiled wryly at the irony of that thought.

"If only—it had all been different," Anna said heavily. "Oh! I can't bear to think of forgetting all this, Noel, of perhaps not being able to remember about you or about Ruth and Glynmareth! I feel that—fate might have been kinder to us," she added brokenly.

He did not mean her to forget, but he could not tell her that now, and he cursed Sara Enman for her interference.

"We can only work these things out when we come to them," he said. "This afternoon I am going to take you to Alnborough to your father."

A wave of deep color stained her cheeks.

"Was he really ill, Noel, or did he not answer my letter because there was something wrong—because he did not wish to see me?" she asked. "I've never been able to understand why my people didn't report my disappearance to the police," she went on unhappily. "It would have saved you so much unnecessary troubles and all these long, wearying journeys."

"Your father has been ill," he said. "Desperately ill, but he is well enough to see you now. Whatever he felt in the past, Anna, he wants you to go back to Alnborough now."

"I see," she said, looking down at her clasped hands, but not completely convinced, because there had been just a suggestion of hesitation in his voice. She would not persist with her questioning, however, because she was already grateful beyond measure for all he had done for her.

When Ruth made her appearance they decided to spend the morning going over the castle. It would fill in time, Noel said, and he had always wanted to see the place. There was, he believed, a particularly well-preserved dungeon, and the castle itself was in excellent repair.

"Ruins need to much imagination from my point of view," he confessed, "but I can people a reasonably preserved castle down through the ages. I'll go round and get the car, and you had better change those fancy shoes of yours, Ruth, for we'll have to walk when we get there."

Ruth left Anna to wait for them in the lounge. The big, oak-panelled room was deserted at that hour, and Anna sat down near one of the deep mullioned windows, conscious once more of the feeling of familiarity which she had experienced the afternoon before at "The Schooner". If she had lived near here, if Noel was right and he had traced her family, it would be quite natural, but nothing could account for the unhappiness which assailed her each time she considered the past in relationship to her own family.

Something like dread stalked her mind when she contemplated her return to Alnborough, the grim old house which Noel believed she had described so faithfully, and she could only account for it by supposing that her relationship with her family had not been good. That fact alone distressed her anew as subconscious protest rose to deny it, and a deeply abiding love seemed to be entangled in her impressions of Alnborough and the past.

That these impressions were emerging, slowly but surely, from behind the veil of forgetfulness, could not be denied, however. She felt far more sure of herself now, sure of the way to the future, and only the cold fear of forgetting the present which Sara had implanted crushed hope down in her heart. When she tried to analyse it she saw it as a fundamental fear of losing the love she had, fear of losing Noel, although she had no real right to claim his love.

Despair so great that it almost shook her fine courage gripped her in its relentless stranglehold and she got to her feet with a movement as if to escape, and then she saw the other girl standing in the doorway looking in at her with naked hatred in her dark eyes.

It was someone she knew. Uncertainty and bewilderment choked the expression of surprise back in her throat and she put both hands up to it in a protective gesture as the intruder came towards her across the thick pile of the carpet.

"Jess——!"

The one strangled cry was all she uttered. The name had burst in her brain like an exploding shell, leaving a havoc of confusion and darkness behind it after that first blinding revelation of light.

"I thought your memory wasn't all that far gone!" Jess Marrick sneered. "You remember me, and you remember what you did, sneaking off with Ned—you and him planning everything while you slept under my father's roof and he wrote to me like a lover! And now you want to come back, don't you? Something's gone wrong, and you want to come back!" Jess laughed sharply. "Well, you never shall! My father can't do without me at Alnborough now, and he knows it! The farm means more to him than his life. It would kill him to part with it, but he needs me to run it with him! You were the one who ran the house, but anyone could do that. I helped him to run the farm," Jess boasted. "I was as good as any man out in the fields, and I still am, but the day you come back to Alnborough, Anna Marrick, I leave it!" Her lips twisted with passionate denunciation. "You can take your choice," she flung at her sister. "You'll kill my father if you got to Alnborough, *because he will be forced to leave it if I leave!*"

The harsh, brittle voice rang in Anna's ears with no very clear meaning behind the words except the fact that she was being denied the right to return home, denied the right to memory and the past.

"You can't do this, Jess," she appealed desperately. "I've got to remember, and only you can help me! I've got to go to Alnborough, as Noel says——"

"He's in love with you!" Jess accused. "Anyone could see that yesterday when he tried to make me do his bidding, but he knows now what you did to me and Ned Armstrong——"

Anna covered her face with her hands.

"Jess, please—please try to let me think!" she cried. "Please try to help me! I have tried to help you. Oh! why doesn't it all come back to me? Why can't I tell you all I want you to know?"

"Because you are ashamed of what you have done!" Jess assured her. "And whatever has happened between you and Ned, it serves you right! You want to crawl back and be accepted again, don't you? But you won't be! I'll stand in your way if it is the last thing I do, for I hate you with an everlasting hatred——"

"Be quiet, you little fool!" Noel came striding past her and went to Anna, but he turned on Jess almost immediately, taking her by the shoulders and shaking her with a depth of passion rarely seen in him. "You don't know what you are talking about, and you have no decision to make," he said. "It will not matter in the slightest whether you leave Alnborough or not. I shall take Anna there this afternoon and you can listen to the truth with the rest of us or not, just as it pleases you. And now," he added, releasing her abruptly, "if you have any sense of pity left, you will go and leave us to look after your sister."

Jess stared back at him with concentrated hatred burning in her eyes, but she knew better than to renew her tirade against Anna in his presence.

"Don't go," Anna said haltingly. "Jess, if you would only try to understand—how difficult it is just at first—adjusting everything. It's like—feeling one's way through a jungle, hoping that civilization is coming nearer all the time, yet never being quite sure, never being able to see anything clearly for the dense undergrowth. It's—praying that you're going to win through, praying for the return of life as you know it, yet—yet——"

Noel moved and put a protecting arm about her shaking shoulders, drawing her back to the chair she had left.

"Take your time," he advised.

"It's—coming back," she whispered. "Noel, I knew her —I knew Jess!"

"Yes," he said grimly. "It's just a pity she succeeded in slipping in when my back was turned. All right, Jess," he added, turning to the other girl, "you needn't make the effort to understand if it's too much for you." His voice altered suddenly, becoming surprisingly gentle. "You won't believe it, but perhaps I can understand how you feel just now, how far from forgiveness you are at this moment."

176

"I'll never forgive her!" Jessica Marrick cried again. "I've vowed never to speak to her as long as I live!"

"Never is a bitter word," Noel told her, "and life is long. You'll learn to love again, Jess, and live to forget all this."

He led her to the door, returning immediately to Anna's side with all his concern etched in the deep lines around his mouth and eyes. Her own face was colorless, drawn into the lines of perplexity he hated to see, but he knew that this was the supreme effort, the final endeavour that must bring results.

"She hates me," she whispered. "You could see that, couldn't you, but I tried to help her. Oh! if only I could think why she needed my help so much! If only I could understand why! It was about Ned."

"Jess and Ned were to have been married," he prompted quietly while his own heart contracted at the irony of the situation, of helping her to remember this part of her story which he prayed might be wrong. "Their wedding was planned, Anna. Do you remember that?" His voice reverted to the old note of authority. "You must remember! You were to have been her bridesmaid, I suppose."

"Yes—yes!" She drew in a sharp breath, one hand still clasped to her throat as if she would force the words out in the way. "It was all planned. My mother was dead and Jess had been so good to me—looking after me all these years. I was bewildered, Noel, when my mother died. It didn't seem possible that someone I had loved and relied upon for all the comfort and happiness that came my way should suddenly have been taken from me—cut down at the height of her own happiness."

"You were very fond of your mother," he suggested, "and Jess was kind to you after she died. You were, in fact, a happy and devoted family, who would have gone to any lengths to help one another."

She nodded, accepting the authenticity of his statement with an eagerness he had never seen in her before.

"I worked in the house because I was more like my mother and Jess liked the outside jobs. My father taught her to do everything about the farm, as he would have taught a son. A son!" She paused, searching diligently for the connecting thought. "When Ned first started coming to the farm to see Jess we resented him a little. I suppose. Perhaps I was even a little jealous, and my father thought he was going to break up the happiness we had built round ourselves at Alnborough like a wall, but soon my father was accepting him as a son, as an addition to our small family circle. The fact that he went to sea made it simple enough, for Jess could still be at home a great deal of her time. We would not really lose her!"

"Did your father ever suggest, at any time, that Ned Armstrong might leave the sea and come and farm at Alnborough?" Noel asked, watching her closely, and whatever reaction he had expected to follow his remark he was certainly not prepared for the complete upheaval the suggestion appeared to create in Anna's mind.

She stared at him for a moment without speaking, without seeming even to see him, and then her whole face seemed to break up, quivering pathetically, while her hands fell to her sides and were clenched tightly there in a desperate effort at composure as memory came rushing back, sweeping everything before it.

"That was it! That was what caused the trouble, but it was Jess who talked Ned into the promise to leave the sea. She over-ruled all his objections, all his desires, but the sea won in the end!" Her face was as pale as a ghost, but her eyes were keen with understanding. "Noel," she said uncertainly, "the sea won—in the end."

He took her hands in his holding them firmly as he turned her round in the chair to face him.

"Don't think about that yet," he commanded. "You knew Ned felt like that about his career—about giving it up for Alnborough. Was it because he wrote to you and told you, Anna? Was it all in that letter you tried to burn the day you went away?"

"Yes," she agreed without hesitation, taking his knowledge for granted. "Ned told me he had changed his mind, not only about giving up the sea but about Jess, too. He said—he said he couldn't go on loving anyone so possessive when he knew he couldn't give her everything in return. He said that his chosen career meant more to him than any woman he had ever met and he couldn't give it up."

"Was that all?"

Her mouth twisted painfully, but the words could not be stopped now. They came tumbling out, one after the other, as if time was limited and so much had to be said in the shortest space of time.

"He was terribly upset. He said he would give the world to be able to change back to loving Jess again, but he just didn't know how. He said he would try to explain everything if I would only agree to meet him, but he would not come to Alnborough. Perhaps he feared a scene with Jess —he had always a hasty temper—and I thought that sounded cowardly at the time, but I was foolish enough to think, too, that I could persuade him to change his mind again if only I could see him and talk to him."

"And so you went to Swansea instead of going to your holiday hotel?"

She nodded.

"I decided to telephone to them to say I would be late, and then Ned said he could get me there in reasonable time, so I didn't. He had bought a second-hand car in Swansea and he said we could talk it all over on the way north to Harlech. He was going on to Liverpool to join another ship there."

Noel's face was almost as pale as her own now, but he held her firmly.

"How far did you drive on the journey? A long way?" he suggested.

"We left Swansea quite early. My train got in early in the morning and Ned met it with the car. He looked dreadfully—haggard and untidy, as if he had been up all night, and he was terribly unhappy. I felt sorry for him. He was so deeply concerned about what he was doing, but—he just couldn't go on with the marriage. And after a while I saw that I couldn't argue against such black despair. He just didn't love Jess any more."

"Anna," Noel asked quietly, "was he in love with you?"

She gave him his answer instantly, clear and decisive as all truth.

"He was never in love with me. We had been good friends, that was all—good friends for a very long time. I would have welcomed him as a brother if he had gone on loving Jess."

179

"And since he couldn't do that, your mission was hopeless," he concluded. "Anna, do you remember your mother's ring?"

Deep distress lined her face again.

"My father gave it to me to give to Ned before the wedding because it had always been said among us that the first bride should wear it, and I took it with me to Wales, thinking that it might help me in my argument for Jess. I thought—I must have thought that I could influence Ned in that way, but it was no use. When a person has made up his mind about a thing like that—about not loving someone sufficiently—nothing will sway them—not pity or sentiment or anything like that," she added. "I didn't even show him the ring once I realized how hopeless everything was."

"You put it back in your pocket and it was found there with your other possessions," he said.

"I don't know——"

For the first time she was thinking about the ring, thinking directly about herself, and she stared down at the thin gold circlet on her finger and began to twist it round and round in confusion. He put a firm hand over hers to stop the confused gesture.

"Never mind that now," he said. "Where did you leave Ned Armstrong?"

Her fingers gripped hard on his as Ruth came in at the door and he nodded to his sister to stay where she was. Little beads of perspiration were standing out on Anna's brow now and her voice began to shake.

"I didn't leave Ned," she said unsteadily. "We went together—to the edge of the sea. There was no other road ——"

Noel got abruptly to his feet.

"All right, you can forget about that now," he said. "The essentials are all here, Anna." He bent down and took her hands again, drawing her to her feet. "My dear, I've got the right to look after you now, thank God! Try to remember that there's nothing more to fear."

Ruth came to his side, her kind eyes full of concern.

"Is it all right?" she whispered.

"Practically." His tone was buoyant with relief. "Much better than I could have hoped for, in fact, but I still think

I should take her to Alnborough. I think, too, that we might go right away. If we're quick enough, we may even get there ahead of Jess."

Ruth could not understand his reason, and she was more perplexed when he decided to take a road along the coast instead of following the main highway, which he knew. He was driving much faster than he normally did, too, and he had insisted on Anna's sitting beside him in the front of the car.

They came upon the sea at last, looking down over sand dunes covered with rough grass; from there they climbed on to the cliff, and the dunes finally gave way to a rocky coastline with a steeper drop to the sea. Noel began to increase his speed and almost instantly Anna covered her face with her hands.

"No! No!" she protested. "Noel—stop! Please stop! The road——"

Her cry ended in a shuddering sigh, as if all the breath had gone out of her, and she lay back against the cushioning with her eyes closed, the blue veined lids trembling spasmodically. Noel slowed the car and turned to look at her.

"Anna," he demanded ruthlessly, "you saw that car go over the cliff. When did you leave it?"

"I jumped. I saw the road all broken away ——"

"And Armstrong couldn't stop in time! He braked and slowed up, but it was too late—for him." He was forming his own impression, fitting in clue after clue to make an acceptable whole, and he knew that it coincided with the picture shaping in her mind. "That could have meant a traumatic," he muttered. "The blow as she fell from the car, but thank heaven it's all coming back naturally!"

He looked at Anna again, critically, and Ruth spoke for the first time.

"Is she all right?"

"I'd like to take her somewhere where she could rest for a while," he said. "It looks as if we had better go back to the hotel."

"Or on to Alnborough," Ruth suggested. "Take her home, Noel, and leave Jessica Marrick to me. I passed her in the entrance hall of the hotel just now and she glared hatred at me, though she couldn't possibly have known who I was, but I knew her because she was with a young man who called her Jess—the farming type."

Noel hesitated.

"It's the only way," Ruth urged. "Anna will want to go home."

He let in the clutch and the car slid away down the hill, away from the sea towards the open moor.

"You're right," he said. "We'll take her home. I'm sorry for Jess Marrick," he added, "and I'm possibly going to have the thankless task of proving to her how wrong she has been, but I've also got to convince her that the man she still loves is dead, drowned off the Welsh coast when a car plunged over a cliff in the darkness! I'm not exactly looking forward to that bit!"

"Will we ever have proof!" Ruth wondered.

"I don't know. I don't really think so, but I'll phone Dennis tonight and see if he can put any inquiries on foot before we get back. He was as interested in this case as I was."

Ruth's heart soared in spite of herself and the color was still high in her cheeks when they reached Alnborough.

The house was quiet, as it had been the day before, but Noel drove straight in through the white gateposts this time and drew up on the cobbles before the back door. Ruth sat quite still while Anna got slowly out of the car, her face trans-figured in a sudden gleam of bright sunlight as it broke through the morning haze. She looked a new being, radiant in her self-possession, although there was still a certain amount of nervousness in her eyes as she approached the house. This was home! There was no doubt about that. Her whole expression proclaimed it and she almost ran the last few steps to reach the door.

Noel walked after her into the big, cool dairy with its stone floor garlanded in carefully piped scrolls and the butter churn scrubbed and airing in the corner where she had turned it so often. The morning milk had gone out and the pans were scalded and set up on their ends against the whitewashed walls.

The scene in the hotel lounge had faded a little now, and the old love and companionship was crowding out all the harshness and the pain of bitter recrimination. She turned eagerly toward the door leading into the kitchen, and then she seemed to remember Noel for the first time. Holding out her hand to him, she took him with her into the old familiar room, which he also knew, her voice choking as she said:

"I've come back, Noel! I've come home."

Her eyes were on all the dearly beloved objects about the place and they were shining, all her uncertainty gone.

"Your father's waiting for you upstairs," Noel said. "Don't forget that he's been ill, my dear. This meeting— after so long—may be a tax on his strength."

He was giving her responsibility, knowing that it would counteract her own feeling of strangeness if she had to think of another's welfare, and he followed her up the stairs with a lightness in his tread that he had not known for weeks.

At the bedroom door he halted and she went in alone.

"I'll be here, if you need me," he said.

Abraham Marrick was seated in his chair beside the window, and he looked up, expecting to see Jess returned from her unheralded visit to Alnwick, but instead it was Anna who stood there in the doorway, Anna, who was so like his dead wife that he had found it the harder to forgive her for the misuse of her mother's ring. But all that had been forgotten now. He held out his work-roughened hands and she came to him instantly, locked in the shelter of his arms for a full minute before either of them spoke.

"Ay, lass, you had to come back!" he said. "We couldna get on without ye!"

He let his hand stray over her hair as he had done when she was a child, conscious of all the harshness gone out of him with the old, familiar action. His lost lamb had returned, and he would shelter it, however lame!

It was some minutes before Anna remembered Noel, but he came to the door as soon as she called his name.

"May I come in?" he asked.

"Come in lad! Come in!" the farmer hailed him. "I've been thinking about you all morning—ever since you left here yesterday, in fact!"

Noel smiled down at him, his handsome face reflecting the relief in his heart that these two had come together without question, and with a simple trust restored.

Later, when he told Abraham Marrick the truth, the old man's concern was immediaely switched to his elder child.

"Jess'll take this hard," he said. "She'll find it difficult to credit at first that Ned Armstrong's really dead. I suppose," he added with a pathetic hopefulness, "there couldn't have been any mistake? He couldn't be injured—badly injured, I'm meaning?"

"If that had been the case he would have been taken to a nearby hospital and we would probably have been notified when we made our inquiries about Anna," Noel explained. "Anna's luggage would have been found in the car, too, but nothing like that has happened. Everything has just disappeared—gone into the blue with no trace."

He did not want to discuss the accident with Anna fussing about the room putting it in order, because he knew that a repetition of all she had gone through would only distress her needlessly. He was glad that she had reacted so naturally to her return to Alnborough, taking up her old responsibilities as a matter of course while Jess was away, and deep in his heart he had to acknowledge that a miracle he had prayed for with all the faith left in him had actually taken place before his eyes.

By all the rules of ordinary amnesia, Anna should have forgotten her sojourn in that space of time carved out of her ordinary living when she had become one of their community at Glynmareth. It was what Sara had hoped for, he realized, without troubling to acknowledge why, but something had worked a miracle.

Could he hope that his love had conveyed itself through the haze of returning consciousness, penetrating the dark curtain of Anna's unawareness by the sheer force of its longing, demanding her love in return?

There seemed so much to sort out between them, but at least she remembered. He could thank God for that.

Presently, remembering Ruth waiting patiently in the car he left Anna with her father and went down to his sister.

"I think Anna would like you to come in," he said. "She's with her father at the moment, but I'm going to prescribe some rest for the old man as soon as she comes downstairs. He's had enough emotional disturbance for one day!"

"Everything has gone off all right, then?" She asked. "Somehow, I felt it would, although I must confess that the session out there on the cliffs almost unnerved me!"

"It was easy," Noel assured her, "compared to some. Reaction, of course, depends largely upon a patient's own temperament, and Anna isn't the dramatic type."

"But Jess is!" Ruth said. "I wonder when she'll come home?"

"I mean to be here when she does," he said. "I'm not risking any setbacks at this stage."

"Apart from Jess upsetting her, you think Anna should be all right?"

"There's nothing at all the matter with her now. She's got back her memory and she's as normal as you or me." Noel took out his pipe for the first time that day. "She hasn't even the usual blank spot concerning the time between," he added with such relief in his voice that Ruth heaved a sigh of relief, too.

"Can I say thank heaven for that, Noel?"

"You can," he told her. "It might so easily have been the other way round."

When Anna came down she insisted that they should stay. She was gay and smiling in her new-found happiness, and even the shadow hovering at the back of her eyes could not dim the radiance of her face as she moved about the familiar room, touching this and that as a blind person might who had suddenly been given back the sight of her eyes.

"Surely you can spare twenty-four hours, Noel, even though you are a busy doctor?" she asked.

Noel agreed.

"I'd like to stay, if you can cope with us. But talking of doctors reminds me of another one I know!" He grinned across at Ruth. "I'll have to relieve Dennis some time, you know!"

"Dennis will cope," Ruth declared. "Though I think we should go back to the hotel and phone him."

"I want a word or two with him," Noel decided. "Anna," he asked suddenly, "if we found difficulty in clearing up the facts about the accident would you come back to Wales and help out?"

She paused beside the dresser, her fingers closing on its carved edge.

"You mean—go over the ground with you to—to where I think it all happened?" she asked.

He nodded as he watched her.

"I'm hoping it won't be necessary," he said, and Anna's heart contracted with relief and also with pain at the thought that the end of this day might have brought her so much and lost her much more.

That glorious sense of freedom she had experienced with returning memory was clouded over a little by her love for Noel and the thought of their inevitable parting, for she knew that he must go while she would stay here with her father and Jess. This was her home, and he had brought her back as he had promised.

Was that to be all? Was that to be the end of their loving, the end for Noel and the beginning of long heartache for her? She remembered Jess with compassion, realizing how much her sister must be suffering at that moment, but she was in no way nervous of their meeting except that she had no grain of comfort to offer Jess. She was convinced now that Ned Armstrong was dead, but she felt that Jess had never really accepted the fact. Love held on to hope for so long, as her own heart clung to the hope that her friendship with the Melford's was not going to end here and now that Noel had seen her through those dark days of her forgetting.

The lucidity of her thoughts was almost too clear; the past no longer a mystery, the future something she strove to grasp pathetically with hands that trembled.

When Bill Cranston's car drove along the narrow road to the farm and her sister got out and slammed the door she went slowly to meet her, realizing by the expression on Jess' face that the coming interview was going to be far more difficult than she could have imagined. She was convinced, however, that nothing short of the truth would be possible between them at this stage and she could not pretend that their relationship was other than strained.

"You've no idea how sorry I am about all this, Jess," she began. "It has been—difficult for me, too, you know. I had no idea who I was or where I had come from when I was picked up in Wales."

Jess glared at her with no sign of softening in her eyes.

"So your doctor friend told me," she said icily. "He was most concerned about you when he came here last week. You certainly get the men with your air of helplessness! I've heard before that it works every time!"

"Jess," Anna appealed, "please don't let's quarrel over something that is far too big for petty spite! Ned is dead," she added flatly. "He never loved me. I can swear to you that this is true."

"But you couldn't convince me with all the glib talk in the world that he died loving me!" Jess cried. "Something happened to change him, so what was it? He turned to you for sympathy. Why didn't he come to me?"

"Is that why you hate me so much, Jess?" Anna asked quietly. "It was—inevitable, in a way," she went on when her sister did not answer. "You see, we had all known each other for so long and Ned and I were good friends—because of you. He had no one else to turn to, so I suppose I was his natural choice."

"He discussed me with you! He told you he had stopped loving me! He ran to my sister to tell her the things he was not man enough to say to my face! Well, if that was Ned Armstrong I'm better without him! I'm glad it's all over," Jess cried passionately. "I'm glad there won't be any more heartache and tears—because now I know! There are other people—there's someone else who will love me in the way that I want, and maybe I'll be glad in the end that Ned Armstrong didn't come back!"

She flung past Anna into the dairy, her head held high, the stormy glint of tears in her eyes that a fierce, unbridled pride would not let her shed, and Anna followed her and stood beside the bench where Jess had flung down her parcels.

"You know you don't mean that," she said gently. "Oh, Jess! if I could only make you understand how well I know about—all this—about how you feel now, the utter hopelessness and the bitter despair! I've felt all that during the past few weeks for a different reason and—love may have passed me by, too——"

Her voice broke, but Jess Marrick could not concern herself with another's sorrow in that moment of her own most bitter grief. Her pain was the blinding kind that shut off insight and did not know the meaning of compassion. Yet Anna's sincerity could scarcely be doubted, and Jess turned after a second or two and looked across the bench at her with a questioning expression in her eyes which banished some of the dark anger from her face.

"If you really didn't want—Ned for yourself," she asked slowly, "why did you go off and meet him like that without a word?"

"How could I tell you the truth when it came to me in that way?" Anna asked honestly. "Jess, I know it is terribly difficult for you, but please try to believe me when I say that Ned was deeply unhappy about it all, that he had fought round after round the issue for weeks, but still couldn't reach any other conclusion. He could not—he would not marry without the love you had a right to expect from him."

Jess flushed darkly, but this time she had nothing to say. Then, quite suddenly, she collapsed into the wheeled-backed chair beside the bench and buried her face in her hands.

"I knew how he felt!" she cried. "But I would not accept it! I knew on his last leave, and I ignored it. I talked him out of telling me because I was so sure that I could settle everything in my own way, and—afterwards I hated you for knowing all about it, for sharing my shameful secret!"

The stark, unexpected confession dropped into a deep silence, broken as Anna bent closer to her sister and said kindly:

"There's no shame attached to losing someone you love, Jess. So many of us have to face that bitterness, and courage is the only answer. You always had plenty of courage in the old days," she went on quietly. "Don't let this spoil your life now."

Tears were seeping through between Jess Marrick's work-roughened fingers, the slow, difficult tears of a hard nature that accepts grief harshly, and when she lifted her head her face was disfigured by them.

"It's easier for you," she said. "You never loved anyone like that."

Anna did not contradict her, and after a while Jess got to her feet and began to fumble with her parcels.

"Bill Cranston wants me to marry him," she said.

"Maybe you will one day," Anna answered, "but not just now. It will take time for you to forget Ned, to look at all this without bitterness."

Jess turned towards the window, staring out at the distant moors.

"I should thank you for trying to bring him back to me," she acknowledged almost resentfully. "I see now that you did."

The sullen admission was all the appreciation Anna was likely to receive for her effort, but she did not want to be thanked for what she had done. The family ties which she had accepted from infancy had made that the most natural thing in the world and she had not hesitated when they had demanded the effort from her.

"I suppose," Jess said, nodding towards the closed door of the kitchen, "these people will be staying for a meal?"

"I would like them to stay," Anna said. "They have been so good to me, Jess."

The meal Jess insisted on preparing was plain and not very attractive. She had none of her sister's finer points

189

and considered the household tasks as chores which had to be overcome in the shortest possible time, but Anna would not interfere with her preparations once she had made the offer, and she let her preside at the head of the table when they finally sat down.

They washed the dishes together afterwards, while Ruth expressed her deep interest in the running of the farm and melted some of the ice from Jess' manner.

"I'll show you round," she offered unexpectedly. "I'll be making butter tomorrow and I'll show you how it's done, if you like. Town folk always like to see these things."

Noel smiled across at Anna when they had gone.

"And now it's up to you!" he said. "I'd like to see those moors of yours—particularly that spot you described when you wrote about your home."

"High Garnet?" Anna said disappointedly. "It's over seven miles away."

"That won't matter. We can take the car."

They motored towards the sea, to a high tableland where the rough grass crowned the outcrops of rock and shale, and where the breath of the sea came, salt-laden, from the north-east, and Noel slowed up almost by instinct on the brow of a hill.

"This is it," he said. "This should have been where I found you, Anna!"

She turned to look at him, her eyes shy but steady on his.

"It was, really," she said. "I think I must have put all my heart and all my love into the description of High Garnet, Noel."

Gently he drew her to him, taking her hand, and more gently still he turned it over and drew the wedding ring from the third finger where she still wore it. He put it in his pocket without a word, but he kept her hand in his as he looked down towards the sea.

"Anna," he said at last, "I want you to come back to Glynmareth one day—in your own time. You know that I love you. I've never been able to hide it, and there's no reason why I should hide it now." His voice vibrated on a

190

note of passion as he turned to take her in his arms, his dark head bent suddenly to claim her lips. "Tell me that I needn't wait too long," he demanded. "These past few weeks have been near-purgatory enough!"

"You needn't wait, Noel!" she whispered. "I'll come! Oh, my dear! I'll come!"

His lips sought hers again and again with a passionate tenderness of possessing.

"If I had lost you," he said huskily, "nothing would have been the same again. It's been a strange interlude, Anna, but it's over and we belong together now!"

"Yes," she said gently, "we belong together! I think we always have."

CHAPTER TWELVE

RUTH AND NOEL returned to Glynmareth the following afternoon, Noel with Abraham Marrick's blessing on his union with his favorite daughter and Ruth with a feeling that she was treading on air.

"Who would have thought," she observed to Dennis Tranby when they met, "that all this tangle would straighten itself out so satisfactorily?"

"And give you to me!" He caught her hand. "Ruth, isn't it time that you and I got married after all these years? You've not got an excuse in the world now that Noel's going to marry Anna in the shortest possible time and they will be going to Bristol to live. But you know you could never have left Glynmareth!" he added with an assurance strange in him. "You're part of it, my dear, and it of you! Just as I am. The life here is essential to us both."

"Yes," Ruth admitted, "I know. I'll marry you whenever you like, Dennis. Glynmareth—and you mean so much to me," she added unsteadily, "that part of me would always have remained here no matter how far away I might have gone."

They were married before Noel and Anna, on a day when a fisherman picked up an oblong sheet of metal which had once been a car's numberplate. It was Noel who took it to the police and had it identified as the number of the car which had been sold to Ned Armstrong in Swansea.

"It's the final clue," he told Anna with deep satisfaction in his voice. "The end of an episode."

"Poor Jess!" Anna whispered compassionately. "She fought a losing battle against the sea. It had claimed Ned so long ago. It was his only true love!"